NINE TENTHS
OF THE LAW

Claudia Hagadus Long

Kasva Press

Make its
bowls,
ladles,
jars and
pitchers
with
which to
offer
libations;
make them
of pure
gold.

תִּישְׂעוּ
וִיתְרְלְעָק
וִיתְפְּכוּ
וִיתוֹשְׁקוּ
וִיתִיקוֹמוּ
דְּסִי רֹשָׁא
בֵּהֶן זָהָב
הַשָּׁעַת רוֹהֵט
סֹתְא

St. Paul / Alfei Menashe

To Ada,
Enjoy!

Book design & layout: Yael Shahar

First edition published 2020
Kasva Press LLC
www.kasvapress.com
Alfei Menashe, Israel / St. Paul, Minnesota
info@kasvapress.com

Nine Tenths of the Law

ISBN
Trade Paperback: 978-1-948403-16-0

Ebook: 978-1-948403-18-4

9 8 7 6 5 4 3 2 1

DEDICATION

To my mother,
memory suspended like the day,
a bridge between night and dawn.

Aurora,

Named for the dawn, Mother, you died in darkness. You didn't have a memorial. You didn't have a *shiva*. The rest of us let you down, didn't we?

The sun is shining today in California. The lemon tree is dripping with Meyer lemons and sparkling raindrops from last night's storm. You loved the fact that I could grow lemons. It was the most exotic thing you could think of, coming from the flat plains of Poland, where the snow could come up to your waist and there were still horse-pulled sleds when you were young.

You never told the world what really happened to you. Your courage. Your decision to brave it out with the Nazis. What they did to you, a beautiful Jewish girl of fifteen, too beautiful to kill, too smart to be wasted in the fields. How they mutilated you. How you fooled them. How you survived. Can you give me that permission?

You have a great-granddaughter now, did you know? My daughter has a baby girl. She doesn't look like me, but she's strong and has brown eyes like you and I do. Your great-granddaughter's middle name is in your honor, and the life-thread goes on.

Love,
Zara

Chapter I

My name is Zara. I was born Zara Persil. Now I'm Zara Persil-Pendleton. In college I said that Zara was short for Zarathustra. That's the kind of pedant I was.

While ostensibly I've followed my husband Sam on his sabbatical to New York City, I've really come to New York to find my mother. She's been dead for three years and her restless spirit plagues me with newsreel-style visions, jumpy, crackling, terrifying. My mother haunts me because I failed her, failed her in the way the world failed her, although with the best of intentions. I just don't know yet how I failed and how I could have done otherwise, but still she haunts me, and she will, I'm certain, until I figure it out. Too late to save her in any case, but maybe I can appease that wandering spirit, and do right by her.

My sister, Lilly, lives in Katonah, one of the more northern suburbs of New York City. Lilly's a middle-school teacher. She's far taller, far more buxom, vastly more stylish than I am. She also has Anne-Frank eyes, not the hard ones I got. Even as she nears sixty she's got thick almost-black hair to the middle of her back. Sure, Lady Clairol helps, but you can't entirely fake this. She's got mile-long legs too. She considers it her life's work to make the most of her looks, and, as an extra-credit project, to make the most of mine as well.

Three weeks after we move here, my own daughter Angie comes to visit with her daughter, my perfect granddaughter Meghan Johanna.

New York City is an amazing place with a four-year-old. Blasé from her own urban environment in San Francisco, Meghan takes most things in stride, but she's amazed at all the yellow taxis and the hot dog vendors. Now that Angie and Meghan are here, Lilly and I make elaborate plans to show them the town.

"You going to actually wear that, Zara?" my sister says as we get ready to leave the apartment.

"No, I'm just trying it on before putting it on the Halloween scarecrow."

"Pull your hair higher on your head. It'll make you look ten years younger."

"If I pull it any higher it will break off."

"Have you tried a keratin rinse?" Lilly says, easily casting her eyes over the top of my head.

"Have you tried balancing your checkbook?" I reply.

After we cover Central Park, the Disney Store, and the trash chute near the elevator, Lilly and I take my daughter and granddaughter to visit the Jewish Studies Museum. I'm surprised by Meghan's excitement at the prospect, until I realize she's excited about going to a "juice museum". They're showing "Treasures of Lost Poland: A Retrospective". We spend some time looking at the older items in the regular collection, and eventually make our way upstairs to the Retrospective. And there it is. I feel a shimmer in the air around me, a chill that's somehow warm and also, somehow, green. My body tenses, my gut flutters. I feel the coolness of the glass as if I were touching it. And I hear my mother's voice: *That was mine.*

———— ·⊹⸦❖⸧⊹· ————

When I was twenty-one I lived at home with my parents for a year, in the toney suburb they'd moved to when they left Manhattan for the third time. In addition to my job teaching English as a Second

Language at the local high school, where I was propositioned daily ("Hey Miss Pencil, you wanna go out into the parking lot and fuck?" "No, I want to stay inside and work on punctuation.") I also kept my mother company. It was in that year that I really became close with her. She had suffered a blood clot, and though it was a serious situation she felt fine, and her doctor recommended frequent long walks once the immediate danger had passed.

We went to the Bronx Zoo, we went *plein air* painting — she painted, I glowered and flipped off people who shouted things from the road — and we went to the Jewish Studies Museum in Manhattan.

I'd never even heard of the Jewish Studies Museum, but I followed along dutifully when she suggested it. We took the train into Manhattan, and because she was supposed to walk we strolled up Fifth Avenue, looking in the windows of the fashionable stores, until the stores petered out, and the gorgeous old houses began; then we cabbed it the rest of the way to a small building across from Central Park. This was in the late seventies, and it was the first time I'd ever encountered a security check at a museum. Usually prickly about her privacy, my mother handed her bag over without a word, allowing it to be opened and all of its contents examined. I followed suit, and filed away the memory. It was still dangerous, in my mother's mind, to be Jewish.

I followed her as we acknowledged various exhibits: clothing, jewelry, dioramas of "real Jewish life". She evidently had a specific purpose, though, one that she had not disclosed to me, but these outings were for her health so I didn't ask a lot of questions. We took the elevator up to the third floor, stairs not being included in the doctor's walking prescription. Here was a display of Jewish ceremonial paraphernalia, including plates and cups ornately worked in silver and gold, bejeweled and carved; and menorahs, candlesticks, oil lamps, and bowls for ritual hand-washing. As we walked along looking at the dazzling display, my mother pointed out workmanship details.

Then she stopped in front of a glass case containing a menorah. The hand-lettered placard said, "Hanukkiah. Poland. Circa 1930."

"This is what I wanted to show you," she said. I knew there had been a reason. "You see that? My family had one."

"A menorah?"

"A menorah exactly like that one. See that turquoise enameling? That's a lost technique. No one does that anymore. See the pattern? It's like your ring." I was wearing the family ring, worked in blue enamel.

I looked at the ring she had given me when I was eleven. It had tiny gold stars and planets orbiting a seed pearl in a sky of turquoise blue. The pattern was repeated on the menorah. "We had one just like that one," she said for the third time. She put her hand up to the glass case, her lips parted.

The penny finally dropped. "Do you think it's yours?"

We were both very quiet. Finally, she said, "I don't know how it could be. It's here in the museum. I would never — "

"We should tell them," I said.

She shook her head. I knew why: If we told *them*, we would be telling *them* that she was Jewish. And even thirty years after the end of the war, she couldn't do that.

I should have taken her hand. I should have embraced her. I should have marched up to the museum's head and told him that it was our menorah. Mom still had her hand on the glass, not quite touching the only piece of her past she had seen since coming to America. It was there, on the other side of that barrier, and I failed her.

I didn't put my hand on hers, I didn't suggest that she sketch it or paint it, I didn't suggest that we ask Dad to offer to buy it. In fact, none of these things even occurred to me. I only thought *No, then they would know.*

"It must have been a pretty stylish pattern," I said instead. "Number One in Vogue for Menorahs." As usual when things got serious, I made a joke. She nodded, and I thought she looked relieved as her armor sealed up again.

I never told Lilly about that visit with our mother to the museum, and I never told anyone about the menorah. Now we're standing in front of it and my mother is speaking to me from the grave.

• ⪢◆⟨●⟩◆⪡ •

"I'm going to get it back," I say. The shimmering diffuses and is gone.

"Get what?" Lilly says.

I snap towards her — I've almost forgotten she's there. She raises a perfect black eyebrow.

"You see that menorah?" I say to Lilly and Angie. "The small, carved gold one, with the beautiful turquoise insets? It's ours."

"How do you know it's ours?" Angie asks.

"What's ours?" At four, Meghan is at the parroting-everything-she-hears stage.

"That menorah thingy," Angie says.

"Don't say *thingy*," I chide.

"Don't dodge the question, Mom. What do you mean, *ours?*"

Lilly and I exchange cautionary glances. The habits of secrecy die hard, in the form of never giving your real name, and extends to not wanting to tell my own daughter. But I do. "Your grandma told me."

"What, in a dream?"

"No. I saw this menorah with her more than thirty years ago."

"Uh, they change the exhibits, Mom. They don't keep stuff for thirty years."

"I know that, Angie, but this is a retrospective. They're showing pieces from a previous exhibit, thirty years ago. And I came here with your grandma, and she...she showed it to me."

"So, this was Grandma's?"

I nod — I'm relieved that she believes me. "You see my ring, the pattern on it? It's the same one, and I guess it's unique. She recognized it, and brought me to see it. But your grandma was too scared to ask for it back."

"Why was she scared?" Angie asks. "Grandma was so brave, what could she be afraid of?"

"We should forget it," I say, almost reflexively, certainly defensively. Lilly comes to my rescue. "The war made people afraid of so much, Angie." She looks at the menorah, and I see her own hand come up to touch the glass.

"She was braver than anyone I've ever met," I say.

"Oh, Mom, I know that. She was super-brave in the war. But I also know that it really messed her up," Angie says, trailing her own fingers on the glass case. "It blocked her off from the world for the rest of her life ever after."

That's a long speech for Angie. Angie's a gal of few words. I want to hug her, but of course I don't. I don't do public affection displays. I touch her hand instead. But Lilly suffers from no such self-restraint, and she pulls Angie into her big embrace. Angie grins at me from behind Lilly's bear hug. I shrug. Now I have to be brave. I can't let Angie down.

"Come on, you guys. There's a time and place for everything." I take one last look at the menorah, its tiny stars and planets of gold in a turquoise sky swirling up and around each candle-holder, with little seed pearls on the central *shamas* candlestick. *That's mine*, I hear again. I shiver. "We'll come back. Let's go home to the apartment and make some dinner."

"Gramma was a super-hero," Meghan says, and takes my hand. "Can we see the juice now?"

"You need to see *The Lady in Gold*," my sister says. "It's all about getting the art back."

"Or *Monuments Men*," my daughter chimes in.

"I hate movies," I say.

"We know."

"I'll read the books." I can see the eye-rolls, even with my back turned.

I'm making kasha with pork chops. Yes, I know. *Treyf.* But we don't care. You take thin pork chops, brown them in a little olive oil, take them out, sauté onions until golden, add powdered thyme, and a can of beer. Salt and pepper the chops, put them back in the pan and cook them slowly until the chops are super tender. If the beer's bitter, add some more salt and some broth. If the sauce is thin, thicken a little with flour. Serve with kasha.

I got my mother's cooking gene. "I'm not a kitchen patriot," she'd say. She would cook any style, from any country. And she'd cook pork. No shellfish, though. For that, you eat out.

⁕ ⁑ ⦁❖⦁ ⁑ ⁕

My mother's name was Aurora Judita. Named for the dawn. Not a common name for a woman born in Poland in 1927, and definitely not for a Jewish woman born anywhere in the twenties. It may have saved her life, and it also may be why my sister and I have such unusual names for girls born in the conformist Fifties, when being *average* was the goal for anyone not connected with our family. We never went in for the grey flannel suit. The red feather fascinator, maybe.

My mother had a complex / rich / unknown / unknowable / vibrant and probably terrifying inner life, but her exterior was pure Chanel. Her war-ravaged beauty had hardened into crystal and been draped in silk by my doting, jealous father. But crystal cracks, and sometimes the hot, angry liquid leaked out and caught her family in its sticky trap before hardening again, this time with pieces of our lives frozen in amber.

In photos she was an inscrutable beauty. If the camera doesn't lie, it is still an unreliable narrator, never showing you what's behind the lens or inside the subject, and here the subject herself existed only to hide. I avoid pictures from back then, from the time before Manhattan. There's too intense a feeling of loss in those old photos.

When Aurora lost her mind in the end, into the sticky web of Alzheimer's, we grieved the loss of her intelligence, as she had allowed it to define her. We certainly didn't regret her loss of her own memories; in fact, we felt that was possibly the only consolation. That her heart was laid bare by the crazed cracks of her crystalline armor didn't console us either, and her fierce love of us, now on naked display, scared the crap out of us. Now in her death she approaches me, when I can no longer fight her off, and demands her due.

Aurora loved to cook turkey. Once, when we were small and lived in an apartment building in Nuevo Laredo, we kept a turkey on the rooftop. At Thanksgiving, she wrung its neck. With her small, graceful artist-hands she twisted that sucker to death. "I used to compete with them for food," she said. It looks like she won.

Once Angie and Meghan go back to San Francisco, I'll read the books about heroic efforts to get Jewish art back home. Meanwhile, there's a big city to explore, and while they are still here I can hope that Mom's restless spirit stays quiet.

Chapter 2

My sister's name isn't really Lilly, it's Lilliana, named for my grandmother. She was spared being actually named Leokadia, which was my grandmother's real name. Lord help us, middle school was hard enough.

Ah, Lilly. Lilliana, Leokadia, Leah. Lilly took Leah as her Hebrew name one day on a plane as she was flying back from finalizing her first divorce. Seated next to a wigged Orthodox woman, Lilly poured her heart out, telling this total stranger in absurdly unstylish clothes how Mark had done her wrong, had ignored her to the point where Lilly had no choice but to have a torrid affair with a twenty-one year old photographer, had goaded her into putting his bicycle and tools out on the lawn in the rain, along with his work clothes and his typewriter — this was a while ago — and the notes to his dissertation, and how he had gotten the car in the divorce. How that resulted in her acknowledging her Jewishness or choosing her name is still a mystery, but Leah is a good choice for Lilly. Never loved by her husbands, bearer of many sons, scorned by her parents in favor of her blonde and semi-infertile younger sister, yes, Leah suited her just fine.

Lilly's had it hard in life, not that being me is a bed of roses. When I had trouble getting and staying pregnant, Mom was less than sympathetic, even despite her own terrible loss. *I don't know where you get that from. All a man had to do was hang his pants over the end of my bed and I got pregnant.*

Why the obsession with names? Because names were one of the talismanic ways my mother used to keep us safe when we were born. Growing up on both sides of the border of Mexico and Texas, sometimes in Nuevo Laredo, sometimes off of Loop 410 in San Antonio, the other way we stayed safe was to never mention the fact that we were Jewish.

We were not only Jewish, we were a very special kind of Jewish: the kind that descended from Jews who fled Spain and Portugal during the Inquisition but didn't go to Morocco, Amsterdam, or the New World. No, our contrarian, non-conformist ancestors went to Poland. There they were welcomed by the king, who promised that if they converted to Christianity they would be given land, but if they didn't, they would still be allowed to remain as artisans and workers in precious metals. Some of my ancestors actually owned land.

We have Spanish eyes. My mother once asked me if I thought she had intelligent eyes. I remember looking at them and saying, "Yes. Intelligent and hard." Those hard eyes, rather than the liquid brown Ashkenazi eyes, also saved her life.

This outpouring of recognition of reality comes late in life for me. There were decades when I couldn't even say the word *Jewish*, never mind associate with it. I can recite the entire Latin Mass, I speak fluent Spanish, I consider myself bi-cultural Latina, even though I have only remote Spanish ancestors.

I actually have a Hebrew name. It's Zachrona. It's not a real name, but again, my parents weren't into traditional names. It's a form of "I remembered." Lilly may also have had an original Hebrew name, but no one can remember it.

My mother was a Holocaust survivor. It took me decades to be able to even say those words: *My mother was a Holocaust survivor.* And I'll say it now any way I want to: whether sufficiently reverently or not, or with a broken heart. She's gone, and it is my name's commandment to remember.

Lilly calls in the middle of the night. I answer with my heart in my mouth. "Sorry, I forgot about the time difference," she says.

"There's no time difference. I'm here, remember?"

"I know. That's what I meant."

"Jesus Christ, Lilly. It's after midnight. What are you doing up?" No use going over the time issue.

"I couldn't sleep, so I thought I'd natter with you. It used to be nine, remember, when it was midnight here? You were the only one I could call. And that damn cat of yours would yowl into the phone while we talked. Tiger-balm, we miss you! I guess I got used to it."

"Take a Xanax."

"I'd rather have a drink."

"Have a drink then."

"I don't sleep since Mother died."

"I sleep better now that she has," I say.

"Zara…"

"Sorry. But it's true. All the years of waiting for the phone to ring, *ready* for the phone to ring. I would dream that my text went off and I'd have to check my phone to see if it was true. Now I sleep fine."

I don't really. But I don't call people up at midnight to "natter".

"Did I wake Sam?"

"No, he doesn't go to bed until three." I'm married to a night owl. At home we hardly share a room anymore anyway, so even if he went to bed when I did he wouldn't hear the phone. Here, most nights he unfolds the sofa bed when Lilly isn't staying over. Lilly doesn't know that Sam and I sleep apart. No big deal, it's just that he snores like a freight train. He's louder than old Tiger-balm was, may he rest in cat-peace. Lilly'd understand, but I don't want to give her the satisfaction. I'm the one who was lucky in love. The Rachel to her Leah.

"I'll let you go back to sleep."

"It's okay, I'm awake now anyway. And I don't have an early day at work." Since I don't have any work.

"I was thinking about the menorah. Or what did you call it? The Hanukkahya?"

"*Hanukkiah*. Menorah for Hanukkah. Me too."

"I wrote down the name of the people who lent it to the collection," Lilly says. "The card said, *On loan from the collection of the Lev Zimmerman family*. I think we should contact them."

"Oh, sure. Call them. Write to them and offer to buy it. Just say, *hey, we liked your menorah and would like to have it*."

"Why not tell them it's ours?"

"Because if they don't hang up on the spot, if they'll even consider a sale, they'll raise the price. They'll realize we *really, really* want it."

I can hear Lilly's mind turning this over. "You think so? I think they'll just give it to us."

I shake my head. "You're so innocent sometimes."

"You always have to make a joke out of things," Lilly says to me.

"That's because if I don't laugh I'll cry."

"Maybe you should cry. Have an honest emotion sometime."

I much prefer not to. "Maybe the world doesn't have to know every emotion that flits by my tender heart," I reply. "Facebook doesn't make enough emoticons for me to have a proper public emotion. I don't see a *smiles sarcastically* face, do you?"

But we're really close. So close that we know exactly how to trigger one another. So close that we don't.

I blink. "I see mom's ghost," I say into the phone. I hear Lilly's sharp intake of breath and I add, "She's an extremely well-dressed visiting ghost." I omit the terror-inducing crackling visions that leave me shaking and sweating and starving for the truth.

"My god, Zara."

"Yeah. So, yeah. We need to get it back. I think . . . I think this time I'll finish what Mom was really asking me to do thirty years ago at the Jewish Studies Museum."

"I'm right there with you," Lilly says.

Of course Lilly's going to help me because after all, if it's my quest, it's hers. And no one does a quest like Lilly.

The next morning, I wait for Sam to leave, and then I start looking up the potential owners on the internet. There are quite a few Lev Zimmermans in New York City alone. And there's no reason to think that the owners even live in the City, so I use other criteria to narrow my search. I ignore the grocer in midtown and several of the Lower East Side types based on their Facebook profiles. No one that young owns, never mind lends, a collection of Judaica to the Jewish Studies Museum. I narrow it down to an art collector, a lawyer, two rabbis, and someone whose occupation I can't discern but he seems to have connections to a large and evidently prosperous congregation near Newark, New Jersey.

For some reason, I'm embarrassed to be looking. I don't want Sam to see me looking into the menorah. Some remnant of fear, or maybe it's shame, clings to me. He's a good man, and he'd probably have some great ideas for figuring out who the owner is, but I don't want to ask.

Sam is completely enmeshed in his sabbatical. At home, he's a professor of economics, but since the last election he's also been part of the Coalition for Electoral Rights, known colloquially and on blogs all across the country as the Rights Coalition. It's a supposedly non-partisan group that ensures access to voting, but operates almost like a private CIA. His Rights Coalition's real mission is to fight the slow destruction of democracy by infiltrating shadowy organizations that create fake social media personas, following big money sources to off-shore accounts, and dismantling the structures from within. After spending the last three years working almost day and night, teaching at the university by day and working most nights for his Rights Coalition, he's gotten a teaching sabbatical at Columbia University. The Rights Coalition got a lot of press at the end of last year, and he and his colleagues had to go underground for a bit, so this move could not have come at a better time.

The change of venue has also helped Sam worry less about me. I have been plagued with my mother's memories, to the point where they've become an obsession. Sam encouraged me to do yoga, meditate, see a shrink, and even take martial arts classes, all to manage the fact that the memories have become more real to me sometimes than my own work and home. All of his encouragement has been lovely, but I think his own preoccupation with the current state of our government has warped his perspective. Sam is sure that coming to New York will *get me out of myself.* If he only knew.

I'm a legal investigator. Not the kind that tracks down criminals or sleuths out fraud, but the kind that gathers facts for basic employment and insurance claims. My career is pretty transferable, but the work sources aren't. I've got a law degree, and I can investigate workplace discrimination complaints anywhere, since I don't actually practice law, but the business is built on referrals and I don't really know anyone in New York anymore. I've been gone for over three decades.

But one of the real delights of being in New York is the luxury of seeing Lilly whenever I want. She's almost like a twin conjoined at my arm, or some other form of attachment. We've seen each other almost daily since I got here. The sabbatical comes with an apartment on 94th and Madison, which is the Upper East Side, even though Columbia is on the other side of Central Park. We're a short subway ride from Grand Central Station, and three blocks from the Jewish Studies Museum.

Most of my time has been spent unpacking, figuring out where I can buy groceries, and pretending to look for work. The groceries are the same challenge they are in every big city, with bodegas and mini-marts on every corner, but real grocery stores, with multiple fresh produce aisles, are hidden under buildings and behind offices, and getting your food home requires biceps of steel or a taxi. Finding work is easier, as in easier to give up on.

Lilly gets here around ten, bearing bagels. They're smaller and denser that the California version, and actually have a taste.

"Why would so many mothers want to name their sons Lev?" I say as Lilly and I look over the list.

"Trotsky."

"Trotsky?"

"Yeah. Leon Trotsky. You know. Russian. Communist. Horror show."

"No, I know who Leon Trotsky was." We're almost sixty and she acts like I'm twelve, so I sound like I'm twelve when I say it.

"Well, Lev is Russian for Leon, more or less. Trotsky's given name was Lev."

Lilly knows all things Russian. My mother used to say that she was the only one in the family ever to go to Russia voluntarily. My mother spoke Russian almost fluently. Add that to the list of things that saved her life. Lilly speaks better Russian than my mother did, but it never did *her* a bit of good.

"Still," I say, "unless the guy was born in the twenties, who the hell would name their kid after Trotsky?"

"In Russia they would have. He was a big hero then, and besides, they might think it would help them blend in."

My mother took a typical Polish Christian name, Zosia Warszawska, when she walked out of the Ghetto into occupied, but non-Jewish Warsaw. Not that *Aurora* would have given her away, but a girl named Zosia, the common nickname for Sofia, wouldn't stand out. For once in her life she needed to be average. Maybe Lev's parents wanted the same for him.

* ⊰•◦◦•⊱ *

The windows of the apartment face west and the afternoon light is streaming in. The furniture, most of it streamlined early-modern-and-angular, most of it not ours, takes on a golden glow. Lilly is on the sofa with her laptop, and her dark hair flows like obsidian. She's wearing a long burgundy sweater over leggings that make her legs look endless. She tucks those gams under herself and peers at the screen.

"Was that the same name on the card when you saw it with Mother?"

"That was over a quarter of a century ago," I say.

"I would have remembered." That's true. She would have.

"I guess we need to contact all of them." I can't believe we're going to do this, but I've *promised* my mother. At the moment in the museum it seemed inevitable, in the middle of the night it seemed right, but now it's also ludicrous.

We consider email versus snail mail for the three out of five Lev Zimmermans I was able to find on LinkedIn. "Email's more impersonal," I say, "but it's also quicker."

"We can write on beautiful stationery," Lilly says. "Dear Lev, we crave your menorah. Please give us your menorah, and we'll be forever grateful. Love, the Persil sisters."

"Our emails could go straight to spam, along with other life-enhancers. *Lev! Grow your menorah! Just send two boxtops… Don't disappoint Mrs. Zimmerman! Super-size your menorah today!*"

"Uh, didn't we want to buy it?" Lilly says, wiping her eyes.

"Oh yeah, I forgot."

We settle on email for the ones whose emails we have. "Dear Mr. Zimmerman. Our family immigrated from Poland after World War II, leaving behind everything that they held dear."

"No," Lilly says. "That sounds a little too Nigerian Prince."

"Yeah, and besides it should be *emigrated.* Try again: 'We saw the beautiful collection of Judaica at the Jewish Studies Museum, including the Hanukkiah that your family so generously lent to the exhibit. We immediately felt a connection to the menorah, and would like to know if you would consider selling it.'"

"I guess that's straightforward," Lilly says, "but I'd still want to put in that we think it came from our family."

"That sounds like blackmail. In *Monuments Men* it was looters who took the art, Nazi looters. Wouldn't this imply that we think Zimmerman's a criminal?"

"You've got a point. Besides, all we have is your memory," she grimaces, "and Mother's word."

"No," I say. "Mom recognized it, and so do I."

"How can you recognize it?"

"The ring, dummy." I show her my ring. It's been on my pinky for almost fifty years. "See the pattern? I thought you saw it when I showed you the menorah."

Lilly squints at my ring. She's been squinting a lot. She looks at it from the side.

"Look," I say, frustrated, "get your reading glasses. The pattern. The two planets, one on top and one on the bottom, and the four stars. In the turquoise enamel. They don't do turquoise enamel like that anymore."

"Okay," she says.

"Moving on. So, *Poland after World War II*. Put the part about emigrating after *exhibit*. Mom's family must have had such beautiful things. It must have been horrible to lose it all. Before they started losing their lives, of course."

"Really, Zara. Don't be flippant."

"I'm not. You know, at first they really must have thought that they were going to just have to live a more narrow life, not that they were going to lose everything, and then starve, and then be taken away. It's gradual, you know? And then, one day, you realize that it's never going to be over."

"Or that it's totally over."

"Her father was going to take them to Switzerland," I say, as Lilly sets the table.

"Yeah, but he got sick. His kidneys failed and they didn't go. Mother told me."

I feel the usual jealousy. "Mom never told me anything. At least not about that. The only person who ever told me anything was Dad."

Lilly busies herself with folding napkins. She never talks about Dad. He's now in the category of what we don't talk about. The war. The Holocaust. The baby. Dad.

"I suppose Mom's father was our grandfather, but I never think of him that way. Mom's dad was a socialist," I say to distract myself from my own faux pas.

"Dad hated me," Lilly says.

I can't find an answer to that.

Chapter 3

Lilly tells me to meet her in front of the clock at Grand Central Terminal. It's still a thrill to be here, after living in California for more than thirty years. I look up at the sparkling gold-painted constellations in a sea of aqua so like my ring. And the menorah. I seek out Orion in the great green-blue dome. Looking up leaves me feeling a little dizzy and I reach back and steady myself against the metal schedule display. A man in a dark green windbreaker puts his hand on my arm. "Steady there, lady," he says. I smile my thanks and check my bag for my wallet as soon as he's passed by.

I leave my post in search of the restroom, and find one on the lower level, where the food court is. A gaggle of fifteen-year-old girls is blocking the entrance, long straight hair gleaming against the faux-fur edging of their jacket hoods, ignoring the derelict peeing against the WET FLOOR cone outside the men's room, the last three yards to a more conventional urinal somehow uncrossable.

I dry my hands next to a sign in red and black: No Bathing, No Laundry, No Changing of Clothes, No Smoking. It brings to mind the poems I used to write. My mother even painted some of my poems, before life got too serious for serendipitous pleasures, before I left for California for good. Where are those paintings of poems now, the words swirling on lacquered crumpled crepe paper, granting the words an intensity I hadn't given them? Probably at the dump, along with everything else Dad got rid of when he sold the apartment, when Mom got sick.

I return to the clock, and the people swirl by as I stand against the kiosk, a rock in the river. So many people, all with someplace to go. I watch the women especially. Women dragging heavy suitcases down or up the stairs; women clicking by on thin-heeled boots; I'm looking to see what's being worn. My mother used to say that: *what's being worn.* I never really can tell.

Lilly comes in from Katonah on the train. I'm the one living uptown, in the sleek apartment this time, though she's the New Yorker and I'm the West Coast transplant. Lilly always knows what's being worn, and today she's determined to help me wear what's being worn. I'm dreading it.

All my life Lilly's had a thing about how bad my clothes are. Mom had a thing about clothes. It seems everything in New York is related to my mother. I went three years after her death never thinking about her, at least not more than two, three times a week. Now in New York I seem to see her everywhere, in every stylish woman, in the street artist, the blonde girl in the grey pea-coat singing an aria in the tunnel in Central Park — though my mother never sang in Central Park, Lord help us.

"Remember the trips to the dressmaker?" my sister asks as we head to the stores. My mother used to take us to the dressmaker in Nuevo Laredo every season for a new dress.

"God, yes. I was never more miserable."

Lilly grabs my arm as I venture into the crosswalk, saving me from a bicyclist who would have smashed my legs with his wheels. "Don't they have to stop?" I ask.

"The dressmaker visits were the high point of my life," Lilly says. "I always felt so sophisticated."

"I felt itchy."

"Mother used to tell me about her trips to the dressmaker when they were still in Lodz," Lilly says. "Before the disastrous move to Warsaw. She used to go four times a year, at the beginning of each season. She and her mother would get entire new outfits for the seasons."

"Leokadia," I say. "I guess the fashion sense got passed down with the name." We never call Leokadia *grandmother* because we never knew her. "I think they could have survived if they'd stayed in Lodz."

"Who knows," Lilly says, pulling me into a boutique. It's no more than a narrow storefront, stretching far back into the brightly lit distance, but unlike a San Francisco boutique which might feature two perfectly styled mannequins in stark designs, here the shelves along the walls are crammed with every imaginable weave of sweater, cut of blouse, drape of jacket and scarf.

Lilly pulls down a heavenly-soft black sweater with flowing sleeves and a deep, almost navel-grazing V neck. "Look. See this sweater? You can wear it with anything."

I finger it. We're all allergic to wool: my mother, my sister, me, my daughter, my granddaughter. The sweater's something other than wool. I check the label. Angora. "It's rabbit," I say, putting it back on the shelf. "Who wears rabbits?"

"You eat them, don't you?"

I pull a brown fluffy sweater down and hold it up against myself. "Where did you find that?" Lilly says.

"Top shelf."

"Amazing. You can't even see up there, never mind reach, and you manage to find the only earth-toned sweater in all of Manhattan." She takes the sweater from me, folds it expertly, and replaces it up where I can't get it. "Try this instead."

"Do people wear anything other than black here?"

"A pair of red heels and you're set."

"I don't wear heels," I say.

"Neither do I," she admits. "Now that I don't mind being six feet tall in heels, I can't wear them anymore. But you should."

I pay for the black sweater and we head back out into the cool air. I can smell pizza over the steady down-notes of exhaust and pee that make up the city's perfume. "Wasn't that easy?" Lilly says.

We go into a Starbucks for coffee. It looks like Starbucks everywhere. They probably don't need to pay for heat: hundreds of laptops provide all the light and warmth necessary. "Remember when we'd go into the City to Christmas shop and stop in a Chock full o'Nuts? Remember how freaking cold it was?"

"It still gets that cold," Lilly says, "but now we can get decent coffee."

"It was decent to us."

We settle into our own lattes, mine made with almond milk. "Any answers to the emails?" Lilly asks. She licks the foam from the wooden stirrer.

I shake my head. "One bounced, one of the rabbis. We should check if I got the address wrong. Otherwise nothing."

"You'll have to find phone numbers, call them."

"Why me?"

"Well, for one thing, you're not working. For another, this was all your idea."

"I am too working. It's just slow. And you're not working either. At least not every day."

"Let's call them after we get done shopping."

I groan. "I thought we *were* done."

Back at the apartment, I make a cup of coffee for myself with my new automatic coffee maker, and watch the little pod make its Rube-Goldberg descent into the used pod holder. I offer Lilly tea.

"It's after four, Zara. Make me a drink."

I pull a bottle of Domaine Eden Cabernet out of the cabinet. Sam likes good wine, so we have some pretty nice bottles. I can tolerate about a glass a week. "Wine?"

Lilly nods, staring at the laptop screen. I manage with the cork-screw and pour her a glass.

"Have one with me," she says, not expecting an answer. "Okay, here's a phone number for the rabbi."

"Why don't we wait and see if the others answer?" I say.

"Chicken."

"Rabbit."

"Angora."

"Turkey."

She laughs and spills a little wine on the oatmeal-colored carpet. "Shit, Lilly," I say. "Now we'll never get our security deposit back." I put some club soda on it and dab it with a paper towel. "Look!"

Lev the Lawyer has answered our email. "Ms. Persil, I regret that I'm not the owner of the menorah you mentioned in your email. It sounds beautiful. Good luck finding its owner. And by the way, I believe you may have better luck going through the museum rather than sending out random emails to people. There are a lot of Zimmermans in New York. Best, Lev Zimmerman."

"Uh, duh. I guess we should have thought of that."

"Let's call the rabbi anyway," Lilly says. "He might be single."

Before I can chicken out, I grab my cell phone. "Should I block my number?" I ask.

"Naw. If you do, he won't answer."

I punch in the number and wait. It rings six times and goes to voicemail. "The mailbox is full. Goodbye."

"Loser."

We craft an email to the museum. We had seen the exhibit on its last day, but that had been only two weeks ago — so it would be reasonable for the curator to know which menorah I was talking about. I look up the possible staff and find the most likely candidate. *Hello, Ms. Goldberg. I visited the "Treasures of Lost Poland" exhibit two weeks ago and was struck by the beauty of the enameled hanukkiah from the collection of the Lev Zimmerman family. My sister and I are*

curious to know more about the object, its history and provenance.
Could we make an appointment to speak with you, either in person or
by phone? Zara Persil-Pendleton.

"Let's call the others," Lilly says after her third glass of wine.

"Sam will be home soon," I say. "I need to get dinner on."

"You've been here six weeks," Lilly replies. "Don't you know how
to order out yet?" She clicks on the computer a bit. "Give me your
credit card." I hand it over. "Done. Chinese in thirty minutes."

Sam's not crazy about Chinese food.

It turns out not to matter. I get a text, he'll be home really late, eat
without him. I text back that Lilly's over and she ordered Chinese.
"So it all worked out," he texts back. I guess...

Lilly's on her cell phone. "Can I speak with Lev, please? ...Lilly
Persil." She covers the little hole where the voice goes in and says to
me, "The wife, maybe?"

"Sounds old," I say. "Which one did you call?"

"Mr. Zimmerman? My name is Lilly Persil. We sent you an email
about a menorah." She listens. "Oh. Sorry. Never mind then. Sorry."

But she doesn't hang up. He's still talking. She's nodding, even
though he can't see her. Finally, she puts the phone down and hits
the speaker button. A man's voice comes through. "...So when
the committee heard about my troubles they took away my board
membership. I ask you, Mrs. Pencil, do you think that's fair? No?
No! Neither do I. They could have been more careful with their
books, I say. It was a small loan, and I was going to pay it back, no
problem. I'd paid back all of the other little loans, and in fact, one
time I paid them even more than I borrowed, because the horse
came in first. And to threaten me with the police? Me, who kept
the temple's books for fifteen years? The *police?*"

I've got my hand over my mouth so I don't guffaw. I hit *mute* just
as Lilly starts to talk. "Now, Mr. Zimmerman, that can happen to
anyone." She should know. Lilly and finances don't exactly get along.

"Are you there, Mrs. Pencil? Can you help me?"

"Come on, Lev. Get off the phone. The chairman will be here soon!" a woman says in the background.

"No, Marcia. There's a lady on the phone who'll help me. Isn't that right, Mrs. Pencil?"

Everyone calls us Pencil instead of Persil — they have since elementary school. "I'm not sure I can," Lilly says, still on mute so Zimmerman can't hear her.

I reach over to un-mute the call, but I hit *end* instead. Lilly snorts wine out her nose, just as the doorman buzzes us — the Chinese food delivery has arrived.

⊹ ⊰•◆⊃◑⊂◆•⊱ ⊹

"Three down," I say, and serve myself some tea-smoked duck.

Lilly pulls the scallops towards her. "Two, no?"

"Three, unless we find another number for the missing rabbi."

"If you're going to give up just because his voicemail's full, we'll never find this menorah. I mean, what if he owns it and we don't find it just because his email bounced and he doesn't check voicemail?"

She's right. "And it's ours. We're going to find it. Pass the scallops."

Chapter 4

It's a breezy Thursday afternoon. Lilly lets herself into the apartment with the key I gave her the second week we were here. Her cheeks are flushed from the wind and her hair is held down by a pink crocheted cap. I recognize the hat: I made it for her for the first Women's March. She's picked up the color with a pink ribbon holding back some of her dark locks, making it both a political and a fashion statement all at once. When she arrives, I'm lying on the couch with a translated version of Julio Cortázar's *Hopscotch*. I've been lazy all day, feeling guilty about being lazy, dispirited by my lack of focus.

"How did it get out?" I ask, sitting up on the sofa. Lilly knows what I mean. She always does. "If the Nazis took all the nice things the Jews had, did they take them back to Germany when they were chased out of Poland? And if so, how did the Zimmerman family end up with our menorah?" My mind has eliminated any doubt that it's ours.

"Maybe Mother's family got the best things smuggled out with someone else. Or sold things for money to eat with when her father wasn't allowed to work anymore."

"And the Zimmermans bought it? Unlikely. They'd be in desperate straits too, and besides, the Nazis would have taken their stuff too, whoever they were. Did Mom ever say anything to you about sending things out of the country with other people?"

"No."

"They must have," I said. "That's got to be how I got the ring."

I've been wearing the ring since I was eleven. The ring part is thin 10-karat gold. I know this because it's etched with that inside. It's bent where the ring goes between the fingers on both sides. The oval in front is blue enamel with veining that comes from the enameling technique. At the top and bottom are small gold circles, solid, and at the northeast, southeast, southwest and northwest are tiny gold five-pointed stars. In the center, held by gold prongs, is a tiny seed pearl. I used to think I could see where the ring had been by staring into the pearl. I've replaced the seed pearl four times as it has worn away over the years.

When I was eleven I wore it on the ring finger of my right hand. Now I wear it on the pinky of my left, next to my wedding ring. I lost it twice — once in a pile of leaves when I was twelve, and once at the beach in Lake Tahoe. Each time I found it by miracle. Mom said it was the family coat of arms, which was ludicrous, since Jews didn't have coats of arms, heraldry, or even — certainly not in Poland — the right to bear arms. Somehow the idea made her happy.

My father called Aurora royalty. Equally ludicrous, but it informed our view of her, and her projection of herself. She should have been a princess, or a queen. There was definitely something regal about Aurora.

⸺ ❖ ⸺

I twist the ring on my finger. "Okay, then how do *you* think it got out?"

"Her aunt must have taken it," Lilly says. Mom's Aunt ChaCha, Lilly informs me, was the much younger sister of my mother's father. "She left for Paris on what was supposed to be her wedding tour, in 1939. Of course, they never made it home."

"Why would she have taken it?" I ask. "And how do you know this? Did you ask her?"

Lilly has managed to track down every surviving tendril of what was once the family tree. "She's been dead for thirty years. I asked her daughter."

"She has a daughter? Like, a cousin of ours? How have I gotten to my late fifties without knowing this?"

"I told you. You said you didn't care."

That seems plausible. It's easier to face not having family if you don't care.

"Is she on Facebook?" I ask.

"Of course. Hannah Bellon."

"Wait. Seriously? Hannah Bellon is our cousin?"

Lilly puts down her book. "Get your fucking head out of the sand, Zara."

I'm shocked. Lilly never uses the f-bomb. "What's got you?"

"You've talked about nothing but this damned menorah for three weeks now, but you've never shown even a drop of interest in our family before. You know I told you about Hannah."

She did. In fact, Hannah friended me on Facebook. But I thought that she was friending me as someone who liked the same poetry sites she did, or maybe Cortázar's novels — not as family. "Hannah lives in Israel," I say.

"They have email there."

"Since when are you sarcastic?"

"Since you stuck your head in the sand or wherever. I don't get you. You always act like you're so much better than us, you're so aloof. Like Mother. You think you're some kind of, what, nobility." I feel the room shimmer, a cold, arctic blue, but Lilly goes on. "Well, we plebes down here have family."

"I don't think I've ever said anything that gives you the right to think that." Even my voice is icy.

"You don't have to. You never, ever, communicate with our cousins."

"Third cousins, or something."

"Whatever. You see?"

"Why do *you* care so much? Mom never did."

"Because they're our blood. The same genes run in our veins." I don't correct her science because the tip of her nose is reddening. "Mother thought she was better than all of them, and so do you." I can't defend myself. I don't even try. I reach for her beautiful hair, hair from Dad's side, and stroke it. Dad couldn't handle this big, beautiful black-haired daughter, who was so much like him it was terrifying. When he looked at her he looked in the mirror, only female. Why couldn't she have been the son...? I move on by force from that line of thought.

"Maybe they cut *her* out," I say. "In fact, they probably did. I know that's one reason I want the menorah. Mom wanted it, but her fear was greater than her desire. The menorah tied her to her own mother, to Leokadia, to her own past. Now it ties me to her." My throat closes but I refuse to cry.

We sit in silence for a bit longer before I get up. "I've got to start dinner." Chicken paprikás. The final *s* is pronounced as *sh*. It's Hungarian, as was our father. I make it better than anyone in our family ever did. But I use yogurt instead of sour cream, and Lilly says it makes it taste different. *Dietetic.* Sour cream upsets my stomach.

I make real dumplings with it, not noodles or rice. Lilly watches me. "You do that every night?" I know she means do I cook every night.

"Not as much now unless I've got the grand-baby. Sam works late a lot."

"I know how that is. It's hard to eat alone," she says. "Not worth cooking just for myself."

I don't want to agree with her. "No, I think we're each worth it."

"But when Sam's at work, you don't cook. You just said so."

"We go out when he gets back." I'm lying. She doesn't bother to call me out on it.

"Mother cooked every single night. Even when dad was being a jerk." She keeps bringing him up. Has he become safer to talk about than Mother?

"She said it was her job. 'Just because your father is angry doesn't mean he doesn't go to work. Just because I'm angry doesn't mean I don't cook.' Either she had an overdeveloped sense of duty or she was deep into depersonalization."

"Or gratitude."

Sam comes home in time to eat with Lilly and me. I've told him about the quest, and his main reaction was that it would keep me occupied. "I was worried that Zara wouldn't have anything to do while we're in New York. Not that anyone can be bored here," he told us. I resented the condescension but I didn't say anything in front of Lilly.

He looks good, his greying hair well cut, his New York clothes fitting sharply. In my mind he never ages. "How was the lecture today?" I ask. Part of the sabbatical at Columbia is lecturing on political economics.

"These kids are super bright," he says. "It's a privilege."

"Sharper than the kids at Cal?" I ask.

He shakes his head. "It's different. They're more, I don't know...incisive. Their questions are sharper. Or maybe it's just their voices. Political studies seem more global here, and certainly more euro-centric than Asia-oriented."

"Any pretty professors?" Lilly asks. I glare at her but Sam just smiles.

"Plenty. And just the way I like them. Plenty of short Jewish professors, all smart and tough, like Zara." He winks at me. "And a few single men, too. Want me to introduce you?"

Lilly sits up straighter. "Absolutely! When? Want me to drop by your office Monday afternoon?" She almost crawls across the table onto Sam.

"Whoa, slow down! Anyway, I thought you were teaching."

"I had a leave replacement — I filled in for someone who was out on maternity, but that ended last month. Now I'm just tutoring and substituting. So I've got plenty of free time. So, shall I come by on Monday or Tuesday?"

That's Lilly. In her mind it's been decided.

"Why don't you come to the Holiday party with me and Zara instead? That way you can be all dressed up, make a great first impression."

Sam, always the politician, knows just how to smooth the waters.

Lilly goes to bed early, the holdover of decades of being a middle-school teacher, up at the crack of dawn. She's staying the night; her neighbor has fed and walked her dog for her again. She sleeps on the fold-out in the living room, so Sam and I retreat into the bedroom. It's as large as the living room is small, and I've arranged two good chairs under two good reading lamps, along with a work table and a little bookshelf under the window. I look out at the night sky, greyish-yellow from city lights. Below, the thick river of cabs has thinned to a steady trickle. "Are there really lots of pretty professors?" I say.

He looks up from the paper. "Of course. And beautiful students too. I could go to jail for thinking half the things I think at the university. But that shouldn't make you jealous."

"I'm not jealous," I say, and I think I'm sort of not.

"How's the quest going?" he asks with a little smile. Again I resent the implied condescension, but truthfully, it's become my whole focus.

"We're kind of stymied. No answers to our emails to the Lev Zimmermans of this world, and nothing from the museum, either. I know what the next step is, but I'm hesitant."

"What's the next step?"

"We need to go to the museum, corner the curator in her lair. And maybe actually go and knock on the various Lev Zimmermans' doors. It's much easier to do things by email, but as I know so well, personal interviews are so much more effective in an investigation."

"Speaking of which, any work?"

I shake my head. "It's all in the connections. I don't know that many employment lawyers out here, so I can't get the referrals. Big surprise, right?"

Sam gets up and comes back with his wine glass refilled. "You don't need to do investigations here, you know. The sabbatical plus the rent from the house more than covers everything."

In fact, the rent from our California house covers my full salary — that's how crazy things are in California now. And the university pays our rent here. "Net, we're making money," I say. I haven't really tried hard to get work, and Sam knows it.

"Then concentrate on the quest," he says, going back to his paper.

I pick up the crossword puzzle. One of the benefits of living in New York is getting the Sunday Times puzzle the week it's released, not the following week. "My mom used to do the Sunday Times puzzle," I say.

"I know."

"But it was in a foreign language for her."

"Yeah," Sam says, immersed in his article. "Amazing."

"This quest is bringing up all kinds of stuff," I say.

Sam glances up. "Like…?"

"Well, it turns out that Lilly and I know almost nothing about our family history. How can that be?"

He puts down the paper. "*You* don't know much. Lilly does."

Even Sam has noticed. I defend my ignorance. "She doesn't really, though. There are things my mom told me that she never told Lilly. And my dad never told Lilly tons of things he told me. Not that he was the most reliable narrator," I add.

"He may have told them from his point of view, but he didn't lie," Sam said.

"True." I sit quietly, looking at my puzzle. Sam looks at his paper. But we're both tuned to one another. "Everything here reminds me of Mom."

"That's the whole point, isn't it? You're meant to be here."

Chapter 5

I make coffee for us. Lilly is reading the morning paper, Sam is looking at his phone. I serve the coffees and pull out scones from the oven. I put them on the table, and open a jar of Sarabeth's lemon curd. I adore Sarabeth's. I want to live in their restaurant, but instead, I get to live a block from it. I buy their lemon curd and reheat their scones.

"Any raspberry jam?" Lilly asks. I put that out too. "So, what should we do today?" she asks between mouthfuls. "Call the museum?"

"It's closed. Shabbat."

"Sabbath," Lilly translates unnecessarily for Sam. He probably knows more Hebrew than she does. "You don't have to say Shabbat, you know," she says to me. "You can still speak English, even if you've gone all Jewy on us."

"What do you mean by that?" I say, irritated. I know perfectly well what she means. Ever since I did my bat mitzvah, or *became a bat mitzvah*, more correctly said, at the age of fifty-three, Lilly's been teasing me. I figured if an entire generation died for this, it had to be worth preserving. On the other hand, the same might have been said about the Confederacy, and look where that got us.

Still, I had done it. I'd learned Hebrew, studied the Torah, become acquainted with all of the rituals, both liturgical and secular, that set our people apart. While my bond to my ancestors strengthened, I also began to see how the eccentricity of some of the customs made our presence in everyone else's countries anathema.

And they certainly irritated the daylights out of Lilly.

"Inconvenient to have Shabbat on a Saturday," Sam says. "Well, I'm going over to the university. Plenty going on there. You two have fun."

Part of me wants to kick Lilly out so I can offer to go with Sam. If I suggest it now, she'll want to go along, meet some *cute professor* type. Before I can hint, Sam's got his New York coat on. It's a long navy-blue wool coat, the type that he'd never need in California. It's November, not quite cold enough for the natives to wear that kind of coat, but he looks terrific in it. And he's not used to the cold.

As soon as he's gone Lilly gives me the look. "He's fooling around, Zara."

"That's a horrible thing to say!"

"I know the signs. God knows, I know the signs."

"Yeah, from both sides of the bed."

"Not nice, Zara."

"Oh, don't be delicate. You just said my husband is cheating on me. And I'm supposed to tiptoe around your feelings?"

"I'm saying it for your own good. I'd sure hate to be the last to know."

"Easy enough to cloak nastiness in virtue."

Lilly gathers up her stuff. "I'm going home. When you're civil I'll be back."

I don't answer. She actually leaves.

So now I'm just feeling bad. I look at my ring, and the same weird chill and green warmth come from it. I get up and make another cup of coffee, just to make the chill stop.

You just know different things.

I whirl around. I heard that, clearly, in my mother's voice. The chill is gone, the green warmth has vanished, and there's no one in the apartment but me. I can feel my heart pounding and I worry about atrial fibrillation, mitral valve problems, all the hereditary ailments that beset my mother, that lately have taken up residence in me. Mom would have said, "You never went through what I went through. You won't have the same problems," about my heart irregularities, the way she did when I had paralyzing anxiety after a lunatic attacked me with a bottle in my twenties. It cured me but fast. After all, how could one little random crime compare with an entire holocaust?

———————

I stare into the ring, into the pearl. I can feel where the ring has traveled, and the room gets dark and cold. The walls fade away and I fade away with them. I'm in a town in Europe — I know it's in Poland — and it smells like blood and horses. It's cold out but the day is sunny. I can hear my mother's voice in my bones.

Our town had stood up against the Nazis. We were only two hundred strong, but they numbered thousands. Jews and Christians fought alongside one another, resisting as the last holdout of the Poles against the invaders. No, not every Pole resisted. Only later did they learn that the conqueror they accepted wasn't like the rest of the long line of oppressors Poland had suffered. No, this particular invader took the soul with the body, wasn't content to rape and pillage, but enslaved young girls and castrated men. But our little town resisted. Of course we were defeated. And now our men are in a line around the town square. I am in the square, as we all are, ordered to attend this humiliation, and I clutch my mother's hand. Her brother is among the soldiers. The winning Nazis have lined all the surviving town soldiers up in the streets, and now they hand a gun to our captain. Shoot every fifth man, and the rest can live. Refuse and they all die. The Nazis understand mental torture as fluently as they speak physical cruelty. The captain meets every man's eye, even before he shoots. My mother's brother, my uncle, is among the unlucky.

I'm shaken and weak when my vision clears of the horror I've just seen. I've had these episodes before, but nothing like this. It's as if my mother is living in my bones and talking through my heart.

The apartment is suffocating. I need air, but I'm afraid to move. I reach for the phone to call Sam, but stop. What if Lilly's right and he's off with some pretty professor? I won't call him. And I can't call Lilly after I more or less threw her out.

The feeling is passing, though, and I need a cup of coffee and I really need to get out. I put on a light jacket, and my hands are still sweaty enough to stick to the sleeves. *This is idiotic*, I mutter. If I don't go out I'll go nuts.

Outside the building the cold air focuses me, and the honking of taxis and trucks draws me back to the present. I walk along the edge of Central Park. All the leaves are gone and the grass is dead, but it's still greener than the California I left at the end of August. It's like the old Mamas & the Papas song, *California Dreamin'*. It doesn't rain back home from the end of April to November, and in the past few years it didn't rain much from November to April either, so any kind of greenery makes me nervous. *Going to be a bad fire season*, I think when I see the grass grow. All that grass will die in May, and be tinder in October.

It's cold — to me it's freezing — and I'm not dressed properly. You'd think with all this sun out it would be warm, but it's about fifty out. I shiver. I've forgotten what the East Coast is like.

Along the edge of the park there are tables full of books, dusty used volumes no one wants. I trail along the tables, hardly glancing at titles. I come to a table with books in Spanish. *Los marranos*. The Pigs — the insulting name for the converts from Judaism to Christianity in Spain during the time of the Inquisition. I stop and pick up the thin volume, and the pages fall out onto the table. One falls to the dusty ground. I look up at the bookseller. He's my age, late fifties, but he's lived a harder life. His skin is darker than Lilly's and as lined as a walnut. I'm the color of a blanched almond, and we're all nuts.

He has a mustache that's half grey, half dried spittle, and his hair is poking out of a hat in sharp grey and black points. "You broke," he says.

I know he means the book. "Nope, it was broken about fifty years ago," I say. I snatch the page from the dirt and shove it back between the covers.

"Two dollars."

I reach into my purse and pull out a five. "No change," he says. I put the book down. But I want the book, and I would have paid five bucks if he'd named that as the price.

I stuff my five back into the purse without bothering to put it back in my wallet. I shake my bag until I hear the change bouncing around in the bottom. I reach in and grab a handful. Counting it out I see that it comes to a dollar seventy-eight. I shake and reach some more, coming up with two dollars and eleven cents total. I hand the whole thing to him. "Tax," I say, and walk away with the book, just a little ashamed.

I walk back to the apartment, stopping at the Korean corner market for an apple and a Three Musketeers bar. I hand the clerk the five that I had in my purse, and he returns a quarter, without ringing me up. I open my mouth to say something and then shut it.

Upstairs in the apartment I open the book and rearrange some of the loose pages. I read perfectly in Spanish, and almost fluently in French, though I'm out of practice speaking it. Lilly, of course, reads and speaks perfect Spanish and French and can read and speak Russian and German, get by in Polish, and when she spent a week in Iceland she could actually make herself understood in that insanely difficult language as well.

Mom spoke six languages, something else in the long list of things that saved her life. She was fluent in English, Spanish, French, Polish, Russian, and German. I have no idea if she could read Hebrew, ever spoke Yiddish, or even knew any Ladino. I never asked her, and until today I've never asked myself why I didn't ask. Something else Lilly might know.

I open the book. It starts in 1391 with a vicious auto-da-fe during the time of Henry of Castile and Leon. The Jews whose lives were spared were converted "at the point of the sword". Those Jews, called New Christians, were not readily accepted by the Old Christians, and among the other ugly terms they were called pigs, *marranos*, for the pork they were forced to eat. I fall into the history, and soon it's almost four in the afternoon.

We're fools, I think, to squabble when so many suffered so much more. *My point precisely*, I hear my mother's voice again. I pick up my cell phone and call Lilly.

"Hi sweetie," she says. One thing about Lilly, she doesn't stay mad long.

"Hey. We shouldn't quarrel," I say, right to the issue.

"Oh, we didn't quarrel, I just had to go home for the dog."

I blink. She's unreal. Half of me wants to say *Wait a minute, of course we did! You said Sam was cheating on me, which is a horrible thing to say!* And the other half wants to let it go, like she's doing. I go with that. After all, that's why I called, wasn't it? To make up? Or was I hoping for an apology — or a retraction?

"You know what we should do?" I say instead. "We should do a marathon share. You tell me everything you know about Mom and the family history, and I tell you everything I know. So we can have, you know, a full set."

I feel that chill again, and this time the heat is red, orange and yellow. I start to sweat, and I wonder if I'm sick or having a mini-stroke or something.

Oblivious, since she can't see me, Lilly plows right in. "Lots of wine will go into that. We could do it here, and I can get the picture albums out."

My heart's pounding and I'm feeling a little nauseous. "Wait, what? Picture albums?"

"You don't know about Aunt ChaCha's picture albums? Of course you do." She starts talking about the albums. She borrowed them from Hannah about two years ago, then forgot to return them, and Hannah never asked for them back.

"Hannah lives in Israel," I croak out. "How could you borrow them?"

"She lived in New Jersey for years, until she got fed up with the American suburban life,. I borrowed them before she left."

I've steadied myself against the kitchen counter. The feeling is subsiding, and the color aura is fading. I grab a can of very stylish fizzy water from the fridge while she talks. I pull the tab and take a sip before I interrupt. "Isn't ChaCha kind of a strange name for a Polish Jew born in the twenties?"

"God, you're dense," Lilly says. "It's not ChaCha like the dance, silly. It's Ciocia, it means Aunt. Her real name was Neomi."

Oh.

"How would I know about the albums? What's in them?"

Lilly sighs. "We'll need even more wine than I thought."

Sam calls at six asking if I want to meet him for dinner. "You can bring Lilly if you want, but there won't be any cute professors with me," he says, and I can tell he's tired of having her with us all the time.

"No worries. She left a few minutes after you did."

"She did? Why? I thought you two were going to hang out all day. That's why I went over to the university. If I'd known she wasn't planning to stay around I would have. Stayed around, that is. Why didn't you tell me?"

"No, she just ended up leaving," I say. I can't tell him that we got in a fight because she said he was having an affair. "She had to go feed her dog."

He accepts the lie. "Well, I'm sorry I missed the chance to spend the day with you," he says. *You're wrong*, Lilly, I think. He mentions a restaurant we can meet at. "And I heard some fascinating talks today. I'll tell you at dinner."

As soon as I hang up Lilly calls. "Come tonight. Just jump on a train. We can have a sleep-over!"

"I'm meeting Sam at a restaurant, so I can't. Besides, we had a sleepover last night, remember?"

"Sam? You still married to that guy?"

"Knock it off."

"I'll get the albums out, and we can spend the whole day on it tomorrow. What time can you come?"

I feel myself slipping into her wake, being dragged along by her enthusiasm. "I don't know ... how about Monday? Are you working Monday?"

"I am. Aren't you eager to see what I have? It was your idea, after all, remember?"

"What was?"

"To share information. I want to show you the pictures. Jesus, you're skittish! You're still afraid of what you'll find out, aren't you?"

"What are you talking about? Why would I be afraid?"

She doesn't answer.

"Lilly, if you don't have a really good reason to say something, how about you don't say it?"

"Okay, come Monday after I'm done with school, and we can do it then." I hate the disappointment in her voice, and remind myself that all I did was express my preference for when we would get together.

"See you Monday."

Am I scared to find something out? I wait for the chill and the colored heat to come up, but they don't. What could I possibly find out that would be so bad, and how would Lilly know it? But Lilly talks to people, so who knows. I put on a black silk shirt and black trousers, the New York City uniform, and venture out into the night.

Chapter 6

On Sunday morning I leave the Times on the glass dining room table that came with the apartment, I leave a capsule in the new coffee maker, and I leave Sam sleeping in our bed. It's ten already, but he's always been a sleeper. I was too, until Angie was born, and I never got it back. It's another beautiful, cold fall day in the City. Even the sky crunches like the dry leaves on the ground in Central Park. I have a grey fleece jacket over my sweater and leggings, and a gold scarf around my neck. I pull on the gloves that Lilly gave me last week, black with faux fur trim, and walk the three blocks to the Jewish Studies Museum.

I've bought an annual pass but they still search my bag, send me through the metal detector, and check my ID before I can approach the desk. Charlottesville, with its marching Nazis, its *Jews will not replace us!* and the image of a car plowing into the crowd standing in opposition, killing an innocent young woman — it's all very present in our minds. Our temple at home has security guards all around the perimeter during High Holy Days. Last week two of the synagogue walls were spray-painted with swastikas. Again. I don't blame the museum one bit for its intense security measures.

The exhibit left weeks ago, but according to the website there are three curators, and someone will know what I'm talking about. "You'll need an appointment," the woman behind the desk says. She's about my age, but she treats me like a kid asking for a favor.

"I emailed to ask for one, but got no answer. Can you tell me which of the three curators curated the 'Lost Treasures of Poland' exhibition that ended two weeks ago?"

She fumbles with the directory for a bit. Her pale cheeks redden. "I'm afraid that curator isn't with the museum any longer."

"Really? So quickly?"

"I'm sorry. I can't help you. Maybe come back on Monday and speak with the Director."

"Can you make the appointment for me?" A line of museum-goers has formed behind me, surely with questions regarding the location of restrooms or other basics. I'm creating a nuisance. The woman writes something on a piece of paper. It's a woman's name and the museum's phone number and extension.

"That's his assistant. Call her." She turns her head to look past me. "Can I help you?"

It's clearly my cue to leave.

I go upstairs and look through the permanent collection for a while. I've seen it before, and it still gives me the creeps. Our entire history is collected in paintings and ceremonial objects, all with a legacy of tragedy weighing them down.

I pause before a Hanukkiah and read the description. It's in the shape of a house, with an ornate balustrade and an odd clock with Hebrew markings on it. The little pots at the bottom — all missing now — would have contained oil, and the placard says that they would have been shaped like little lions. The flames would have come out their mouths.

My god, what an effort someone made to create this little piece, what imagination. I want, in my sinews and blood, to hold my mother's menorah this Hanukkah. I wipe away a tear before it shows.

Another placard says the museum has over eleven hundred Hanukkah menorahs. Eleven hundred surviving pieces of ceremonial legacy for a holiday that was minor at best until it had to compete with Santa Claus. Eleven hundred surviving pieces that were of a quality sufficient to merit inclusion in the museum.

I bought my own menorah at Cost Plus more than twenty years ago. It's covered with multi-colored wax from all the birthday candles that have done ceremonial duty over the decades. Angie didn't even know that "real" Jews don't use birthday candles until she was about fourteen. *You know, Mom, there are real candles you can use in these things. I know, Angie. Have a chocolate quarter.*

We celebrate Christmas big-time at our house. Not only is Sam a Methodist, but growing up, even in my parents' household we had a tree and presents. My father went all out, loving the pageantry and opportunity to buy the biggest tree on the Christmas tree lot, and choosing elaborate presents for my mother. We would get plenty too. *Feign interest,* Mom would say when anyone else was opening a present. I said it to Angie. She now says it to her own daughter, my perfect granddaughter Meghan. *Feign interest.* It sounds like an Irish revolutionary.

For Hanukkah, Angie always got a book and a pile of *gelt*. Also from Cost Plus, the chocolate coins weren't necessarily the kind with Jewish symbols on them. Often they had fake George Washingtons or buffaloes. The *latkes* were real, though.

With eleven hundred menorahs, would the museum director know which one I was talking about? Of course, most of those weren't in the special exhibits, and my quarry had come from a particular collection; surely they had a digital record that would help identify it.

As I'm leaving I notice the open hours: Monday through Sunday, but closed on Wednesdays. Not on Saturdays. On Saturdays, entry into the museum is free. So much for Shabbat.

On Monday I call the Director's secretary, and it's easy enough to make an appointment for Tuesday afternoon. He's had a break in his schedule, she says, and would be happy to talk to me about how the museum chooses and creates particular exhibits. Yes, they have digital records from past exhibits, but he wouldn't be the person to show them to me. For that, I'd need to get his clearance to speak with one of the curators. And unfortunately, the curator who handled this exhibit is no longer with the Museum. Which I already knew. And she's so sorry, she just realized that he had booked a meeting for that Tuesday, could she get back to me? And she hangs up, without taking my number.

I call her back, get voicemail, and leave my number. Is it me, I wonder, or is something weird going on?

I haven't spoken to Lilly since Saturday, almost forty-eight hours, possibly a personal record. She answers immediately. "Zara! Are you okay?"

"Why wouldn't I be?"

"We haven't spoken. I was so worried." Forty-seven and a half hours, to be precise.

I fill her in on the Director business. "What would you do if this were an investigation you were conducting?" she asks. "Just go over there tomorrow?"

"Nah. Of course, if someone won't see me for questioning in an employment investigation it looks really bad for them, so usually they can be convinced. Shining me on, that's another matter. But here, yeah, now that you mention it, I think we should just go over tomorrow. Show up. But do you think something's fishy?"

She starts to laugh. "Something's fishy…"

"Something's fishy…very fishy…" I'm giggling.

It takes a sister. Which is why, when Lilly and I used to squabble, Mom used to say *She'll be the only one who'll remember your childhood.* And now, she really is the only one who remembers.

"Remember how Mom used to say that fish in America came in a cardboard box?"

"Yeah, it was the frozen box o' fillets. She was so disappointed."

When I was in Germany, one of the families I was quartered with got me a fish for Good Friday. We were all hungry, all the time, but the mother caught a fish in the stream and brought it back for me. "We know how important it is for you Catholics," she said. I had no idea how to prepare it, but the mother cooked it in a pan with water and salt and some leaves the family used to pick in the forest. We ate it together, the German family and I. I still pray every night for them.

"You there, Zara?"

"Bad connection," I croak.

This time there's a man at the desk. He barely looks up from his book, says "Down the hall, stairway's on the left," and goes back to his reading. Those are the directions to the amazing deli and the ladies' room in the museum's basement, but no matter. I've got Lilly. And Lilly has something neither Mom nor I ever had: a sense of direction.

"If the restrooms are this way," she says, looking around, "the offices must be up these stairs."

"Why?"

"Because it's a small building," she says, "and they'd run the plumbing stacked that way. The offices have to have rest rooms, right?"

"The entry from the stairs is probably locked," I say. Lilly smiles. She watches until she sees a blonde woman with a name tag on a lanyard enter the nearest elevator and motions me to follow her in. I do, and we go up to the third floor. The elevator door opens into a small foyer, and we get out with the blonde, who uses her ID to open the next door.

The door is marked *Private, Staff Only.* She pushes it open. I hold my breath and slide in behind her. Lilly holds the door open and I freeze, petrified of a siren or alarm, but nothing happens. That's because the next door we reach is locked. Lilly knocks, hard. After another attempt the door opens and a tiny, black-haired woman opens it. She can't even be up to my shoulder, and she's wearing jeans and a Super-Girl t-shirt. I haven't seen a Super-Girl t-shirt in years. She looks up at me, and further up at Lilly.

"We're here to see Director Rosen," Lilly says.

"Four o'clock," I add. It's one of my favorite investigation techniques: truth. It *is* four o'clock. That much is true. And we *are* here to see him.

"Oh, sorry. They didn't buzz me from the desk."

"Actually, he did try. He said that we should go on up and he'd buzz again," Lilly adds. She has a very accommodating relationship with my friend Truth.

"Well, come in. Walter just went down the hall a minute. He should be with you shortly. Coffee?" We're in.

The offices are far from posh, more standard-issue cubicles and small conference rooms with white laminate tables. We stand near the entrance until Super-Girl motions us forward to an actual and appropriately-furnished office. A man comes out from behind the desk.

Walter Rosen is about seven feet tall. He's blond, and fairly trim for a man about our age. He looks a little taken aback when Super-Girl announces us. If she hugged her boss it would be illegal in six southern states plus Utah, but they're clearly used to their Mutt-and-Jeff situation. "Ms. Persil?" he says. "I wasn't quite…"

"I'm sorry," I say crisply. "You were expecting a man, perhaps?"

"Oh, no, no, no…" he tries. "It's just, I was given a different name." He picks up his Daytimer, looks at it, puts it back down, looks at his phone. "Well, do come in, Ms. Persil, and Ms…."

"Pendleton," I say. No sense in making this any worse with the sister act.

"We're sisters," Lilly says.

I step in front of her so as not to belt her, and take a seat. She follows.

"So," Walter Rosen says, lowering himself into his seat. "How should we begin?"

"I think," I say, "by clearing up this misunderstanding."

"I'm terribly sorry," he says. "It's just when I was told that an inspector would be coming to speak to me, well, I suppose I'm guilty of stereotyping, because I expected Roger Krause to be a man, and in uniform."

Inspector? Why would he be expecting a police inspector? Although that could explain how willing the assistant was to let us in. "Oh, no worries," I say quickly, covering my confusion. "Roger's on his way. We're just here to take care of preliminaries. From a more Jewish point of view."

"Of course," he says, and his brow relaxes. "More of a family approach."

"Indeed," I say, wondering what the hell I'm talking about. "So, let's start at the beginning, from *our* point of view. We are actually more interested in helping you than finding fault," I add. These are tried and true openers from employment investigations — though I usually know what I'm talking about. "The collection..." I pause, hoping he'll jump in and take the lead.

"Yes," Rosen says. But my hopes are quickly dashed when he says, "Ask away."

"I've never been able to get over the fact that the primary coordinator for Hitler's art thefts was named Rosenberg," I say, mining my *Monuments Men* reading. "You'd think..."

Rosen finally takes the bait. "It's terribly unfortunate. And my name was shortened from Rosenberg as well, so I've always resented that."

"No relation," I smile.

"Of course not!"

"Interesting how many treasures were stolen. Major works of art from the Rothschilds and other famous collectors, down to tiny artifacts from unknown families."

Rosen leans back. "You do know, don't you, that we check very, very carefully before we put anything on exhibit. We would never exhibit something knowingly stolen. Or rather, that we knew had been stolen. Or, better said, that had been stolen or bought from a theft." His fair skin is flushed.

"The curator," Lilly says, "is no longer working here. A rather abrupt departure, so soon after such a successful exhibit as the 'Lost Treasures.'"

"I can't discuss personnel."

"Oh, we certainly don't want you to breach any confidentiality, at least not until Roger gets here," I say smoothly. "Just, given that she's no longer here, it's a little more difficult to trace exactly what the research was before you chose the items for the exhibit."

We'd never intended to conduct an interrogation. Lilly and I had pictured a cozy meeting, telling our story, shedding a few tears, asking who Lev Zimmerman was, but this strangely adversarial discussion has taken on a life of its own. I wonder if I can redirect it. "Perhaps working from a different angle would be easier. Let's take a small, unimportant item from a personal collection, and you can tell us how it came to be exhibited."

"Fair enough," Rosen says, but he doesn't look happy.

"I understand that the Museum has over a thousand Hanukkiahs," I say. "For such a minor holiday, it's interesting that so many were crafted and wrought as works of art."

He nods. "Some are truly remarkable."

"So let's take one of those."

Lilly reaches into her messenger bag — her three-hundred-dollar messenger bag — and pulls out a note pad and a pen. For the time being she's letting me do the talking.

"Of course, you'll want to talk about the one in the Zimmerman collection," Rosen says.

"Of course."

"Well, that's the problem, isn't it?"

It is? I don't dare ask what he thinks the problem is. Ah, but Lilly dares.

"Here's the thing," she says. "Quite frankly..." she adds. I feel the chill, and the warm air that follows is a coral shade. *As soon as someone says Quite Frankly, you know they're lying.* But I can't stop Lilly. "Quite frankly, we think that the menorah that was on exhibit was part of our own family's collection. We want it back."

You were wrong, Mom, I think. *This time Quite Frankly led to the truth.*

But Rosen is old-school. "Really? Now that's a weak ploy. Why don't you two just come on out with it. You want to know why Marie Goldberg was fired, and you want to know whether we've recovered the treasures, including the gorgeous turquoise inlaid menorah, and the answer to your second question is *No! We haven't.* And we probably won't ever recover it. And as to Marie, we didn't fire her. She left. So yes, she's suspect number one. And if you think I was taken in by your sister act, or your purported affiliation with the police, you're nuts. I knew from the moment you walked in the door that you're working for Zimmerman's lawyer. Well you can tell him to go ahead and sue the museum, and if he thinks that we'll pay him a dime, he's wrong because Zimmerman knew all along—"

Rosen's voice is cut off by the buzzing of his phone. "Lieutenant Krause is here to see you."

Lilly and I stand up. "Thank you for your time, Mr. Rosen. We'll be in touch," I say crisply.

We walk swiftly towards the door, but I turn and see Lilly give Rosen a quick wink. He gasps, and I try not to. We go into the anteroom and see a small, out-of-shape man in a grey suit standing in cop-stance, feet apart, hands casually behind his back. He gives us a professional once-over as we go past and we escape into the hall.

Wordlessly we head back down the stairway. "I gotta pee," Lilly says.

"We can go at the apartment."

"No, I've got to go now." She pushes the door of the Ladies' Room open. Exasperated, I follow her in. I want to get out of the building, but she's right. We need to walk out casually, and having to pee only makes us look more desperate.

As soon as she comes out, she says, "Well, that went well."

I start to laugh, and then I can't stop. She's laughing too, and I say, "Thank God we peed first!" Now she's hiccuping. "Let's go before we get arrested."

As we're slipping out the front door under the baleful eye of the security guard I say to Lilly, "I can't believe you winked at him."

"He wasn't wearing a wedding ring," she answers. "You never know."

<hr />

We sit at Sarabeth's with decafs and scones. My hands are sweaty and I'm retroactively shaky. "You were brilliant," Lilly says.

"No, you were," I say back. "*I didn't fall for your sister act!*" Lilly snorts and almost chokes on the scone. "Careful," I add. "Not worth dying over."

"The Monuments Men thought the art was." Lilly saw the movie, which was evidently far more exciting than the book. The book is dryly captivating, from an intellectual point of view.

"Yeah, but that was big-deal art and Roman ruins and basilicas and all. So... Marie Goldberg was the curator. And the Zimmerman family is pissed. So not only is there a provenance issue, but it sounds like our sweet Marie has gone off with the goods."

"That's problematic," Lilly says. "Makes it hard to get it back."

"On the other hand, if there's been a theft, then it's public, and we can ask questions more openly. We can ask for police reports, find out who Lev Zimmerman is, make sure the powers that be know that we have an interest in the investigation, and let the pros take over."

"Or we can hire an investigator ourselves... Zara! You're an investigator! You can investigate the crime."

"I'm an employment investigator, not a criminal investigator. I don't have a PI license, and I'm not even on my home turf. But if we could find Zimmerman — maybe he'd hire me... No, that's ridiculous," I correct myself. "Besides, didn't Rosen say at the end that he thought Zimmerman was in cahoots with Marie?"

"He certainly implied it. It's really too bad, though, that we couldn't have approached Walter in a more friendly, confidential way."

"Walter, is it now? Have some pride."

"He's about seven feet tall. Almost a foot taller than I am. How can I resist?"

I shake my head. "You've got post-menopausal hot pants." She's actually had hot pants all her life.

"Jeez, I haven't heard *hot pants* since Mother in her heyday."

We're both quiet for a moment. "Hey, Lilly, I got a question."

"Yeah?"

"Do you see Mom's aura?"

"What?"

"Her aura. I keep seeing her aura. Ever since I got to New York. Or no, ever since we took Angie and Meghan to the museum."

"What's Mother's aura look like?" Lilly asks me. I can tell she's indulging me.

"First I get a chill. Then I feel warm air, and I sense a color. Different colors. When we were in Rosen's office she was coral. Yesterday she was lime green."

"Well she's improved your color sensitivity."

I don't insist.

"You know she hated to be called Mom," Lilly says, changing the subject.

"I know," I say. "I tried not to. We had a deal. I didn't call her Mom, and she didn't say *hmmhmm* when I was talking to her. I'd forget. She would too."

"What's wrong with saying *hmmhmm?*"

"Because it meant she wasn't listening to me."

"She probably couldn't understand what you were saying, you talk so fast," Lilly says. "I realized after I started teaching that she had an aural processing problem."

"Oh sure, that's why she spoke seven languages."

"You can have both. A facility for languages and a processing problem." Lilly's a teacher, so she knows these things. "Remember how hard it was to talk to her on the phone?"

It was true. "It always sounded like she was reading a book or doing her nails while she was talking to you. Like something was distracting her."

"That's because she couldn't process unless she was looking at you. And you talk so damn fast that half the time she had no idea what you were saying."

"Well, when you were younger you bounced around so much. At least I stood still. You're the one with ADHD."

"Yeah. A six-foot-tall girl with ADHD in the sixties. It wasn't easy, but Mother didn't try." Lilly juts her lower lip.

"Poor baby. First world problems," I say. We've degenerated into sibling squabble, only with grown-up words.

"You know, I hate that expression," she answers. "You know why?" I could guess. "Because I live in the first world. And I'm fucking sick and tired of my problems never being important enough. They're all I've got."

I reach across the table and hold her hand. "Seriously, you're right. Compared with starvation and war, yeah, our problems are minimal. But we spent our whole lives having our problems minimized. Sometimes that gave me perspective, and sometimes, you know what? It made me hate myself. Because not only was I miserable over my problems and my heart-pounding anxiety, but I despised myself for having it. I didn't earn it. I didn't deserve it. And no matter what happened to me, it was never, thank God, as bad as what happened to her. So how dare I be anxious!"

Now Lilly's holding *my* hands. My face is hot and I'm going to cry. Right there in Sarabeth's. And I feel the chill.

Chapter 7

"Lilly, do you see them on beautiful days?" I look across the fading grass and I can almost hear Mom's voice. It doesn't intrude, it's just there.

It was on a beautiful day like this one, on the first of September, when the Nazis marched into Warsaw.

"No," Lilly says. "I don't see them at all. I hear them, though. I hear boots." Lilly and I are walking through Central Park, it's cold and bright, and we're holding hands. Just like in San Francisco, in New York City no one even gives us a second look.

"I smell sweat, I smell fear. Can you imagine? I don't think anyone knew, even then, how horrible it would be. I think they all believed only as far as they could project."

Yesterday I was safe in my home. I went to the market, I went to school. In school we learned Russian. Today, I'm still in my home, and I still went to school, but our teacher, Sister Bernadette, said we would learn German. I was delighted. I love to learn new languages. Sister was crying, but she wiped her eyes, said a prayer — a really long prayer — and then we began our first German lesson.

Her voice weaves through my own and I grip Lilly's hand. It has not been this present before. The park shimmers and Lilly pulls me to a bench. We sit close, waiting for the colors to return to normal.

"We never know more than we can project," Lilly's saying, "except the rare few who can really see forward."

"Not us," I add. "It was a beautiful day in San Francisco when the president was elected. I wore black the next day. And yet, I thought, it's America. Nothing really terrible can happen. They must have thought the same."

Lilly lets go of my hand and wipes hers on her jacket. The mere mention of the current political regime makes her nervous. The parallels make me even more so. "Maybe," Lilly says, "but they'd been through World War One, so you'd think they would have guessed. Or maybe not. Maybe they just didn't know. Maybe they didn't think that the Germans were so bad that time."

"Mom's father guessed. Or supposedly guessed. And wanted to take them away, but he got sick. What deadly consequences of getting sick."

"No more trips to the dressmaker, no more special meals," Lilly said.

"And eventually, rounded up, forced to leave everything they had, and Mom stopped being allowed to go to school. She and her mother were made to work in a factory for the Germans."

"By then, I think Mother's father was dead."

We're trying to tell each other the story, trying to fill in each other's gaps. Which warped, edited version does each of us know? And we both had unreliable narrators tell us in the first place. Our stories flow over each other's, wrapping around each other as they manifest to us, out of chronological order, but we rarely get very far. Too often our stories dissolve into questions, tears, and changing the subject. "And then the horror began."

My father was dead, my mother was already gone. I didn't know where they had taken her, along with the other older women. I was now alone. The German overseer said to me, "You're special. You're so pretty. Don't worry, pretty peach, you're my special pet from now on." I was fifteen. I knew what he meant.

I didn't look Jewish. I could pass. That day, when we all left the factory to go to our living quarters, I just kept walking. At the edge of the ghetto I took off my star. I lifted my chin and walked with my hard, Spanish eyes, away from the ghetto, the Germans, and everyone who knew me. I walked to the Ursuline convent, slipped into the church, and spent the rest of the evening there.

I never saw anyone I knew again.

"She could speak literate Polish, which many Jewish girls couldn't do. She had been attending the Ursuline academy, and knew Catholic customs. She could speak Russian and German, and French too. How did she learn English?"

"I think she just picked some up later," I say. I don't know. Amazingly, neither my sister nor I have the remotest idea how my mother first learned English. But she knew enough by the end of the war to speak to the commander of the American battalion. "She was like you. Ten minutes and she was fluent."

We walk silently for a while, until we find ourselves outside the Jewish Studies Museum once again. It's been a week since our visit to Walter Rosen. "Shall we drop in on him again?" Lilly asks.

"What the hell for? To get ourselves arrested?"

"For what? We didn't do anything."

"I guess not. I mean, we didn't impersonate a police officer, or whatever this Roger Krause was supposed to be. But no, I still don't want to drop in on our man Rosen. Even if he is seven feet tall."

"Oh, come on," Lilly says. "You're still a big chicken. Or a little chicken, which is worse."

"Too bad."

"Well, I'm going in to see him." Lilly strides through the doors before I can stop her, and walks right up to the security guard. I practically jog to catch up. She's taking off her coat and opening her bag as I join her. We show our membership cards and walk right past the information desk.

"Excuse me," the woman behind the desk says. "That's a private area. The exhibits are over this way." There's always someone different at the desk.

"Oh, thanks," Lilly says, "but we have an appointment with Mr. Rosen."

"I'll have to phone you up," she says. "Your name?"

"Lilly Persil," she says. I would have given a fake name, but I'm not Lilly. I'm just her short, blonde sidekick, running after her like Chicken Little, terrified that the sky will fall on me for breaking a rule.

"It's going to his assistant's voicemail," the desk-woman says. "I'll try again in a few minutes."

"I'll just use the second-floor rest room and by the time I get through you'll have announced me," Lilly says, striding to the door with me at her heels.

I'll admit I'm impressed. Petrified, but impressed.

For the second time, we go up the stairs, walk through the door marked *Private*, and this time go straight into the reception area for Rosen's office. Former Super-Girl is in a Michelle Obama t-shirt with the logo *When They Go Low* across the bottom. God, that makes me nostalgic.

"Hi again," she says brightly. "I'll tell Mr. Rosen you're here."

"No tricks this time," Lilly says to me.

"As if!" I'm offended, but there's no time to assert my virtue. Rosen strides out, his white face pink. He stops right in front of us, and given the height differential I'm staring rather awkwardly at his tie-tack. Lilly, however, is not.

"What the hell are you two doing here again?"

"Walter, sorry to barge in on you," Lilly says. "We really, really need to talk to you."

From my angle I can't see her face, he's standing practically on my feet, and with the folding waiting-room chairs behind me I can't back up. It would be awkward but possibly useful to climb up on a chair, and if I were thirty years younger I would have. But I don't have to see her face to know that Lilly's batting her big, liquid brown eyes at him. I can tell from her voice.

"Really *really* need to talk to me? Great. How about making an appointment like a decent human being?"

"We did try," I pipe up. They both ignore me.

"Here we are," Lilly says. "No time like the present, I guess."

"Okay. Come in, but make it quick."

We scurry in and sit down. Well, I scurry in, and Lilly waltzes in, in three-four time.

"Mr. Rosen," I say.

"Now we're back to Mr. Rosen."

"Just trying to be polite," I say.

"Polite people make appointments."

"Polite offices let people make appointments instead of telling people that people are booked, and hanging up on them," Lilly says. Not elegant, but we all know what she means. "But that's water over the bridge."

"Under the dam," I say, "as it were." I don't know why this guy brings out the best in me.

"Enough of this," Lilly says. "Walter, we have a confession to make. We really are sisters."

"And? That matters to me why?"

"No, not at all, I just want to straighten everything out," Lilly says. "I want you to be satisfied." Both Rosen and I cough a laugh. He and I exchange glances in a moment of shared amusement. I glance at Lilly and see that she's pleased.

"Can we get to the point, ladies?"

I'm letting Lilly handle it. She brought this on us, and I, complicit as usual, am tagging along for the show.

"Here's the thing," she says. *Not 'Quite Frankly'*? Mom's voice is again in my ear. "We really are sisters. Our mother was one of the few in her extended family who survived the Holocaust." My sister doesn't say *Shoah*. I don't usually either, but here I would have. Street cred.

"I came here with her the last time you had an exhibit like the Treasures, back about thirty years ago," I say.

"We've had it every decade for forty years," Rosen says.

"Sorry, I live in California. I only was here then. In any event, we saw the menorah, the one that in this exhibit was labeled as from the collection of the Lev Zimmerman family. I don't really remember if it was labeled that way the time I saw it. In fact, I'm pretty sure it wasn't."

Lilly turns to me. "I thought you couldn't remember. How come you're remembering now?" Christ, I wouldn't have asked that in front of Rosen.

"Dunno," I say. "I just do. But anyway, our mother, of blessed memory," I throw that in, "recognized it. It came from her family."

"Why didn't you or she speak up then? It would have been a lot easier than it is now, if it's even the same one. You only saw it once, right? Thirty years ago? And now, what? You think it's yours?"

"Good point," I say. I can't really tell him why Mom wouldn't have spoken up. "It was a different world then. No one talked about returning the stolen personal items to the victims or their survivors. No one talked about citizenship for their children. People only started talking about restitution in the past ten years or so."

"So why didn't you come forward ten years ago?"

"It never even occurred to me. It wasn't until I saw the menorah last month that I even remembered."

"Oh, very pressing indeed."

Lilly jumps in. "We saw it, we recognized it, and we tried to make an appointment to see the curator. We were ignored, hung up on. We tried to make an appointment to see you. We just about had one, and would have come in quite respectfully, as we are now, but suddenly we were turned away again. We can't just sit and wait forever. And so here we are, barging in on you, trying to tell you that this menorah is ours."

I'm impressed. I can't tell if Rosen is, but he's leaning forward. Lilly leans forward too. She's taken off her jacket, and when she leans forward, a whole lot of cleavage leans with her. Rosen notices. He pinks up and leans back. I can almost hear Lilly thinking *Gotcha*.

"So, how can you prove it's yours?" he asks.

I take a breath, and take my gloves off. I'm still not used to this New York cold, and I've had them on since Rosh Hashanah. I take off the ring I've worn since I was eleven, and hand it to Walter Rosen, head of the Jewish Studies Museum. Will he know what he's looking at? I am almost certain that he will.

"What's this?" he asks without even looking at it.

Okay, maybe not.

"My ring. My mother gave it to me when I was eleven. Please examine it." He holds it between thumb and forefinger, away from himself, like a bug.

Why won't he even look at it?

He hands it back, but I don't reach for it. He puts it on his desk. "Proves nothing."

"Look. At. It."

"Please," Lilly adds.

We sit in silence. Finally, he picks it back up again. He pulls a jeweler's loupe from his top drawer, holds it to his eye, and examines the ring. I watch his chest for clues from his breathing but I see nothing. He does take a while, turning the front oval around, looking underneath at the strange hollow beneath the crest, comes close up to the enamel. He puts it back down on his desk.

"Beautiful old work. Turquoise enameling, not seen much anymore. Probably no real auction value, but rare."

"This isn't Antiques Road Show. I'm not trying to sell it. It's the same pattern as on the menorah."

He turns to his computer screen, clicks away a bit, until the menorah is there, larger by far than the real thing, on one of his two big monitors. He zooms in slightly on the pattern. I can feel my heart, so loud in my chest that I can hardly breathe. There it is. The pattern.

I start to sweat and I shiver. The chill and the turquoise-colored warmth are overwhelming.

We had been told that no one could leave the house. We are confined to our homes as the Nazis go door to door. No knocking, our doors are to be unlocked. Two men enter, shaved heads, uniforms, speaking an ugly guttural German, not the beautiful language I am learning in school. My mother and I cower away, but my father, ill and frail, steps forward. In his aristocratic German he asks what they could need. It is the polite form but he isn't toadying.

Shut up, the Nazi says. Then he sees me. I'm thirteen, still plump, not quite a woman, but almost. You, he says, come. You can be our tour guide. I look at my mother, her big, soft eyes are wide. She puts her hand on my arm and the soldier crosses the room in two strides. He back-hands my mother, my beautiful, delicate mother, across the face, and she falls to the floor. My father rushes to her, and her mouth is bleeding. Come, dumpling, the Nazi says to me, give us the tour.

The living room, I say in perfect German. So, you speak the language of the pure, he says. I nod, ja, and then, the dining room. He begins to fill a bag. It is labeled with our apartment, our last name. He takes everything that is beautiful. Look at this Jewish shit, he says, taking our menorah, the one we use for Hanukkah, the one with the same pattern as my ring. I gave the ring to Ciocia Neomi when she got married, and mama was furious, but now I'm glad. The soldier throws the Hanukkiah into the bag. Now and then he gropes my arms, my little breasts, but I am only scared. I don't know enough, yet, to be horrified.

Lilly is standing over me, there's something wet on my forehead, and a monstrous pink-faced man is looming over me. I push my hands out to block them and realize that I'm in the museum director's office. I struggle to sit more upright, and Lilly puts her arms around me. I look around. "What the fuck?" My voice is quietly raspy, and the words hurt my throat.

"She's come to," Lilly says unnecessarily.

Rosen hands me a cup with water but my hands are too shaky to hold it. Lilly holds it to my lips and I take a sip, then another. Finally, I begin to feel embarrassed. "What happened?"

"I don't know," Lilly says. "One minute you were looking at Walter's screen and the next thing you were making kitten sounds and pouring sweat."

"Jesus," I say.

That goes over well.

"You've done this before?" Rosen asks. "I was about to call 911."

"You came to just before he dialed. But you didn't seem to lose consciousness, just went weird on us. Like you used to when you were a kid."

"She did that when she was a kid?"

"Yeah. That's how I knew it wasn't a stroke or anything. Even when she was a teenager she used to pass out if she saw blood, or if there was any violence on TV. She hasn't gone to a movie in twenty years."

"Not true. I saw *A Man Called Ove*. The original one in Swedish. And *Grandma*, the one with Lily Tomlin."

"Really? I'm impressed." She picks up a pencil and begins to poke it down her cleavage.

I start to laugh. "One ringie-dingie…"

"*Saturday Night Live*, circa nineteen seventy-five," Rosen says, and he's actually not bad-looking when he smiles.

"You should smile more, you look so nice when you smile," Lilly says, deadpan.

"Huh?"

We don't bother to explain. Any woman would get it. And then I realize I have to pee. Really badly. Or throw up. "I need to excuse myself."

"We'll be right back," Lilly says, and helps me up. She holds me as we walk to the door, me wobbling and she trying not to fall over from laughing and holding me up. We make it to the ladies' room just in time.

"Jesus, Zara," Lilly says when we come out. "What the hell triggered this one?"

I try to explain about the chills and colored heat. "You know how I asked you if you're getting weird sensations and hearing Mom's voice?" I say.

"Yeah, Zara, and I'm not. And you know that she didn't like to be called Mom."

"You've mentioned that. As did she. Anyway, this isn't the time. I had one of those, I don't know, visions. Spells. That's what happened."

"Umm hmm," Lilly says, and I want to belt her. "So you had a little hissy in Rosen's office just when he was warming up to us. Terrific."

"It's not a hissy. It's like an out of body experience. And besides, I haven't had a full-blown one like this in decades."

"Well you picked a crappy time to have one now. He was just looking at your ring."

"Shit," I say, "I left the ring there. We've got to go back."

"Of course we're going back. We were just getting started."

"I wasn't going back in there . . . I mean, now I am; he's got my ring."

"And stop swearing. You've said more bad words in an afternoon than I say in a year."

"You teach little kids — of course you don't swear. Hold up," I say as she goes striding off with her long legs, "I'm still a little queasy."

When we come back in, Rosen is looking at his computer screen. He does not look good. "Look at this, Lilly," he says. Oho! I think. They're getting mighty chummy now. She scoots around his metal desk until she's leaning over his shoulder, her breakfront of a bosom grazing his arm. It must be a hell of a website they're looking at — he doesn't even acknowledge the girls.

"Man, that's awful," Lilly says. I start to get up. "No, Zara. Don't look."

"What? What is it?"

"It looks like Marie Goldberg's dead. Like someone killed her."

"That's horrible," I say after I catch my breath. "How?"

"Not too squeamish for details?" Rosen says.

"Not as long as I don't have to see them," I say, untruthfully. "I'm an investigator for a living," I add.

"Really," he says.

"It's from the local news station," Lilly says, and reads, "A woman killed near Cranford, New Jersey, has been identified as Marie Goldberg of Fort Lee. Her partially clad body was found in the wooded area near a playground attached to a local Jewish pre-school."

"Oh my god," I say. "Your curator."

Rosen looks positively ashen. "I should have told Krause," he says.

"What do you mean?" I ask very softly.

"Krause. The cop that came to see me the same day you did. He wanted to know why we fired Marie. I told him it was because she took pieces from the collection. Including your piece."

"Wait, I don't understand. You knew she had stolen parts of the exhibit? You must have reported it to the police, no?"

He looks miserable. "That's why I thought you were from Zimmerman's lawyer's office. I got a call from them; they said that when his collection was returned there were missing items. They gave me time to find the missing pieces, they didn't want to go to the police and embarrass the museum, with all the rampant antisemitism these days. The country's going to hell."

"Damn right it is," I say. He ignores me.

"And I asked Marie to double-check. She worked for us for five years — I trusted her completely. And then, she was gone. She didn't show up for work, and she didn't call in, and she didn't answer her phone. The next thing I knew, a police inspector wanted to see me. And you two."

"That's awful. No wonder you were so annoyed with us. What did Roger Krause ask about?" Lilly says.

"He asked about the missing artifacts, so I knew that someone had gone to the police, without giving me a chance to find them. I figured it was Zimmerman. I asked Krause not to let the press know, and he just shrugged, said he wasn't in the publicity department."

"And you didn't tell him that Marie had disappeared?" I say.

He shakes his head, and looks again at the screen. I crane my neck and Lilly turns the screen away from me.

"And I'm guessing you didn't show him the video, either," I add.

"Video?" Lilly asks, her voice high.

"You know about the video?" Rosen is pale with shock. "Who the hell are you, really?"

"It's okay, both of you. I'm an investigator, like I said, and every place, certainly every museum, has CCTV, right? Everything's on security cameras these days. What's the retention period?"

"So you don't really know." Rosen seems relieved.

"How long?"

"None of your business."

"It is now."

He stands up, dislodging Lilly from over his shoulder. "You really need to leave now."

"But we can help you," I say, "if you'll help us. Please."

"Well, I can't give you your damned menorah, that's for sure."

"Unless we help you get it back."

"You get the items back, I'll help you talk to Lev Zimmerman's lawyer," Rosen snaps.

"Thanks," I say. "but what if this Zimmerman killed your curator? I mean, to get his artifacts back...no, that's idiotic." Rosen obviously agrees.

"My ring?" I hold out my hand. He looks on his desk. He lifts the blotter. He checks under the papers scattered about. "Oh for

Christ's sake," I say, realizing how much I swear like a Christian. "Look on your chair."

He bends down and starts checking the seat, while I go onto my hands and knees to look under the desk. I feel around and can't see it. Then Rosen grunts. "It's over there." He reaches into the crack between the plastic chair mat and the green and yellow carpet. Somehow my ring has gotten slightly under the mat, where one of the little points digs into the pile. "Ow," he says and pulls out the ring.

He hands it to me, both of us still on the floor. "Thanks," I say. "Be careful getting up."

We both rise gingerly, neither of us nimble in our late fifties. Lilly reaches out as if to help him, but he's got his dignity and masculine pride to pull him vertical.

"Here's my phone number," she says, handing him a slip of his own paper with her name and cell on it. "What's your direct dial so we can communicate? Email too," she adds.

He hands her a card and she slips it into her three-hundred-dollar purse. I know it's three hundred dollars — she told me. Then she holds out her hand again, this time to shake his. When he clasps her hand she puts her left over his as well, in an intimate two-handed shake. I have to look away to hide my smile. She's got her own agenda, and she knows how to follow it.

"Come on, Zara," she says, as if I were the one prolonging the meeting. "I'm sure Walter's got more than enough to do today. And isn't Sam waiting for you tonight?"

Yeah, she's letting him know she's single and I'm not. "He sure is. My husband," I add, in case he's being oblivious. "He's a visiting professor at Columbia this year. It's very exciting."

"Take care," Lilly says, as she edges me out the door. "I'll be in touch."

This time we leave the building with dignity. After all, we've been meeting for almost an hour with the Director. We're VIPs. In the time we've been inside, clouds have moved in and the wind has picked up. I shiver and pull my jacket close as we head two blocks uptown towards the apartment. The streets look different as the weather turns, and people move even faster than usual. I'm not the only one pulling my jacket close, though I'm in the minority in that I'm wearing a fully quilted Uniqlo winter coat. Most people are in sweaters, hoodies, or fall blazers.

"What are you going to do in the winter?" Lilly says when I shiver.

"Die."

"Baby."

When we get up to 94th we leave Fifth Avenue and the park and head east. At Madison I say, "Sarabeth or home?"

"Sarabeth," Lilly says, and we head back down Madison. The windows are steamed and a blast of warm air hits me when I open the door. At this hour, though, there are no lines, so we sail inside the warm and welcoming restaurant that's become my second home. Again we order coffee and cakes. I'm amazed that I haven't gained a ton in the two months I've been here, between Sarabeth and stopping my karate workouts, but then, we walk everywhere — I can't imagine driving in New York — so that probably keeps the weight off.

"So," I say once our coffee is set before us, "that was not what I expected. I seem to say that a lot these days," I add. "Nothing is as I expected."

"What's going on with you?" Lilly says, ignoring my philosophical digression. "What the hell are these seizures, or visions or whatever the hell you're having? Have you been checked out by a doctor?"

"No, and I'm fine. I don't know what's happening, but it's really kind of cool."

"Strokes aren't cool."

"I'm not having a stroke and you know it. I've had these little episodes since I was a kid — you said so yourself."

"Yeah, but you said yourself that you haven't had one that bad as an adult. Look, I know how stubborn you are, but you're here in the heart of the greatest medical community in the world — so use it. Get an appointment with someone. Can you use the Columbia medical system?"

I nod. We have our regular insurance, plus we have the Columbia benefits. "Then get an appointment. A neurologist, or a GP at least, to see what's going on with you. You still take that heart medicine?"

"Yeah. What a crushing blow that was."

Lilly smiles. "It's not supposed to be us, is it? It's supposed to be men. But Mother had the same condition, with the mitral valve prolapse, so I'm not surprised you have it. You're so like her, in so many ways."

I'm warmed by her comments. Also the coffee.

"But you're as stubborn as she was, too," Lilly adds. "See someone. Now tell me about these visions."

We both sigh. We're actual sighers. "Okay. It's true that I haven't had any severe episodes since I was a kid, but I've had things like them. I get cold and start to shiver, and feel dizzy. My heart pounds in my throat and solar plexus, and it's like I'm about to go off the high dive. Then it stops. That's it. But the difference here is that I get hot after, like a hot flash — which I don't get anymore, by the way. Hot flashes, that is. Anyway, so then I get hot and I see a color. That's new. And then, well, this is creepy but also cool. Then I hear Mom's voice, and kind of see her."

I feel like I'm about to cry. Lilly holds my hand.

"You see her?"

"Not really. I sort of envision her."

"As she was at the end, or how? Because I see her all the time, but what I see is when they shocked her when her heart stopped. I'll never forget it. They wouldn't stop. I was yelling, she's got a DNR! Stop! But they kept going, and when she came to, my God, I was screaming so loud they pulled me from the room. I'll never forget it."

Now Lilly's crying and I'm holding *her* hand. I love New York City. You want to break down in the middle of a lovely tea restaurant, go ahead. You want to scream in Newark Airport when you find out that your mother's dead, be my guest. No worries, no one's judging.

"We've got a fucked-up past," I say. Lilly sniffs and I hand her a tissue.

"Is this clean?"

"Mother of God," I say.

She blows her nose. "It isn't now. You know you swear like a Catholic."

"What do you expect?"

"Well, when you went total-Jewess on us you should have learned how Jewish girls swear." She pats her eyes, careful not to ruin her makeup.

"How do Jewish girls swear?" I ask.

"I have no idea. You're the one who crossed over," Lilly says.

"Not crossed over. We've always been Jewish, even when we couldn't even utter the word *Jewish*. And what about you, when you took your Hebrew name? On the plane, remember?"

The chills come over me, but I say to myself, *No, not now. I don't have time for this now*, and they stop. I'd forgotten that I could stop them as a kid. Some of the time.

"Enough," I say. "Let's get this one out, okay? We can stop dancing around this question about who is or isn't Jewish. We've been dancing for almost sixty years. Isn't it time to come to terms with reality?"

"I always did, Zara. You were the one who couldn't deal."

"Because it was complicated. You took the surface and ran with it."

"One way to deal."

"Sure." I don't say, *Yeah, the easy way*, because even I know it wasn't. "We had a choice. Mom didn't. You chose one way, I chose the other. But we're born Jewish, and if some neo-Nazi sends the trains, they'll come for you as well as me. You can acknowledge it or not."

"I do. I celebrate the holidays."

"You eat the holidays. You don't celebrate them," I say.

"You know that we don't have to. There are tons of levels of

Jewishness. Or of Jewish practice. So don't get all high holy days on me. Until ten years ago you didn't know a damn thing about Judaism."

It's true. But I chose to learn. And I know it doesn't matter at all. "The funny thing is, I don't believe any of it. But I just felt that if so many people died for it, one of us in the family needed to carry it on. And that would be me. Obviously." I feel strong when I say it. "I'm Jewish because it's worth dying for."

Lilly and I look at one another, and it's as if we've touched souls. Then the moment passes.

"Anyway, guess what I did while you were crawling around on the ground with Walter?" she says.

"I wasn't *crawling around* with Walter, as you call him."

"It's his name. You want to see it or not?"

"See what?"

She takes out her phone. "Look. I took a picture of the monitor with the menorah, and the notations from the collection showing ownership, provenance, all kinds of things."

I look. There it is. Complete with the pattern of my ring. Our first proof. "Fist-bump," I say, holding up my closed hand.

"Pound it, doggie," she bumps back. That's what you get when you teach middle-school, I guess.

"And now, to find out what happened to poor Marie."

Chapter 8

When my mother was dying, she slipped in and out of lucidity. In the worst of times she called for her father. In better times, she took my hand and looked into my eyes. "Don't let them."

"I won't, Mom. I promise."

I would promise to protect her and she would say, "Promise?" And I would agree.

Last night I dreamed that we were looking at the menorah, but we were in a field and she was painting. "I'll protect you," I said in my dream.

She chuckled. "Don't be ridiculous," she said.

• ⋇ ◦❍◦ ⋇ •

I walked out of the ghetto, still sick from the foreman's words. His special little peach, his dumpling. He was going to take care of me. Mother was gone, Father was dead, and even they couldn't protect me anyway. I was fifteen, old enough to take care of myself, and no one else would. I walked quickly to the convent, slipped into the church. I knew I couldn't stay there, but I had nowhere to go.

Would they hide me, the brave sisters? They had tried when the soldiers came to purge the school. "There are no Jews in this school,

Mein Herr. We are a Catholic school. And we teach our girls in pure German. Right, girls?"

Of course they had called on me, the nuns did, to showcase how well we spoke the new language. I was still nice and plump, and my uniform had been tailored for me so it fit beautifully. I was letter-perfect, as always. "Excellent, Aurora. You may sit down." The other girls' envy at my perfect grades would turn to gratitude. Or at least, so I expected.

"Excuse me, sister," Sofia said. "I don't think Aurora is Catholic."

There was a horrified silence. I felt my stomach drop, but I sat erect. I turned to Sofia and raised an eyebrow, as my father used to do when he wanted to bring someone down from their prideful heights. "Is that what you think, little cloth-merchant's pipsqueak?" Sofia was a small, birdlike blonde whose father was in textiles. The soldier laughed.

"Quite a spirited girl, isn't she?' he said. "Excellent German, young lady," he said to me. "But be careful. Your enemies can haunt you a long, long time."

Three days later, they came to our apartment. I never returned to school again.

Now I was leaving the chapel. It was dark and the sexton had come to lock up. I asked if I could stay and he shook his head. "No vagrants allowed." I rang at the convent door. "No one there anymore," said the sexton as he passed by. "All sent out to the country."

I went out into the cold night, pulling my coat around me. The coat had been new two years before, and was now too short in the arms, but I was much, much thinner now and there was ample cloth to keep the chill out.

I must have walked for hours, and finally, cold and hungry, I sat down on a bench. I had no money, I had nowhere to go, and

I could not sleep in the street. It was starting to snow, little flurries that danced in front of my eyes. I was near the rail station, and there were men coming from the buildings, finished for the night.

I took off my coat and unbuttoned the top three buttons of my blouse.

Men walked by, some looking at the ground, others glancing at me. One or two greeted me in Polish but did not stop. Finally a man, younger than my father but too old to be conscripted, stopped at my bench.

"Evening, girlie. Aren't your titties a little chilly, with your top opened?"

I forced a smile but couldn't repress a shiver.

"Come on home with me, cutie-pie. I'll make you nice and warm."

If he was shocked that I was a virgin he didn't show it. I stayed with him for two weeks, until the night he didn't return.

I snap open the laptop and run a search for Marie Goldberg. I turn up all kinds of details, including her Facebook page — she should have kept her privacy guards up a little higher — and of course, the news article about her murder. She appears to have been about forty, brunette with streaked hair, at least recently, and glasses. She wasn't bad looking, a little overweight, and with a preference for cute-kitten videos. She lived in Fort Lee, and complained on a regular basis about the traffic into the City. Also, in some of her older posts, about the Path train — something I've heard about but I'm still not completely sure what it is. It sounds like a mild amusement-park ride for children, but apparently it gets a lot of complaints.

Marie's Facebook page informs me that she had been a regular attendee at dance-and-poetry recitals in a place called BroomCloset in the Village. I Google BroomCloset and discover that it's a venue for woman- and woman-identifying and gender-queer poets and artists to present their works. There's an open mic on Mondays, live music on the weekends, and something they term "vagina-based art" on Wednesday nights.

I call Lilly.

I meet her at Grand Central and we take the subway down to the Village. The B train is packed to steaming with late commuters, early partiers and people going god-knows-where but smelling of fresh pot, sweat, and wool. Lilly holds a strap and I hold onto Lilly as the train rackets and rattles its way downtown.

Yesterday's flurries didn't amount to anything so there's no snow on the ground, but there's still a sense that autumn is coming to a close and we're in for winter.

"What are you wearing?" Lilly asks.

It isn't the benign question it could be, especially since we're coming up out of the subway into the frigid street, and whatever I'm wearing is probably wrong and can't be changed now that we're here. "Obviously, black leggings, ankle booties and a sweater."

"Let me see the sweater."

I obediently open my coat. "Mother of God. Where did you get that?"

It's a black tight-weave acrylic sweater — I have, after all, caught on to the no-color requirement of New York — with a portrait of a cat glitter-painted full-length on the front. The tail wraps around the neckline, and the cat's mouth is open, teeth showing and tongue, all in gold glitter, no color, hanging out. It does have rhinestone eyes and collar, I will admit.

"Back home. Street fair in Berkeley. Cool, isn't it?"

"No."

"Actually, Lilly, it's perfect for where we're going. How often do you go to this kind of venue? Never, right? And in San Francisco I do, all the time. This is your basic poetry reading attire in San Francisco. I even read some of my own work, sometimes."

"Vagina-based art is your basic poetry reading? Bull."

"Well, okay, maybe not, but I know from poetry readings." I stand up for myself this time. "So let me do the talking."

"Why? I'm not some suburban housefrau."

"Yeah, you are."

"Well, so are you. Turn here," she says.

"No, I think the map said it's farther down. I checked before we left."

"Jesus," Lilly sighs. "Just turn here, okay?"

We do, and immediately arrive at the BroomCloset. It's got twinkly lights around a smallish window, through which I see coffee-shop tables and two women, total. "We must be early."

"Or maybe no one goes to see vagina-based art," Lilly says. "There's a bar across the street, looks inviting. Maybe we can get a hamburger or something."

"No, we've got to go in. And they do serve food."

"Vegetarian, no doubt."

"Yes, and they're probably even willing to serve it to non-vegan barbarians."

"You know, this conversation is totally cis-gender white suburban matron talk. Condescending and stereotyping."

I raise my eyebrows. "You know the term cis-gender?"

"What, do you think I live under a rock? I teach middle school. I know stuff."

We go in, and I say to Lilly, "I guess it's back into the broom closet for us."

"How original," a voice says, and I turn to see a woman who's a couple of inches taller than Lilly, with her hair up in a topknot. She's got black, heavy-framed cat-eye glasses, and is wearing skinny jeans and a kelly-green silk kimono over them. The kimono is open. No bra.

"Hey," I say by way of greeting. "Is tonight the vagina-based art night?"

She smiles and I see that she's blackened one of her teeth. "Yep. Ooh, nice pussy sweater."

"Thanks," I say. *Take that, Lilly!*

"Show starts at nine. Meanwhile, there's drinks at the bar, and the kitchen's open. First time here, I take it?"

"Yeah," I say. I'm not having any trouble doing the talking. Cat's got Lilly's tongue, it seems. "I'm Zara," I say, holding out my hand. "And this is my sister Lilliana."

"Geraldine," says our kimono barely-wearing new acquaintance.

"Call me Lilly," Lilly smiles, and when she takes Geraldine's hand, she goes up on her toes and kisses her on the cheek. *Whoa.* Geraldine kisses her back. "Good to meet you."

We head to the bar, and Geraldine follows. "Take the seats at the end. Especially you, Zara, so you can see. The show's up on the stage."

"Will do," I say. "By the way, do you know if Marie is coming tonight?"

Geraldine stops. "Oh, shit."

"What?"

"You don't know. Oh shit. Fuck fuck fuck."

"Wow, what?" I say. Since I asked if she's coming I have to pretend I don't know.

Geraldine comes around to me, puts her arm around my shoulder. "Hey. I gotta tell you. Marie — no, she's not coming. She passed away."

Somehow I feel shocked, even though I set it up. "No. No, she can't be." I squint to hide my feelings. Tears well up genuinely, even if they're fabricated.

"I'm sorry," Lilly says. "It must be terrible for you." She's addressing Geraldine, who's left my side and has slid onto the bar stool next to Lilly.

"Oh, god, yes. For all of us. Marie was," she leans into Lilly's neck to whisper loudly in her ear, "murdered."

"Holy shit!" Lilly says, loudly.

"Whaaat? What happened?" I squeal. I forget that we're middle-aged, nearly sixty, and of course, that we already know all about Marie's demise. We look younger and we act like we're twelve.

Lilly puts her hand on my arm, and tells me what Geraldine said. I shake my head. "No way. I talked to her last week. She told me about coming here. She can't…when?" I'm playing a part, and it's coming mighty easily.

"You talked to her last week?" Geraldine says, and I wonder if I've put my foot in it.

"I think it was. Anyway, not too long ago."

"Before or after she quit her job?"

"Wait, what? She quit the museum? When?"

"I take it you weren't all that close."

"Hey. We were friends. Not super-close, but enough."

"I'm not judging," Geraldine said.

Not much. "We used to get lunch now and then. I do art, she works, uh, worked at the Jewish Studies Museum, we'd talk. She told me about this place, and the vagina-art, and I said I'd make it down here this week. Not bosom buddies, maybe," my eyes stray to Geraldine's bosom, budding out of the kimono, "but enough. I didn't know she quit. Why'd she leave?"

"Seems her boss was hitting on her. Big time. And hilarious, right? I mean, really, like he couldn't tell she'd never met a dick she liked."

"She should have told me," I say.

"Zara investigates that sort of stuff," Lilly adds.

Geraldine seems to retreat. That happens even though I'm neutral. The word *investigates* spooks people. "Too late for poor Marie," Geraldine says.

"So her boss was hitting on her?" Lilly says. *One track mind, that girl.*

"Yeah, apparently. Big guy, bigger than me," Geraldine says, and the penny drops. Her cheek did feel a little rough. "The guy comes on board, and he's what, new or temporary or whatever, and he shows up with no warning when her old boss went on sabbatical. She was pissed — usually they actually tell the staff when they're getting a new boss. So next thing you know he won't leave her alone anymore.

So, anyway, she quit. And then she got killed, on Sunday." The day before we talked to Walter Rosen for the second time. "Maybe he put out a contract on her."

"Nah," I say. "Jews don't kill people." Geraldine raises her eyebrows. "We're Jewish," I say, by way of excuse or explanation. We can make those kinds of jokes. She doesn't look pleased. "Really, it's okay. But that's horrible about Marie. Was it some random thing?"

Geraldine shrugs. "I don't know any more than what I read in the papers. She was pretty quiet, except when she was performing. We're going to miss her. She really transformed, you know? On stage? She was a different person. And the vagina shows were her favorite. Tonight, it's sort of in her honor. Well, not officially, since we just heard about her, but sort of, honorary. It kills me, though."

I nod sympathetically. "Especially if she'd just quit. She must have been really depressed."

"Oh no! She was rarin' to go!" Geraldine says. I nod, blink, that old silence that says, go on... Geraldine takes the bait. "She said she'd finally hit the numbers. Not really, I mean, she wasn't a gambler, but she'd found something, or someone, or figured her life out. She was really excited about quitting her job. Said she was going to travel, go to Europe, said she wanted to see cool places like Germany and Austria, and those other places everyone's going like Czechoslovakia, even though that country doesn't exist anymore. And Poland. She was obsessed with Eastern Europe, anyway, always was, and now she'll never get to go."

Geraldine wipes a tear from her eye and re-sets her glasses. "Look. The show's starting."

The place has filled up. Almost all women, almost all white or indeterminate, plus a few men, young and slim, mostly hanging around in the back. We're easily the oldest people here, but it isn't a twenty-something crowd either. I watch as an attractive woman in a grey-skirted business suit goes to the stage and takes the mic.

"Hey, ladies. Welcome to tonight's vagina-based art show. We're offering up this show in honor of one of our sisters, who was taken from us violently last weekend. A lot of you knew Marie Goldberg. She was a regular contributor to our art nights, and a knowledgeable and generous woman who never held back. And now she's gone. Our shows won't be the same without her."

"I hope they catch the asshole that killed her," a woman says from the crowd. I scan the group to identify the speaker. She's a hard-looking dark-haired woman who looks like someone from the accounts-receivable department of Hell.

There's a little collective gasp at the realization that Marie's been killed.

"Damn right," says the woman on the stage. "So in Marie's honor, let's give it all we've got tonight."

Applause and *yeahs* greet that. The woman on stage puts the mic back in its holder and takes a roll of paper from the table nearest the stage. A plump young woman gets up to help her, and they unroll what appears to be a poster together. It stretches across the stage and as it opens, it is obviously a vulva, huge, detailed, and realistic. It's no Georgia O'Keefe or Judy Chicago stylization, but more something from a medical text, blown up to a hundred times its normal size.

"Wow," Lilly says to me. "Who knew?"

I try not to giggle, and watch instead as the poster is fully displayed. When it's completely unrolled, the crowd starts to move. A table is placed in front of the poster. The woman in the business suit hands her end of the paper to another woman, and steps in front of the table. She unzips and removes her skirt, and stands in a thong, heels and her suit jacket. Then she takes off her thong. With her hands she pushes herself up so she's sitting on the table. She leans back and rests her weight on her hands, and two other women take her ankles. They lift her legs and spread them wide. The crowd cheers.

"Va-gi-NAH! Va-gi-NAH!" they chant. Other women weave in and out, taking their turns to hold the poster, the woman's ankles, or just to whirl and twirl around the display. I glance back at the young men in the back. They're locked in an embrace, not even looking at the stage.

Now another woman is up on the table, next to the first. She has taken off her pants and is kicking her legs up and down to the beat of the chant. Geraldine approaches her and grabs an ankle. Another very tall woman grabs the other, and help her kick her legs up and down.

A strobe light comes on and the whole display goes into jerky movement. A third woman kneels between the first gal's legs, and plants a kiss smack on her lower lips. I start to stand, I feel a compulsion to join the dance. "Va-gi-NAH!" I chant. Lilly grabs my arm, throws a couple of bills on the counter, and she pulls me the hell out.

⋅⋅—⋅ ⊱═◆ ✦ ◆═⊰ ⋅—⋅⋅

Lilly is singing "Two Ladies" from *Cabaret* in a bad German accent as we walk from the subway back to my apartment. "It's like the thirties all over again," I say. "The contrast between the burlesque and the actual."

Lilly stops singing. "Why did Mother hate me so much?"

Obviously, after we got out of the vagina show, we needed to stop at a real bar, and Lilly's hammered. "She didn't," I say, and unlike our dad, she really didn't. It was far more complicated than that, and this is not the time, I think.

But the show at the BroomCloset has made it clear that there was a lot more going on than I understood: about myself, Lilly, the state of the world, and definitely as to what happened to our menorah. Even Lilly's singing something from *Cabaret* makes that all too clear. It's not a random choice on Lilly's part, even if she's schnockered. It's an acknowledgment that this loss, this quest, and the roots of the

84

theft are all part of history. We can see the future when we look at the past. And lord knows, even the present doesn't look all that good.

Nonetheless, Lilly accepts my reassurance. She goes on to belt out the *Cabaret* anthem itself. "Thank you," she says in German, and then adds something I don't understand. Her few months in Germany of course left her with a working knowledge of the language.

"What?" I ask.

"That's where the dog's buried."

"Oh, the dog's heart!" That's what Mom used to call *the heart of the matter*.

Lilly has a nice mezzo-soprano voice, and people turn to look as we make our way to the building. Funny how you can scream or cry and folks in New York will leave you alone, but sing and they'll turn and watch. She even gets some applause as she holds the last notes of "Cabaret".

We ride the elevator up to the apartment in the unforgiving glare of the fluorescent light, but I see her with fresh eyes. Tall, with thick dark hair that she tends to with monthly trims and generous uses of Root Rescue, she can pass for forty at night, fifty during the day. She's all legs and boobs, and has thick olive skin and full lips. She never leaves the house without lipstick. She's got big brown cow-eyes, and the smallest ears in the country. We couldn't look more different.

"You really should use a keratin treatment. Your hair looks like straw," she says when she catches me looking at her. Even though I'm eighteen months younger, I look older. My light, curly hair has gone dry, and dyes make it break, so I look like an aging Berkeley hippie who didn't get the memo. Sam likes me to wear it long, so I leave it to my shoulders. I'm half a foot shorter than Lilly, with short legs and a flat chest. Rumor had it the mailman was a redhead.

We're both pushing sixty, but only I look it. Neither of us feels it.

She's been married three times, and I've been with Sam for almost forty years. Boobs aren't everything. Fidelity, for example, is a big one.

Lilly and I make tea and curl up on the sofa. It pulls out to make a bed. Sam has texted me that he'll be back around midnight, so Lilly will make up the bed later, as she has about three times a week since I've moved to New York. "I don't want to miss a day with you that I can have," she says.

"Hey," I say. "Can I tell you about the episode I had at BroomCloset?"

"You had an episode? I didn't notice."

Lilly isn't sarcastic so I take her at her word. "Yeah, from the strobe lights. It was about Mom, when she left the ghetto."

"I don't know if I want to hear this," Lilly says. The alcohol is wearing off and Lilly's getting morose.

I, on the other hand, am getting bold. "I think I need to tell you. These are things that happened."

"What makes you think I don't already know? I probably know more than you."

"I think we need to break Mom's code of silence. So we can heal." I reach for her hand. "That's why you still think Mom hated you. That's why I can't grieve her. That's why I have episodes. As Sam says, sunlight's the best disinfectant."

"What a WASP thing to say."

"Sam *is* a WASP."

"No shit."

At midnight, true to his word, Sam comes home. He's jazzed and wants to talk. He went to dinner with members of his department and some outside folks who may be interested in a new company, a spin on his Coalition, and he's talking a mile a minute. He mixes himself a scotch and water and offers me and Lilly one. He knows we'll decline but he's too polite to drink without offering us something.

Once he winds down we head to bed. I can hear Lilly making up the sofa-bed in the other room, while I tell Sam about the Broom-Closet show. He smiles. "Hot!"

We crawl into bed and he takes me in his arms. Before I can check to make sure I have some Glide nearby he's snoring.

Chapter 9

Sam has already left for the university. It's Thursday, and starting tonight he'll be free for over a week, since next week's Thanksgiving. The holiday is super-late this year, almost like it will never come, and the fullness of hope that comes with it is strung out in a long, thin thread, further and further out of reach. I'm looking forward to spending time just with Sam, and even in this crazy political climate, he and I have a lot to be grateful for.

Lilly and I sit on the unmade sofa bed looking out at the sleet falling sideways, coffee cups in hand. The view of the red brick school across the street is almost obliterated. My on-phone weather app calls it like it sees it: *Freezing Drizzle*. "How do people survive this weather?" I ask. Even Sam, who usually either walks the two miles to Columbia or takes the M4 bus, plans to take a cab. "I don't see how he'll catch one in this weather," I say.

"The doorman will get one for him," Lilly says.

"Oh yeah, the doorman," I say. "I'm still getting used to the realities of Upper East Side living."

Lilly doesn't answer. She's checking her phone for the millionth time. "Okay, got it."

"What?"

"A timeline. Look, Zara. Here's the thing. It looks like the exhibit closed the last weekend in October. According to Walter, Marie quit on Friday, two weeks later. We showed up the following Monday, and again two weeks later. And poor Marie was killed on Sunday. Walter admitted that there was video, so I'm assuming that the video incriminates Marie. Marie must have taken the menorah sometime in the two weeks between the end of the exhibit and when she quit."

"No duh."

"Really? You'd worked all that out already?"

"It's like putting together an outfit. You can do that effortlessly. I can do this. And balance my checkbook. Which, by the way, is never overdrawn. So yeah, I can keep track of dates in my head."

"Boy, you sure woke up on the wrong side of the bed. And you can't even be hungover. You hardly drank anything last night."

"Unlike you."

"Unlike me. You're the great Catholic saint."

You're the Catholic, I don't say.

We look out the window some more. Then we both start to talk again at once. "Are you sure you and Sam won't have Thanksgiving with me and Francis X? It's the first time in three decades that we could do this."

"Sorry," I say. Lilly and her youngest son usually go to Vermont over Thanksgiving, and some of her other sons, stepsons actually, and her sons' friends and other attachments sometimes join them. It sounds like a loud time, and based on other meals I've had at Lilly's during prior visits, the turkey may not be cooked through. "I've got to tell you what I'm seeing." I put my coffee down, take her cup from her and put it on the side table. Then I reach over and pull her into my arms and hold her.

"Okay," she says into my shoulder, "tell me. But let go — your shoulder's bony."

"When the spell comes over me, not only do I hear Mom's voice, I see her. Sometimes it's one of her remarks, you know, sarcastic or witty depending on which side you're on."

"Like you."

I ignore that. Lilly is rarely witty, never sarcastic. "And sometimes, and this is the worst — or the best — it's when I actually see her, and she's back in Poland or Germany during the war, and she's telling me what happened."

"Oh my god, Zara. Like a ghost?"

"Well, no. Not really. Since for one thing, it's more like a black and white movie filmed in the thirties or the early forties. Almost like a documentary, drained of its emotion. For another, it's all stuff that I already know. Nothing's being revealed, if you know what I mean. Like, until you told me that it was really flat in Warsaw, in the vision or whatever it was hilly like San Francisco. Now it's flat. It's just playing like a newsreel, but Mom's the narrator. It's definitely coming from inside me. I think. And while the newsreel seems artificial, it knocks me on my emotional ass every time. But I can't stop it."

"Wow. That's wild," Lilly says, her eyes big.

"This never happens to you?" I ask.

"Nope. Not even in therapy."

"Well, no, it wouldn't happen in therapy," I say. "That's a controlled situation, where you're selecting what you want to tell the shrinkette."

"Shrinkette. That's so funny how you call your therapist that."

"She's even shorter than I am."

"Besides, only you control what you tell your therapist. Real people let the feelings flow," Lilly adds.

"Real people?" I try not to let that hurt me. I tell my therapist exactly what I want to tell her. I get up and get more coffee.

"How much are you going to drink?" Lilly says. "That's why your heart skips all over the place, you know."

"That's not what the doctor said," I say, pouring another cup. "Anyway, it's half-caf."

"So *that's* why I can't ever get going here," Lilly says, stretching out on the bed.

"Okay, we've managed to distract ourselves to put off the telling yet again. Do you think all survivors' daughters do that?"

"No. I think they get right to the point."

"Hey. Sarcasm's my field. But probably true, actually. Since Mom never would talk openly, we don't dare."

"Well, here we go."

An hour later, we're both sobbing. "And that's why you think Mom hated you," I say. "Because you could have sex at fifteen because you wanted to, and she, who didn't want to, had to. And everyone says, *Oh, I would never have done that, I would have been a good Jew and gone to the gas chamber with everyone else, you're a traitor, a whore.*"

"Those who never faced Hell have no idea what they would do, or have the courage to do, to survive. Or wouldn't. She was so brave."

"People who don't outright hate Jews want their Jews to be either victims or heroes, and always grateful and humble: fight to the death, and preferably die in the end if you can't come out of it with laurels," I say. But that's not how it really is. It's messy and complicated.

"You know what happened after the guy who was sheltering her was shot?" Lilly asks, even though she knows. She's the one who told me this part.

"Yeah. She went to the German local recruitment office."

"Amazing. She signed up to be a worker in Germany, hiding in plain sight."

I wait for the chill, the heat, the vision, but nothing comes. "Nothing?" Lilly says. I shake my head.

"It must be because we heard the story directly from her."

They sent her to Potsdam, and she worked in the fields. She had a Polish name, Sofia, like the girl who betrayed her, and they called her Zosia. But the foreman recognized that she wasn't a field worker. She spoke German, Polish, Russian. He sent her to work at the hospital, translating. They housed her with a family. She pretended to be Catholic, she pretended to side with the Germans.

They recruited her for Hitler Youth. They examined her and passed her, and said she met the criteria for classification as an Aryan. And she continued to hide. "And then she met the Austrian pilot."

It's late in the afternoon, and Lilly has to go back home. She works tomorrow, and school's in session in New York on the Monday, Tuesday and Wednesday of Thanksgiving week. "Sure you don't want a snack?" I ask. We haven't eaten since breakfast and I'm getting peckish.

"After all the talk of starvation, I'd feel like an idiot saying I'm hungry," Lilly says.

"That's it in a nutshell, isn't it. Nothing we feel will ever measure up, never be real."

"Inherited pain is real," Lilly says.

"Maybe. Unless it's guilt in a pain package. Our generation didn't suffer. We feel guilty about our cushy American lives. So we invent *second generation trauma*. Trauma is so much more valid than guilt."

"God, Zara, you're harsh. There are books written about it."

I know. Brilliant books: Elizabeth Rosner, Helen Epstein. Books that aren't heroic, books that don't bleach the story. But it all makes me angry. "No one seems to recognize the plain old weirdness that goes with this experience, being the child of a survivor, or the enormous complexity of what our parents faced."

"Maybe we're just trying to define that weirdness," Lilly says.

"Okay. A guilt and trauma soup. And there's no paying it forward, is there? You can't suffer a little here, a little there, and call it cumulative."

"No, that only works with smoking."

We walk to the elevator. Lilly is humming under her breath. I listen. "Stop," I say.

She shakes her head. "Sorry, I didn't realize I was doing it." She was humming another song from *Cabaret*, "Tomorrow Belongs to Me".

"You missed something with your timeline," I say as the elevator reaches the ground floor. "Marie Goldberg quit right after we sent all those emails, the ones to the Levs, and to the museum."

"Oh my god, Zara. You're right. Oh my God," Lilly is clinging to my arm, "we may have gotten her killed."

"No. We let her killer know we were aware of the existence of our menorah. Not that we knew it was missing. And it's freaking *ours*, Mom's." I almost said *mine*.

"I would feel terrible if I had a part in her death," Lilly says.

"First-hand guilt."

She glares. "All the more reason to find out what happened."

I walk with her to the front desk, but I'm not going out in that sleet. "It's not rain, it's not snow, and it hurts when it hits you. Do you realize that it's seventy degrees back home? And that there's no school there Thanksgiving week?"

"Nirvana," Lilly says dryly. I think she's catching sarcasm from me.

After the doorman gets her a cab I head back upstairs. My eyes are heavy and sandy from crying off and on as we told each other the stories. I expected a sense of purification once we had gotten the stories out, at least as far as we'd gotten, but I feel shame and exhaustion more than anything else. There are more stories to come. I can feel their weight in my chest, biding their time, ready to swirl my vision and choke me with my mother's pain. Pain, guilt, grief or trauma — it's all there.

In the apartment, I look through the food supplies, trying to decide what to cook. I haven't made dinner for me and Sam in over a week. The chicken doesn't smell right and I toss it, double wrapping it in a plastic bag first. They still have plastic bags here, at least for some things. I rummage through the freezer, but since we've only been here a couple of months, and eat out so much, there isn't the selection I'm used to. Finally I locate a half a package of bacon in the back of the freezer. The chill is from the freezer, I'm sure of it. But the warmth, dark brown, is not.

Johan and I walk in the woods in the early evening. I know how to choose mushrooms, the kind that don't poison one, and there are places deep in the forest where they grow. We've brought a basket. There, in the little clearing, under the fallen tree. We put the little basket down, and embrace.

The moss on the ground makes for a soft blanket, and we lie there, holding each other after we make love. "There's going to be a baby," I tell him. It's the only time in the whole war that I cry. I would have given anything not to get my period during this horror, but no matter how thin I got, I never stopped. The degradation of looking for rags to stanch my flow, every month, even during the long trek from Warsaw to Potsdam, was worse than starvation.

Johan is crying too. I have to tell him. "Johan, my love," I say in German, "I'm really a Jewess." He pulls away from me. He could recoil in disgust, report me, turn me in, kill me. I don't care. I've sold myself to survive, but I can't lie to the man I love.

"Mein Schatz," he says. "I will love you and our child forever. Keep him safe, my darling. If we win, you will live here with me as a Catholic. If we lose, I will go with you to Palestine, and I will convert. Anything to stay with you."

I can survive anything now. It's getting dark, and curfew is approaching. We must get back.

I hear rustling, and a gurgling noise. I pull my dress together and scramble to my feet. It's turkeys, and they're getting the mushrooms. Johan tries to shoo them away, but they get the best ones. I grab what I can, and we hurry back to the town. Tonight we will be hungry.

When my vision clears and my heart slows, I reach a shaky hand into the trash and pull out the wrapped chicken. I kiss it and thank it, as my mother did before she threw anything out. And I toss the whole bag down that amazing New York City feature, the garbage chute.

⋅ ⟡ ⋅

"So how did she die?"

"Who?"

"Marie."

I snap out of my reverie. I've made spaghetti carbonara with the bacon and egg yolks and cheese and black pepper. In Rome there would be five or six egg yolks, but I use two and add white wine. No sense serving up a heart attack. I've filled Sam in on the whole story over our first dinner together in a week, but I've enjoyed two glasses of wine and I'm not concentrating. "I don't really know. The article didn't say."

After dinner, I bring the news clip up on the screen and Sam peers at it. "Nice looking lady," he says.

"Really? She looks like nothing."

He's been married too long to answer me. He clicks around a bit. "Partially clad body. Hmm… Which part, I wonder." He clicks some more. "That's strange. It was pretty cold last week, and she was found topless. Not bottomless. Which is what I would have expected, murderers being what they are."

For a moment I wish I were a man, so I could say things like that and not feel a sick revulsion in the pit of my stomach. "I don't think she took her top off voluntarily," I say.

"It says 'No signs of foul play, but the matter is being investigated as a murder.'"

"Ya think? No, Marie Goldberg went out to a playground behind a Jewish temple and took off her top — "

"And bra. It says here that she was topless. You aren't topless with a bra on."

"Jesus. Okay, so she goes out in the cold night, takes off her jacket, her blouse, her bra, all behind a playground in the middle of fucking winter —" he doesn't interrupt to say that it's the fall, so he survives another night with me — "and then croaks. In the bushes. And the police are only *suspecting* murder?"

My voice has risen to an angry squeak. I breathe to calm myself as my heart starts to pound. With this mitral valve prolapse thing I don't want to stress my heart.

"Let's see where this temple is," Sam says, using his calming voice. "Cranford. Where the hell is that?"

Cranford? I wonder why neither Lilly nor I have thought to look up where she died. "Cranford is where that guy is, the rabbi or whatever, I don't think he's the actual rabbi, the Lev Zimmerman who's in trouble with his congregation for borrowing temple money to gamble with. He's... oh Jesus Christ, I can't believe I didn't think of this. He's one of the Lev Zimmermans."

Sam raises an eyebrow and goes back to the laptop. I feel like a fool. Has this been staring us in the face all week?

"Okay, see here. The Temple Shmuel, where she was found, is near Cranford, and then there's the Temple Ben Yitzhak about a mile away. Lots of temples in that neck of the woods. Which one is the one where your Lev was fooling around?"

"Shmuel."

"What a funny word."

"It's Samuel."

"Then why don't they just call it Temple Samuel? After all, it's a perfect name." Sam smiles.

"Because they use the Hebrew name," I say, "but yes, it's the most perfect of names, Sam." It's so cute.

"So why don't the Catholics use the Latin names? Church of the Holy Sancta Maria?"

"Some do, like Stella Maris, star of the sea."

Sam nods. "Okay, so the closest one to where your friend Marie was found is the Shmuel one. Same one your buddy Lev was involved with. What does that tell you?"

"They aren't my friends. But anyway, Marie steals the treasures, runs off to the temple to — what? Jews don't do confession except as a group on Yom Kippur, and all this happens after the High Holy Days anyway. So it's not like she'd run off to the priest, or in this case the rabbi, out of guilt or anything."

"Look. Here. Here's a little article in the Temple Shmuel newsletter, reporting on their board meeting. Your buddy — "

"Stop calling these people my buddies!"

"Okay, so it says here that Lev is in trouble with Temple Shmuel because he took money from the kitty."

"It says *kitty?*"

"No, it says that money was determined to be missing from the building fund. What's a building fund? What it sounds like?"

"Yeah. You know how I complained that the dues to the temple at home were so damned high because they built the school and the office wings and that beautiful stained glass window? Well, they built it from the building fund, and were charging us after the fact. It was supposed to be like the tolls on the Bay Bridge: once the bridge was paid off they were supposed to be canceled, and now they're six bucks a throw."

"Temples charge by the axle?" I snarl at him. "All right, so maybe Lev here embezzles from the temple building fund, and that's somehow involved with Marie and her theft. In fact, count on it."

"Maybe she was going to sell the stuff she stole to Lev," I offer.

"No, because if he was embezzling money he probably couldn't afford the artifacts. Besides, your mother's menorah, at least, *came* from the Lev Zimmerman family collection. So they were his in the first place, if he's the right Lev Zimmerman."

"Well, we have no idea if this Lev was even involved in all this. All I know is that he was hysterical on the phone when Lilly and I called him."

Sam closes the computer. "I'm going to read for a while," he says, and gets up to pour himself another scotch. I watch him.

"Come on over here and snuggle with me," I say, moving over on the couch. He sits down next to me, puts his arm around me. No way he's fooling around. Lilly must be out of her gourd.

"And after this drink I'm going to bed. Early morning."

"What do you mean, early morning? You're off until the Monday after Thanksgiving."

"Yeah, but there's some stuff I want to look up in the library tomorrow. Figure I'll get an early start, and once I'm back I'm done for a week. Besides, we meet Angie and the gang this coming Tuesday, so it's not like I'll be working when we're with them. Angie's never been to DC — this should be an experience."

This last-minute addition to our trip to Washington for Thanksgiving is lovely, but somehow I feel tripped up. I had been looking forward to having Sam all to myself, and when Angie said that Derek was working the whole holiday, which it seems he always does, and Sam invited her along, with, of course, our perfect and precious granddaughter, I have to admit I was miffed. I'm happy to spend the holiday with them. It's just...

I look over at Sam, and he's fast asleep with his book open on his chest and the scotch, half empty, making a water-ring on the coffee table.

Chapter 10

Mentally I put aside all of the menorah stuff and pack for our DC trip. Sam, Lilly and I all went to Georgetown, and it's amazing that we've never taken Angie to see it. We're meeting Angie and little Meghan at the hotel we've chosen, the Georgetown Inn, on Tuesday. Sam's been almost as good as his word, coming home rather late on Friday, and a little inebriated, but home, and it's Sunday and he's been with me the whole time. We even read the Sunday Times together, just like in my New York fantasies before we came.

"Your blazer is dry cleaned," I say.

"For what?"

"Thanksgiving dinner. I imagine that the hotel banquet will be a bit more formal than eating at home. I'm glad we're doing this in Washington," I add. "Since *forty-five* came into power, I've felt disenfranchised, alienated from my own country. I want my country back."

"Well, he hasn't proven to be a total Hitler," Sam says. "What with the Rights Coalition, he's been really limited in the damage he can do."

"Except to morale, civility, race relations, antisemitism, the environment, and women's rights."

The Rights Coalition, definitely one of Sam's greatest creations, has been working behind the scenes, stymieing the monster when he least expects it. They've defeated him in court, run covert investigations, and it's whispered that they're close to flipping control of the Senate.

"My mother would have been proud of you," I say to Sam. He ducks his head, embarrassed by the praise. "So would yours," I add.

"Thanks," he whispers, and I love him all over again.

"Are you seeing someone?"

"What?" His head snaps up. "What do you mean?"

Why did I ruin the moment? "You know what I mean."

"You mean like a shrink or something?"

I feel myself go still inside. It's my chance to put my head back in the sand, or to say, *No, Sam, I mean another woman.* "Yeah. You seem so much happier here, so I thought maybe, since Columbia has such a big medical facility, that you might have been taking advantage of it."

"Nah," he says, relaxing. "I think I just really like New York."

"I'm so glad," I say. *Chicken,* I say to myself. And then I hear my mother's voice.

Why would you ever ask something like that? If he is, he is. Nothing you can do. Nothing you need to do. Or maybe, you just see someone too.

That's part of her that I never understood.

Once, when we were just married, your father and I were walking across the street in Philadelphia. A cab stopped too close to me in the crosswalk. Your father broke the man's windshield with his fist. That meant more than some silly girl every now and then. He swore he would protect me forever, and he did.

But I still don't. I go back to packing.

We arrive in Washington before noon, too early to check into the hotel, so we do some sightseeing. Sam and I visit the Vietnam memorial and cry at the wanton loss of life. We search for names of people we don't know, but whose names are similar to those we do know, since everyone who is killed in a war survives in those who aren't. We cry for boys with Sam's brothers' names, his own brothers long gone, who lost their lives without a war. We cry for boys, and sometimes girls, with our mothers' names, for our mothers who lost their lives in other wars. We leave a flower for boys with our fathers' names, for fathers who fought in other wars, whose names will never be on a wall.

When we come to the White House, I turn my back on it. For once I am grateful that Aurora never knew the country she chose as it is now. Mom wasn't a patriot. She simply loved this country where she could live without overt fear. She could cover her past with a veil here and never be forced to remove it.

When I came here someone told me that Jesus Christ was a Methodist. In the supermarket, fish came in a box. When I spoke to a group of Jewish women, one asked me if I'd been raped. Could I say, oh yes, three times? In a time where the first question anyone asked about a bride was, is she a virgin? One woman said she would die if she couldn't have a shower every day. That's what they wanted you to do, fool. Die. After they'd worked you to death. A month after I gave birth to Lilly, a woman told me how much more Americanized I was getting, having lost all that weight. When I wanted to breast-feed Lilly a woman said, what do you think this is, the Congo? I didn't understand, and I welcomed friends even if they were of other colors. I invited a jazz musician who was performing in town to stay in our apartment when the hotels wouldn't welcome him. I mispronounced colored, saying 'red' at the end, and one friend said he'd rather be color-red with me than colored with those who could pronounce it. And yet, it was the only country where I could be what I wanted to be. America is the land of the free.

Not anymore, Mom. You would be afraid, Mom. And you would know what to do.

"You know, Zara, I really want you to make an appointment with a neurologist or something when we get back to New York. Those spells are getting out of hand."

I snap out of it and find myself on a park bench holding Sam's hand, and the sun is shining against the Vietnam wall. "That wasn't an episode, really. It was only her voice, not a vision."

"All audio, no video," Sam says, patting my hand. He's humoring me, and I let him. Sam may be right on the surface, but I think it's just the weight of returning to Washington that has broken the dam on my memories.

⸎

I phone Lilly from the Georgetown Inn. "It's like a Federalist Sturbridge Village," I say. "Only there's a cardboard cutout of Jackie Kennedy Onassis in the lobby."

"On so many levels I have no idea what you're talking about."

"Sam says I should see a neurologist."

"Well, Zara, your spells are getting worse. I mean, you never actually saw things before, did you?"

"It's only black and white, like a newsreel. It's not like I'm seeing things in color, or that I think they're real or anything."

"Listen to yourself."

I know they're right. "Don't you think it's psychological? I mean, we never really felt entitled to our neuroses, or our fears, since we never measured up. Maybe now that Mom's gone I'm letting all my crazy out."

"You never kept it in, Zara."

"Hey."

"Well, it's true. And besides, I never felt like I couldn't have feelings or be depressed. So maybe it's you."

After Johan left to return to his squadron, I stopped leaving the apartment except to go to work. I stopped walking in the woods or going to meetings, I only worked and came home. I had a bed on the floor in the corner of the room where the daughters of the family slept, and I put a chair with a sheet over it to block the view. I felt the nausea come and go, but I didn't have enough to eat to actually get morning sickness. And slowly I started to push against my blouse.

Every day I looked up in the sky, and I sent a prayer up to every fighter plane that flew over. I no longer thought in terms of the war ever being over, only looking for the day that Johan would return. At night I would hear the engines rumble and I would pray some more. Not for victory, not for defeat, only for Johan.

When the letter came it wasn't sent to me, of course, it was addressed to the mother of the house. It was from a comrade in arms. The plane had gone down over Holland.

When you have nothing, you care for nothing. When you care for nothing, you feel nothing. I considered finding an abortionist even though I knew that the punishment for aborting was public torture and death. I heard that if I drank a bottle of vodka and jumped in a hot bath I would abort, but there was no vodka, and there was certainly no hot bath.

I stopped eating, but there was nothing much to eat anyway. Finally, I set fire to myself.

• ╫═◆◗❍◖◆═╫ •

We take Angie and Meghan to the Smithsonian, to the National Gallery, to the Lincoln Memorial. Meghan wants a balloon, and we get her ones with American flags on them. The entire corridor from the Capitol down past the White House and through Dupont

Circle is built up with modern buildings and wide concrete plazas, unrecognizable from Sam's and my college days.

"Since 9/11," says the cabbie who picks us up in front of the Einstein statue when we can't walk any longer. "All the big buildings, all for the government. All the poor people, they got nowhere to go now."

"Like any other prosperous city," I say, thinking of the lines of homeless camped for the night on the stretch of Mission Street from 1st to 3rd in San Francisco, and the little cities of tents and blankets under every overpass in Los Angeles.

Meghan wants to see the *prezeebent*, so we drive past the White House. I roll down my window and spit.

"Mom!" Angie says.

"The Polish soldiers used to spit in Churchill's soup," I reply. Meghan spits on the floor of the cab.

"Zara," Sam says softly.

"Sorry, sweetie."

"You should see a doctor, Mom. You just don't look well."

"Your mother has been very stressed by our move to New York," Sam says, gripping the dash of the cab.

"Granny okay?" Meghan asks.

"Of course, lovey-pie," I say. "Granny's fine."

"Try not to use the third person, Mom. Say, *I'm fine*. I want Meghan to grow up with good grammar."

I smile to myself. "You've got it, Angie. I'll try." My obsession with grammar, my father's obsession with grammar, and now my daughter's. I feel the joy of continuity. "Your great-grandpa loved grammar too, Meghan," I say. "Your mama takes after him."

"Where is he?" Meghan asks.

"He's a memory now," I say. I refuse to say stupid stuff about heaven. For Jews, at least for Reform Jews, standard-issue heaven is definitely optional, nor do we believe in a fire-and-brimstone hell.

"Is he in heaven?" she asks on cue.

Oh boy.

At the hotel, we have two rooms — one for us, one for Angie and Meghan. That night, Sam reaches for me, pulls me close. I haven't felt his warmth in ages. Then he kisses me. And slowly, slowly, he starts to make love.

At six in the morning my phone rings. It's Lilly, and I leap up to answer it. "Yes? Hey?" I'm breathless with anxiety, even though Angie and Meghan are asleep in the room next to ours. Yes, I can be terrified that something's happened to Lilly, or to her boys, but if she's calling me... Too much thinking for six in the morning.

"Hi! I just couldn't wait to tell you! I went out with Walter!"

"Wait. You're calling me at six in the morning to tell me this? I thought you'd died and been in an accident or something!"

"No, silly. I didn't die or have an accident. You know, you really aren't very good in an emergency, are you?"

No, I'm not. Lilly is. She gets it done. She takes command. She gets you to the emergency room and she shoves you through the system so fast your clothes stay in the waiting room. She collars the doctors, engages the nurses, inspires the orderlies, and will wrap the bandages herself if need be.

I faint at the sight of blood.

But this isn't an emergency. It's an insult. "It's six o'fucking clock in the morning. Good bye." I hang up.

"What's wrong?" Sam asks fuzzily. The world could be spinning off its axis and he wouldn't wake up.

"Nothing. Lilly drunk-dialed me."

"Oh. Okay."

I lie in bed waiting for my heart to get back to rhythm. It beats out of control these days, even with the pills the doctor gave me. Lilly thinks I should demand another consultation. It's not like there's a Court of Appeals I can go to, I say. I'll just take the pills and see how I am in a year or so.

I'm crappy in an emergency, unless I'm the only one there, and then I'm adequate until someone else shows up. Barely adequate.

But I'm terrific in the long run. I can bring the soup, take the soup away, bring the soup back, during the long convalescence, without getting impatient. With Lilly, as soon as the excitement and drama is over she's over it too.

But wait! Lilly went out with Walter Rosen? I roll over. No, I won't call her back. Besides, she's probably asleep by now, and won't answer her phone. But I have to wonder.

———— ·⊪⊰•❉❍❉•⊱⊪· ————

The table at the Georgetown Inn is set with heavy china with a gold rim. The silverware weighs in gracefully, and the room is thick with lush carpets, opulent wall hangings, and an enormous chandelier dripping crystals. We gather, the four of us, one in a booster chair, for the four o'clock seating. Meghan is in a red velvet dress with little white tights underneath, a traditional "holiday dress" for the four-year-old set. Her auburn ponytail is bound with a gold velveteen ribbon and her dark eyes shine with excitement. There can be no more beautiful child in the world, I am certain. Except, perhaps, Angie.

I look at my daughter, the heiress to my fair hair and Sam's easy-going personality, and wonder if there's another generation of survivor guilt lurking under that smooth apricot complexion. I don't think so. She doesn't even react when Meghan drops a heavy spoon on the floor, other than to reach to pick it up. I start looking for the waiter. "There's another spoon here," she says. "We don't need that one." No scolding, and no wiping the spoon off to re-use. Somehow that all feels symbolic to me.

Sam lifts his glass of wine to start our family Thanksgiving ritual. We pretend we invented it, of course, even though it's done all over the world in various formats. "I personally am thankful for my three beautiful ladies. Zara," he tilts his glass toward me, "Angela, and Meghan. You make my life complete." He sips, and we join him.

"Of course, I'm thankful for all of you, and for Derek, and for you, sweet Meghan," Angie says, raising her wine glass, "and I'm most thankful that we have enough to eat and drink and wear, when so many don't." I smile at my wonderful daughter, and she sips from her glass. We join her.

"Thank you turkey! Amen!" Meghan says, and knocks over her sippy-cup.

"Amen," we all say.

I raise my glass. "It's always hard to go last, when we've all said what I think," I say as usual; and as usual, Angie says, "Gratitude doesn't have to be original."

"Sam, I'm grateful for you as a husband, and for the Rights Coalition. I'm grateful that we're working to preserve our freedom, and that we still have our freedom to preserve. I'm thankful that we still live in this country that's struggling so hard to keep from going off the rails" — as am I — "and for Angie and Meghan and Lilly and Francis Xavier and Thomas and Spot."

"Spot!" Meghan chimes in. We drink. Sam is looking at me sideways. I reassure him with a hand pat. Thank goodness the butternut squash soup arrives and we start our feast.

After dinner we need to walk. It's sunny and warmer than New York was, so we put our jackets on over our finery and head for the hilly sidewalks of Georgetown. As we pass through the lobby, Sam stops. He fishes out his phone. "Take a picture of me with Jackie O," he says, draping his arm around the life-sized cardboard cutout of the classy former first lady in her iconic suit and hat. I snap it, wondering if anyone will ever want a picture of themselves with the current president's beautiful third trophy wife. Probably so, I realize.

The streets look different without the hordes of students and derelicts that filled the sidewalks back in Sam's, Lilly's, and my day. Still steep, sidewalks still boasting unstable cobbles, the roads are now lined with upscale shops interspersed with kebab-on-a-pita and pizza joints. Today there are a few other families, some couples, and the occasional lone worker hurrying either to the dinner shift or home, finally, for a Thanksgiving of his own. Sam picks up Meghan, who wraps her arms around his neck and nuzzles in. It reminds me of the times he would carry Angie with him everywhere — to work, on errands, for fun.

"A great dad makes a great granddad," I say.

"I'm not ready to be a great-granddad," he says, and Angie laughs. She loves jokes like that.

"So, did you talk with Lilly?" Sam asks over his shoulder.

"Not yet. By the time I was ready, she was already in the car on her way up to Vermont with various boys. It'll keep till Monday." There's almost no phone reception at the cabin in Vermont, and of course there's no landline.

"How come Aunt Lilly doesn't have Thanksgiving at her house?" Angie asks. We'd never lived back east before so we she'd never realized that her auntie didn't host like we did.

"She invited us to Vermont, but I wanted to come to DC for the holiday," I said.

"She told me."

I feel like snapping Lilly's head off. "What? She told you that we were invited but I turned her down?"

Angie backpedals, hating confrontation. "No, I think she was still inviting us when she told me."

I let it go. I would never go around Lilly's back and invite her son after she'd declined.

"So why didn't you want to go?" Angie asks. "Is she really that bad a cook?"

"Terrible," I laugh. *And I needed a break from East Coast family. Such as it was. Such as it remains.* "But we'll do Christmas with her."

"And you'll cook!"

"True that."

"Does Lilly make Polish Christmas Eve?"

"She used to, but now she skips most of the cooking 'cause it's too much work. She buys the *uszki* and the borscht and serves fruit cocktail instead of the twelve-fruit compote. And that's about it. On Christmas Day she makes a *bûche de noel.*"

"No fish? No herring? None of that awful sauerkraut and dried peas?"

I laugh. I hate that stuff too. "Nah."

"Does she make a ham?" Sam asks.

"She might. Don't worry, it's a month away. I'll find a way to do the cooking. Maybe a roast beef with Yorkshire pudding."

"I can't believe we're talking about food after that feast we just ate," Sam says.

We walk a little more before we decide to turn back. It's dark and it's gotten colder. "You know, Mom, it's weird," Angie says, falling into step with me as Sam jogs Meghan along up ahead. "Visiting you here in New York, or there in New York, especially now that Gramma's gone, it's really strange. For one thing, this whole Christmas thing. Even though we celebrated it big time, at least I always knew it was for Dad, except the food, of course. But it's more confusing here. I mean, it was always confusing, since we're Jewish, but I never really got how weird it was that Gramma celebrated Christmas, or at least cooked all that Christmas food."

I blow out cold air through my nose. "Yep. That's it in a nutshell. Polish Christmas celebrated by Jews."

"Well I figured since Dad's not Jewish...but neither is Lilly, is she?" Angie has a knack for stating what's obvious to her.

"Nope. She's a baptized Catholic. Like her boys."

"But she celebrates Passover. I know that because she did that one time when we were visiting for Easter." Angie laughs. "Wow, how did I get to be thirty years old and never realize how crazy all this is?"

"Because it's how you grew up. If you grow up with ambiguity you think it's normal — till you find out that it isn't. And then, after a while, you find out that all families are strange."

"Yup. Derek's family celebrates normal holidays, but shoots guns off on New Year's. *Guns*, Mom."

"That's screwed up," I say. "But as long as everyone stays safe..." Which is an idiotic statement.

"They're very careful," Angie says seriously, "but I'm never going to let Meghan be around them on New Year's. I don't want her growing up thinking that's normal."

From the mouths of thirty-year-old babes.

"So, if you get that menorah back in time, I want to use it for Hanukkah, okay?" Angie says as we hold the door to the hotel for Sam and Meghan.

"Sure," I say, but my voice croaks out the word. I turn away to hide the sudden and very unexpected tears. "That's what it's for."

Chapter 11

We tourist around Washington for two more days, and say nothing more about Lilly, the Holocaust, or the missing menorah. It's a wonderful break, and I have no spells, see no imaginary newsreels, and my heart beats a steady rhythm without skips and bumps. We take the Acela train back up to New York on Saturday morning, sitting close to one another and watching the leafless, grey and red-bricked landscape fly by the windows in comfort. Angie and Meghan fly back to California that evening. I cry when they get in the cab to the airport.

"Don't cry, Granny," Meghan says.

"I'm just being a silly Granny," I say, and smile so she doesn't feel bad. I hug and kiss Angie again.

"Bye, silly Granny," she says in my ear. "Take care of yourself and Lilly. Don't get too nuts about this menorah stuff. It'll turn up or it won't."

I hug her once more and she shuts the cab door. I wave until they turn onto Madison.

When I reach the apartment door my text goes off. *I got recep at the restaurant. Can u talk?*

I press to call Lilly while I unlock the apartment door, and let it slam behind me as she starts right in. "I've got to talk fast. I'm having dinner with Walter up here in Vermont."

"He's in Vermont?"

"Yeah. He asked if he could join me, he's staying at the Swiss Chalet Inn in town, not with me, don't get excited. But he's taking me to dinner tonight. He called while I was driving up with the boys, and just said he'd be in Vermont for the holiday. But I've got to tell you about our last date real fast before he comes back from parking the car. We went to the Algonquin because he called and asked me what my favorite bar was in the City. And he bought dinner and drinks. I wanted the shrimp cocktail special but he talked me into pulled pork sliders. Some Jews we are! I had this amazing drink called the Dorothy Parker — it goes down like juice but it's all gin and Saint Germain, with basil. Knocked me on my ass. So anyway, um, he has this amazing apartment on Riverside Drive up near Lars and Katrina, remember them?"

I grunt yes so that she'll continue.

"Anyway, he's totally on board with our finding the menorah. He says Marie took a whole bunch of artifacts, and he thinks she was acting in concert with someone else, and when she delivered the goods the guy must have killed her."

"Oh my god, really? I don't want to get involved in something like that. We should let it go. Let the police deal with it. The whole thing is cursed."

"It's really creepy, I'll admit. But Walter's super hot. We had a really great time. I couldn't help myself, calling you from the train the next morning."

"He made you take the train back at six AM?"

She giggles like she's eighteen instead of fifty-eight. "No, leaving town early was my idea. Some of the boys had already arrived for the Thanksgiving week and I wanted to be home before they woke up. And especially since you're in DC — I didn't have a good excuse for not sleeping at home."

"Sneaky sneaky!" I say. "Anyway, I'm back now. We got back late this morning. I just put Angie and Meghan in a cab to JFK."

"Thomas went back to Chicago this morning — Francis X drove

him to Logan. So, the upshot is, Walter's going to help us find the menorah. He talked to the police; they're investigating Marie's death but for some reason they don't think it's murder. They think that she died from natural causes."

"Right. Half-naked on a winter night in the bushes behind a playground. Sounds completely natural to me."

"Gotta go, here's Walter," she says breathlessly. "I'll get all the information I can out of him."

"Take notes," I say. "Be careful," I add, to a dead phone line.

"Let's get a Zip car tomorrow and go over to New Jersey," I say to Sam a little later.

"Ooh, New Jersey. Sounds so sexy!"

"Gonna cross that bridge to the Jersey side…"

He hums the Springsteen song. "Why?"

"I want to go to Cranford. I want to see that Temple Shmuel, and I want to see where Marie died." Something Lilly said has me wondering. Part of me wants to drop the whole affair, but in my heart, I know my mother is counting on me.

"Leave that to the cops. That shit's dangerous."

"Oh god, no, don't worry. I'm not getting involved in anything like that. Though Lilly says that Walter, the head of the Jewish Studies Museum, says that the cops say — okay, triple hearsay, I get it. But they say that it might not have been murder."

"So she just felt super-hot and took her top off in the middle of a playground at night, then died? Right. Anyway, you should stay out of all this. I don't like the sound of it. Why don't you see if you can get some work instead? The problem is you have too much time on your hands."

"Thanks, Mister Know-it-all. Though you're probably right."

"Why don't you contact some of the people here in the City who do employment law, see if they need any investigations done? Easy enough to do — or I can check in with the Bar Association's Employment section."

"Okay," I say, "but still, I have to find that menorah. You don't understand."

"I do, Zara," he says gently.

"Good," I whisper, "because I sure don't."

"How are you feeling? After the first day you seemed fine on our little vacation."

"I *am* fine. I felt great in DC, by the way. Even with the jackass in residence there."

"He was vacationing for the holiday here in New York — we just traded places. But no spells, right? No episodes while we were in Washington?"

"Not after the Vietnam memorial. But that would throw anyone off. So, shall we get that car?"

I can't do it by myself and Sam knows it. I have no sense of direction and am deeply phobic about driving, even if I did get my license in New York. After three tries. And hit the car I was parallel parking behind during my road test. "Well, I don't want you driving around on the streets of New York, or wandering off to wherever that is in New Jersey by yourself, so I guess so."

"Thanks, sweetie." I go to kiss his forehead.

"I'm going to head over to the university," he says. "See what I missed."

"On Saturday night of Thanksgiving weekend? It's probably locked up like a fort over there."

"Oh, I'm sure I can rustle up something," he says, and already has his long navy-blue wool coat on. He glances in the hall mirror and smooths his hair back with his hand. Once again I hear Lilly's voice saying *He's seeing someone on the side.*

The door shuts before I can say anything.

I pick up the laptop and curl up on the couch. With a few strokes I check the browser history. It isn't even wiped clean. It shows all the searches and sites for the past week, including the hotel, a couple of restaurants, the Smithsonian Museum's hours, nothing suspicious. Lilly's wrong. Sam's just in love with a place where his Rights Coalition and his research are revered. I'm sure of it. I tell myself once more, *don't trouble trouble, till trouble troubles you.* That's Sam's saying, not Mom's. *Your American husband,* she used to call him, with deep, natural affection. He'd think of Americanisms to say to her. *Let's head 'em off at the pass,* he'd say, and she'd laugh.

I scroll back in history to take another look at the article on Marie's death. I click, and absolutely nothing happens. There's no article. I Google it. Nothing. I try Marie Goldberg. Zip. I Google Cranford. That shows up. Temple Shmuel. Nothing but a Cuban-Jewish congregation in Florida. Couldn't be farther away, though Florida sure seems like a nice place to be right now. No matter how I phrase it, the entire story has been wiped off the face of the internet. Even her Facebook page is gone. And that, as we all know, takes superhuman effort.

<hr>

I text Lilly even though I know she's probably still at dinner with Walter Rosen. *All the stories about Marie, including her murder, are wiped from the internet, and so is her Facebook page. Ask* Walter *WTF.*

I don't expect an answer, and really, given how bad the reception is up in Vermont, at least up in the mountains where her cabin is, I may not hear anything at all until she gets back home tomorrow night. Lilly loves her cabin up there, tiny though it is, and over the years she's furnished it with thick rugs, old furniture, wall hangings, and other toasty decorations that evoke a ski lodge in Switzerland. I know, I've seen pictures of both.

I've never actually been to her cabin, though. She bought it back when she was married to husband number two, and got it in the divorce because the economy was so bad it was valued at only ten grand. It's in a group of cabins, so it's more like a cabin condo — she doesn't actually own the land, or even, as I've explained so many times to her, the walls. She owns only from the paint in.

In the winter you park in a clearing in front of the lodge and a snowmobile takes you the additional mile to the cabins. In summer you either walk or there's a dirt bike with a wagon attached for the luggage. Very rustic. But the association has a snowmobile transit arrangement to the nearby ski slopes, and there's a central lodge staffed by young, energetic people in winter and summer, and by volunteers on weekends in the fall and spring.

On the other hand, my rented apartment here in New York City is furnished in minimalist, clean lines, white walls and sleek black furniture, red accents, a painting or two. Internet connection. And central heat.

Lilly's had liaisons and lovers up in the cabin, and has brought her kids and her dogs up too, and it was a refuge for her when things got tough, which was often.

She spends Christmas and Thanksgiving, and sometimes New Years and two or three weeks in the summer, up there. Thanksgiving, she says, is the least popular because there's usually no snow yet, and the cabin kitchens are beyond small. The lodge isn't yet in winter mode, so turkey lasagna is the best you can hope for, and that's if you buy the food yourself. So it's nice that she's meeting up with Walter Rosen and going to the town restaurant. In any case, I don't expect, and don't get, a text back.

Alone in the apartment, I try to think this whole thing through. As best I can see, somehow after World War II the loot the Nazis had plundered was sold or divvied up. I still don't know the distribution channels, and the books on the subject are all about the big, important art, not about the individual, personal pieces stolen from wealthy but unknown families, so they're no help in guessing the trajectory.

There's a Polish website dedicated to the smaller pieces of stolen property, and I scour it looking for clues. Each artifact, each piece of someone's past, tears a hole in a family's history. I find myself examining the pictures, and while not one has the unique turquoise enameling and pattern of my ring, each one seems to bear a trail of grief, cries and screams, blood as it is wrenched from a pleading hand. I try to shake off the misery and concentrate on the beauty of the pieces, the history of loss.

In any event, my menorah — and who knows what else that was taken from Mom's family — ended up in private hands. Somehow, the menorah landed in the Lev Zimmerman family collection. Did they use it for the holiday, or was it so beautiful that it sat on a mantel — or worse yet, in a bank vault where it brought no pleasure to anyone? Eventually, in the eighties, there was the museum exhibit, and the Zimmerman family lent some of its collection to be shown. My mother identified her menorah. And we panicked. And walked away.

This time, I've got to follow through. I've had the easy, comfortable life that she should have had. I have to find and reclaim her menorah, and her memory. Thank god I've got Lilly.

Continuing my timeline, there's the retrospective exhibit, and Lilly's and my visit. Then, I note, my menorah, and evidently other treasures, disappear from the collection, before the works of art can be returned to their lenders. Lilly and I stumble into the scene with our abortive attempts to contact the museum, just after — or is it before? — the thief, or alleged thief, Marie Goldberg, quits her job. She vanishes, and is murdered. Or not.

Why did she steal these treasures? What was she going to do with them? She always was interested in central and eastern Europe, according to the women at the BroomCloset. Was she going to take the things back to their origins? And the BroomCloset...what a strange place.

And then Marie turns up dead, in the same town where one of our Lev Zimmermans lives — the one who does take our call, and who seems to be in trouble somehow. An article in a paper says that Marie Goldberg has been found dead, topless, behind a temple that no longer exists, at least on the internet. The women at the BroomCloset know about the death, and think that she was killed. If she was. The police are treating it as *unknown causes*. According to Walter Rosen, that is.

And then all references to Marie Goldberg, her death, her life, even her Facebook page, vanish.

Who is looking into her death or disappearance? Who is looking into the theft? And what kind of trouble is Lev Zimmerman of Cranston, New Jersey, in? There are so many questions swirling in my mind, as if this were a mystery novel rather than my reality — with a real live (or real dead) woman in question. And I realize that all these concerns are just a cover for the real questions I don't dare ask.

Why didn't we explore the issue back then? Even if we couldn't get it back, why did Mom just turn away?

For the same reason that she never talked about her losses, her family or her pain. We only knew about the dressmaker, the butcher, the food she loved. She ceased to exist from 1939 to 1945. And so, the family treasures, her parents, and her world were a blank in our lives. Until she began to talk in my mind. The newsreels...where do they come from? They are in her voice, and they return with a vengeance that evening.

———— ·⚬⚬⚬⚬· ————

Even though I burn myself, my chest and belly, the baby will not die. Somehow I think the burns will mitigate the pain, transfer it to my body from my heart, but they only compound the anger and grief. Johan is dead. I need to be dead. I run a fever, and the burns begin to smell. I try to treat the burns at the hospital in between translations, but the infections grow.

The doctors I work for know that I'm ill, but we're all ill, and all they want from me is translations. My belly is swelling under my uniform but the dress is such a dismal sack that the change is almost invisible. Alas, the smell is not, and finally Herr Doctor Schmidt pulls me aside. Sofia, he says, you are ill and you are pregnant. I admit to both, no longer caring what happens. We will take care of you. I shiver with fear, the only time I am not in control of myself.

He takes me to a supply closet with a table for bandage rolling and supply counting. Take your uniform off and lie down on the table, he says. I am too feverish to refuse. Oh mein gott, he says when he sees the infected burns. I hope we are not too late. He cleans them with alcohol and the pain is orange, green, yellow, and finally, mercifully, black. But oblivion is short-lived. After he bandages the burns he says, and what about the child? I say, there is no child. Fine, he says, put your feet here.

I scream with pain, out of my mind. He has tied my feet down, and is trying to soothe me as he enters and scrapes. I have never imagined something this horrible as I writhe and howl. But eventually it is over, and I am pouring blood, and he puts something in a towel and the whole thing goes in a bucket. He too is covered in my blood, and he pulls off his shirt and pants and rolls them up. He pulls on an apron from the supplies and leaves the room.

When he returns, he is wearing a pair of uniform pants and is carrying towels and a mop. He dumps them in a corner, and from the pocket of his apron he produces a syringe. The shot is pure morphine, the coveted, rationed and most rare and longed-for supply in the hospital, saved for the most extreme of cases. He has stolen this for me, and the pain and the world recede into dark.

It's the Sunday of Thanksgiving weekend and Sam and I are again reading the *Times* over coffee and scones. The weirdest thing about being away from home for Thanksgiving is the lack of leftovers. Normally at home I'd be making turkey soup, or turkey *jook* — the rice broth that is cooked for about three hours in turkey stock until it's more gruel than anything else. You can top it with crisp-fried onions or mushrooms, add shards of turkey meat, season with sesame oil. Here, we're eating scones and lemon curd.

"We could probably order that stuff from somewhere," Sam remarks when I complain. "You can order anything here, and it shows up." Manhattan is truly amazing that way.

"Do you want to drive over and see Cranford?" I ask.

Sam shakes his head. "Let's stay in and just relax. We can do it next weekend, or you and Lilly can go on one of her days off this week if you don't want to wait until the weekend."

I remember that there's an IKEA near Newark Airport, and Lilly considers IKEA to be the One True Church, but I still don't want to wait. I'm shaken from last night's episode, the horror crowding in and out of my mind. I need to get out, but more than that, I need to keep going on this quest. This quest that has turned into Nancy-Drew-Meets-The-Painted-Bird. "I'm going to take the train then."

"Don't be an idiot."

"I'm not being an idiot. If you don't want to go, I'll just take a train. No biggie. I'll find out what this Path train is all about."

"It's just a commuter train."

"Even better."

I look it up online and it's simple as heck. I don't even get to take the PATH train, which, it turns out, is written in all caps, but the New Jersey Transit line, and it goes from Penn Station, and I'll have to change at Newark because it's Sunday.

"Fine, I'm going over to the university then," Sam says. "Though I really thought you wanted to spend time with me."

Damned if I do, damned if I don't.

Chapter 12

I take the 4 subway from 86th to Grand Central, and the one-stop subway shuttle from Grand Central to Times Square. Today's in-transit entertainment is an old man, maybe my age but he's lived his years a lot harder, with a thick padded cane and thicker glasses. He's Jamaican, he says, and a Vet. His son's a Vet too, served in Afghanistan, and he needs PTSD treatment, but the president won't help the veterans. "The president won't help anyone who actually needs help," I say to him and give him two dollar-coins I got as change in the DC Metro, closing the circle.

It's not worth the trouble switching trains yet again for the few short blocks, so I walk the rest of the way down Seventh Avenue. Unlike Grand Central, Penn Station lacks all charm, and there are homeless people sleeping against the walls everywhere. It's warm in the station, and there are discarded food boxes out of which the hungry will make a meal. Thanksgiving seems eons ago.

There are departure salons for Amtrak, like the one we left and returned on for our DC trip, but the commuter lines are scattered about an enormous, sixties-style hall lined with Orange Julius and tacky stores selling cheap sundries. I find my train.

Charmless though it can be, New York is amazing with the public transit stuff, leagues better than California. From the train window I get to see the marshlands that still define the New Jersey outskirts, along with the refineries, ultra-urban suburbs, and absurd traffic congestion for a Sunday on a holiday weekend. I have plenty of time to figure out my game plan. The trip takes about a half hour, with stops just about every five minutes. I have the seat to myself and the nearby seats are empty except for a teen in acne and a beanie, whose body odor and pot smell wafts over to me every time the door opens. I can hear the tinny sound of his leaky headset over the train noise, but other than that the environment is ripe for rumination.

He was annoying me, making lewd suggestions and sitting far too close to me on the narrow train seat. I passed gas, loud and smelly. He moved away. What was he going to say? 'Fraulein, you farted'?

At first I smile at the memory of the story. One of her lighter moments, I guess. Every time someone broke wind as a teenager I'd think, *Fraulein, you farted.* Then the realization that she could only have been sixteen or seventeen in that story, and had no other defenses available, gives me the chills. I text Lilly, remind her of the story, tell her what I'm doing. She doesn't answer, so I carry on a one-sided text conversation with her, mindful that her son may be reading these if they're in the car.

When I get to the station in Cranston I call an Uber — the irony of the name is not lost on me — and within five minutes a driver signals my cell phone. It's a black Honda. I look at the cars in the station pick-up area, trying to figure out what a black Honda would look like. "Your driver, Mike" says the picture that comes up on my phone. "Mike" is a middle-eastern-looking man with glasses and a New York Mets hat — and luckily, the driver of the black car just up ahead is wearing a Mets cap.

I get into the Uber and tell Mike to take me to the nearest Jewish temple. He looks back at me, and I think he looks frightened. These days, I don't blame him.

"Here," I say, showing him an address on my phone. "That's where I want to go."

"Oh. The old Temple Sam."

Yeah, exactly. "Is it not 'Temple Sam' anymore? What's it called now?"

"Beth Zion."

"Since when?"

"Two weeks ago. Some new people took it over." We glide into traffic. Mike is evidently very well informed.

"Financial troubles?" I ask, nonchalant.

"Oh yeah. Their guy who runs the place, the business guy, well, they say he stole a bunch of money, but he didn't have to go to jail. They just dealt with him. You know what they say. Jews don't kill people, they just make you wish you were dead."

That merits a moment of silence. "Oh? How do you know about the theft? Was it in the papers?"

"Nope," he says, throwing on a turn signal with what I consider to be unnecessary verve. "They circled the wagons. I only know because my wife's sister works there."

I prick up my ears. "Really? What's she do?"

He chuckles. "Very special job. You know how on the Jewish Sabbath they don't work? Well, someone has to clean up after their Oneg, what they call the snacks they have after their service, so they have to have someone not-Jewish to do the work. So my sister-in-law works there on Friday nights and Saturdays. Which works out great because she's got four kids and this way her no-account husband can be home with them now and then."

"So the business manager was caught with his hand in the cookie jar?" I return the conversation to my topic.

"Yeah. Better than where the Catholic priests get caught with *their* hands."

Can't argue with that. "Was that what's-his-name, Zimmerman?" I go for off-handedness, but my heart is flipping.

"Think so. Myra called him Mister Lev. But yeah, I think his name was Zimmerman."

"Was? Did something happen to him?"

"Nah, he just don't work there no more. But a super-nice guy, Myra always liked him. Gave her a big Christmas bonus every year. I guess he gave himself a big one this year, on their high holiday. Too high, if you ask me."

Mike is delighted with his own wit, and I laugh with him. It is pretty funny, actually. But I know I've got a treasure trove of information in Mike so I pick the thread back up. I hope I don't sound so curious he shuts down, but it turns out there's no danger of that whatsoever. "Wasn't there some other crime here too? Some poor woman found at the Temple playground a couple of weeks ago?"

"Oh, man, that was bad. This lady, kind of your age, maybe forty." I smile. "They found her in the bushes behind the little kids' playground. They got one for the bigger kids, but this one's for the pre-school. It's a great pre-school. I'd send my kids there if they were still small. But my youngest is in third grade, so we're beyond pre-school."

"They catch whoever hurt her?" I ask.

"I don't know. We never did hear any more about it. They found her, and that was that. All the women in the area were pretty scared, but it turned out she was from, I think, Fort Lee, and was left here. And they're saying that the cops didn't find any evidence that she'd been killed. So what do the cops think happened? She wandered out to Cranston and took off her clothes and went to die in the bushes? Stupid cops."

My thoughts exactly. "So what else do you do for work, Mike?" I asked, to change the topic and not seem too eager.

"I play soccer. Not for work, it don't pay. So I drive, and I coach little kids, and give some lessons and camps sometime, and drive some more. Okay, so here we are. It's Sunday, though. So they're closed." He laughs at his own joke.

The temple is a solid yellow brick building with large heavy glass doors in front. A cloth sign is draped over the signage. *Welcome to Temple Beth Zion*, it says, with Beth Zion written in Hebrew beneath the English. I'll bet the sign beneath still says Temple Shmuel. Or maybe Temple Sam, as driver Mike called it. I walk around but it's shut up tight. No matter. All the information I'd hoped to get, I already got from my Uber driver.

The wind has picked up and it's plenty cold. I pull my down jacket around myself tighter and take my phone out. Time for the second part of the plan.

Lev Zimmerman answers on the first ring. He's breathless. "Yes?"

"Mr. Zimmerman, it's Zara Persil-Pemberton. We spoke a few weeks ago?"

"Uh, yeah?" He sounds disappointed.

"Were you expecting another call? Because I can call back if you were." I can't, really.

"Uh, no. Yes. I mean, I'm not really expecting a call, it's just that your area code is California and I was excited, I have friends in California, so I thought maybe it was them. But I wasn't expecting them, no."

I dial down my bullshit-ometer and let it pass. "Actually, I was the woman who called you about some of the pieces that went missing from the museum exhibit, remember?"

There's silence on the end of the line. Finally, he says, again, "Yeah?"

"Look, Mr. Zimmerman, is there a place we can talk? I'm not accusing anyone of anything, I just want to know what happened to my mother's menorah."

"Oh!" He sounds infinitely relieved. "Yes, of course. Let's meet somewhere and talk. Where are you? In California?"

I laugh. "No, I'm over at Temple Sam."

"What the hell are you doing there? Sorry," he adds.

"No worries. I came here to look for some answers. Where can we meet? I don't have a car, though, so someplace near here would be great."

He suggests a Dunkin Donuts about four blocks from the temple. I agree. I haven't had a Dunkin Donut in ten years at least. I text Lilly. After all, she deserves to know when I go off my virtuous path.

I'm not sure what I was expecting, but Lev Zimmerman is a knockout. He's got black curly hair, grey at the temples à la George Clooney, he's about five-ten, very nicely built, looks about fifty. He's slightly tanned, and his mouth is shaped like a long bow. A strong chin and high cheekbones complete the model image, and his eyes are a startling blue. He smiles when he sees me, and it's like the sun has risen in Dunkin Donuts. He turns his head to look at the array of fat and sugar lining the wall, and I see a cobalt-blue hearing aid behind one ear. All, in every way, unexpected. It throws off my game plan for a moment. "French cruller?" he asks as he orders one for himself, with coffee, black.

I accept, and ask for coffee too. When I see the kid behind the counter start to pour milk in my cup I call out to him. "Hey, no milk."

"In New York, you've got to specify," says Lev Zimmerman, "otherwise you get regular. Which includes milk. At least, in the old days it did."

I wonder what this specimen knows about the old days.

The hearing aid explains the tinny sound to his voice on the phone, though in real life it's just a bit nasal and slightly too loud. He leans towards me engagingly, fixing me with those amazing eyes. Under the table, I feel his leg jiggling up and down with nerves, but on the surface he's cool and handsome. And he's wearing a wedding ring.

"Well, Mr. Zimmerman —" I start.

"Call me Lev. And I'll call you Zara." He smiles. Wowza. Sounds good to me.

But I pull myself back on task. "Lev," I say. "I know you've got troubles of your own, but I want to talk about my family's menorah." He blinks but doesn't answer. "The one that was on display at the museum."

"I know which one you mean," he says. "The one that disappeared from the collection, along with five other beautiful, irreplaceable pieces. My lawyer and my insurance company are looking into a claim against the museum, but beyond that, money doesn't begin to compensate for their loss."

He looks at me again with those gorgeous eyes, but I'm an employment investigator. I'm not put off the scent that easily. Besides, he's just said those three little words an investigator loves to hear: *my insurance company.*

"They were insured?"

"Of course. Everything is these days. And not just my insurance. The museum has insurance too, but that's for the insurance companies to fight out. It's called subrogation, when one company pays on a claim, and then looks to another insurer to cover their loss."

He doesn't know what I do for a living, so this may not actually be mansplaining. "I forget that you're an accountant," I say, a shot in the dark.

"Not exactly. I'm an independent trader, but my background is in accounting."

"So that's why you were the business manager for Temple Sam." I use the name everyone else uses. My Sam must have had a point. Shmuel just doesn't roll off some people's tongues.

"I hate that name. It was perfectly good as Shmuel," he says. There goes that theory. "But everyone uses the nickname, especially in these, um, troubled times."

I'm glad he seems to be on the right side — my side, that is — of politics. "We all don the cloak of invisibility when necessary," I say. "Not that it works perfectly, but it redirects the eye, like any other magic."

Lev raises an eyebrow briefly. "That's one way to phrase it."

"Tell me what happened," I say gently. I reach my hand halfway across the table, palm up.

"Which story?" he asks.

I don't know what he's referring to so I guess. "Both."

He sighs. "Well, you already know that I was the business manager for the temple. It's kind of a half-time, or less, job, because the congregation is old and not growing. I...well, I made some mistakes when I was younger, which is why I'm not a CPA. But that's not really, well, it isn't completely relevant, but anyway, when I was in my early twenties, I got myself in some stupid trouble, and went to jail for it. That's when a doctor figured out that I was deaf. Believe it or not, no one knew it before then, not even me. I thought everyone was like this. I can't hear anything out of my left ear, and less and less out of the other. The left ear has been that way since birth. Incurable."

I notice that his hearing aid assists the right ear. "So you use the aid for what's left in the right?"

He nods. "So, anyway, I fucked up, excuse me, in school a lot, got in with a rough crowd, was only good at math and gym, but even then I was such a screw-up because of course it turns out that I couldn't hear, but I just didn't obey, and once I got into that habit and got in constant trouble it kind of became who I was."

"Okay," I said. "So how does that affect now?"

"Well, obviously I've overcome some of my past. But not the stigma. I certainly didn't want the temple to know about my past."

"We're not big into forgiving and forgetting, are we?"

"No, the Catholics have it all over us in that regard. Anyway, once I started having some pretty serious losses in my trading, I had some financial pressures that wouldn't quit. My ex-wife needed some medical care, we were living a pretty decent life-style, and anyway, I was coming up short. I borrowed a little from the temple. I paid it back. No one needed to know. And then the exhibit came up. Marie Goldberg tracked me down. My dad had lent some of his nice family artifacts to the museum about thirty, forty years ago, and they wanted to know if I'd do the same. I didn't even know where the stuff was. Dad's in a memory-care facility, and my sister's in charge of everything — thank God, since I probably would have sold some of the artifacts back in the day."

"Artifacts?"

"Or whatever you'd call them. Anyway, this Marie called and

talked to me, and I saw a way out of my troubles. Now I regret the crap out of it. But it seemed so simple then."

"So you got your sister to let you have the family treasures?"

"Amazing, huh? She's got a lot on her plate, and I told her I wanted to lend them to the museum like Dad did, and she was touched. She always hoped I'd reform. And Marie said it would be so easy, just divert a couple of items, make the insurance claim, and then poof, they'd find their way back, on the QT, into our collection. Because my sister would have my ass if we didn't get them back. Not that it would be *my* fault, right?"

I'm getting a little nervous. Thank goodness Lilly knows where I am. I should have texted Sam too. She's still on the road home from Vermont, so I have no idea whether she's even read my texts or not. I ask the next question really, really gingerly. "So what went wrong?" *Besides Marie getting killed, that is.*

I remember the Uber driver's joke and hope he's right. *Jews just make you wish you were dead.*

"I'm actually not really Jewish," Lev says, and I almost spray coffee out my nose.

He actually *could* be a murderer. "Like Son of Sam?" I say.

"Huh?" So he's at least a half a dozen years younger than I am, not to know the reference. When it turned out that David Berkowitz was the man stalking and killing young women and a few men, in New York in the mid-seventies, Jews everywhere were horrified that one of our own could have done this. We were all relieved when it turned out he was adopted. We can be such jackasses.

Lev continues. "My dad was, or is, of course — and no one can be named Lev Zimmerman and not be Jewish, right? But my mom was a Catholic. So technically, even though she left my dad, and me and Marcia, my sister, when I was twelve, and that's when we started realizing that we were Jewish, okay I'm rambling because it's hard to explain, but I always knew, but didn't really, and I was brought up Catholic, if I was brought up anything."

I stare. "Me too," I whisper.

"No!"

I nod. He takes my hand, still extended across the table. I don't pull it away: I want to hear the rest of the story. "The cops don't think I killed Marie, but I've got a record. And there's no one else she would have come to see here, right? But I didn't. And I just had to talk to someone."

Like your lawyer?

"Were you meeting her at the temple?"

"No. I wasn't meeting her at all. We were just at the stage where I reported the theft, she said on behalf of the museum that they'd look into it, and we would wait out the insurance-claim process. I knew it could take months, but I'd worked out the financial issue with the temple, they'd dismissed me but weren't going to press charges — after all, I'd paid them back — even though I had to borrow elsewhere to do it, but I've still got time to pay them back, I mean my new financiers, though the interest is killing me."

"So you didn't expect to see her that night?"

"No way! I read about it in the paper the next day, just like everyone else."

I hope I believe him. He turns my hand in his, pats my palm. Then he stops. His grip gets hard. I freeze too. He carefully turns my ring around, his breath catches, and his sapphire eyes meet mine.

"How did your father get the menorah?" I ask. "Or the other beautiful things in the collection?"

He's stroking my ring, and I know my palms are soaking with nerves. The cruller is churning in my stomach, and I press my knees together under the table to keep from shaking. I need to keep talking.

"It's beautiful," he says, tracing the stars. "Just the same, exactly the same. With the turquoise."

"It's an old form of enameling," I say. "It's no longer done, but they melted the turquoise and mixed it with something — "

"It's a cloisonné technique," he says. "I know what it is."

I hide my surprise. "Was your father in the War?" It's a dangerous question to ask any Jew, but it's the only one that counts now.

"He survived. He was young, and after the Germans came he got away. His family was from Alsace, near the border of Germany and France. It was marginally better there, he lived in the forest, and in little villages. No one else in his family survived, but he was never a prisoner, never in a camp. His mother was shot before his eyes, and his sister — she would have been my aunt — was taken away. She was only fourteen." *Prime age for the delights of those ogres.* "But he managed to escape, I never knew how. He said he learned to live off dirt.

"When Paris was liberated he was there. He married a French girl, and eventually they ended up here. Sort of. In New York. And she died. He remarried, again to a French Catholic, and my sister and I followed."

"Step-brothers or sisters?"

He shakes his head. "His first wife died from something having to do with childbirth, but no surviving children."

I can just imagine. *Something having to do with childbirth* was quite the euphemism. "And now our charming government wants to take us back to those days."

"We'll fight them."

We're quiet for a bit, and I've forgotten that I might be holding hands with a murderer, at a Dunkin Donuts in New Jersey. "So, how do you think your father came to own so many beautiful Jewish items?"

"I don't think, I *know* how, Zara. I've never told anyone, because for the most part no one would understand. But maybe you will."

"Try me. I know better than to judge." I think of Mom. "We've never faced what they did. Only fools think they know what they'd do to survive. Only fools and hypocrites judge."

"I've never been courageous," he says. "Brave, yes. I've got an amazingly high pain threshold. But courageous? Not so much."

"Nor I." I want to press him but I know if I insist he'll resist. And I don't want to make this man angry.

"After the war, he was in Paris, like I said. People were starving. The Americans were there, and yes, they were the heroes, and the Parisians were grateful beyond measure. But the Americans were young, healthy men. They'd seen the horrors of war, but as soldiers. My father would say, *Ils sont grands, et forts, et gourmands. Ils n'ont pas souffert comme nous. Mais ils mangent tout.*"

They're big and strong and gluttons too. They didn't suffer like us, but they eat it all. "Your father spoke French, then?"

"Yeah. We all do. I mean, my sister, me, my dad spoke French at home with my mom. So he hooked up with his first wife, that was Chantal, and like my mom she wasn't Jewish either but she had worked as a maid for Jewish families before the war. She knew where they'd hid things, or at least where they might have hid things if they had a chance before they were dragged from their beds and slaughtered. The Americans were *liberating*, as they called it, everything they could find, which is to say, looting. But they weren't like dogs, just taking what they saw. And the Parisians, seeing that the soldiers would pay for things, especially the officers, found the stashes of beautiful things that the Jews had left behind, and sold them, one by one, to the officers. My dad spoke both French and German, and he helped the officers. And he helped himself — he made a good business out of 'liberation'.

"Later on," Lev adds, as I feel the room wavering, "he made it his life's work to find the beautiful Jewish artifacts that the Germans had pillaged or the Americans had bought when Paris was starving, and reclaim them for his own."

The newsreel is threatening as the chill and warmth combine in a grey-blue haze. I can't let it happen here. But like the haze in Rosen's office, this one is unstoppable.

When I got to Paris I looked for ChaCha. She was gone — they had sent the Jews away in boats on the Seine one night. I remembered the name of her street, because as a child of thirteen it seemed so romantic: Rue Charlot. I found the road and went from house to house. It was the other house, the next one, the one down the end of the block. But finally a woman answered who knew ChaCha — or Neomi, as her real name was — who remembered where she'd lived. I walked by the house, too exhausted to knock.

I worked for the Americans, in a room where we all smoked constantly since they gave us cigarettes whenever we wanted. I translated for the Army. Every language they wanted, I knew. My English got better. My desk-mate, Marie-Claude, was dark-haired and flirtatious. Don't miss the boat, she'd say to the soldiers, reading from a poster. Remember VD!

I went to the hair salon to give myself courage. I didn't know how to ask for my hair to be set, so I said, please wash and curl my hair. The beautician laughed at me. Just here from the provinces, dearie? Yes, I said, the province of Poland.

The woman whose apartment house she and her husband had lived in said she'd left some things when she'd been taken away, and the landlady had sold them one by one to get crumbs to eat. There was a little box left, nothing worth anything. She gave the box to me. In it was a photograph of my parents. It is the only thing I still have of them.

And at the bottom of the box, in the false bottom, there was a tiny compartment, and there was the little ring I'd given her as a wedding present when I was a child, when it was the only thing I had that I could give my Aunt ChaCha. That was the ring that I gave to you, Zara. Don't lose it.

Lev is handing me a fresh cup of coffee. "You really zoned out there," he says, looking at me with anxious and very blue eyes. "You do that often?"

"Do what?" I say, but my voice is a little thick. I take a sip of the coffee, wondering in passing if he's slipped something in it, then shaking my head at the paranoia of the thought.

"No? Well, good, because if you passed out on the streets around here people would just step over you, or more likely take your wallet first."

"It's just the warmth after being cold outside."

"Okay," he says, not buying it. "So, anyway, that's how my dad got interested in our old ceremonial pieces, and made it his business to rescue them from the clutches of the invaders, or their descendants."

I thank Lev, eager to get home. The donut is doing an unpleasant dance in my gut and the coffee has my heart racing unpleasantly, but Lev has something more to say.

"I know it sounds bad, given my past and all, but I can promise you one thing: Whoever Marie was meeting that night, it wasn't me. And whoever she met took your menorah, plus the other things from my father's collection, and I want them back. I want to help, and not just because I helped cause this whole mess. If Marie hadn't approached me about the exhibition, I wouldn't ever have put my dad's stuff at risk. Not because I'm a good guy — you know I'm not. And not just because Marcia would kill me. But because this is our legacy. It's sacred. Kind of like your ring."

I put my coat on and Lev holds the door for me. "I'll take you back to the train station. It's too late and too cold and too dark for a cab."

Do I want to get into a car with this person?

"Come on," he says. "I haven't killed anyone in weeks." He laughs and it's a genuine laugh, and I am delivered safely to the train. But not until I'm inside the station do I exhale.

Chapter 13

About five in the afternoon, after a nice, if chilly, Sunday walk along the edge of Central Park with Sam, I call Lilly. I get her voicemail and I tell her to call me when she gets home. I know she's got Bluetooth in her car, but with her son riding with her she may not want to set a bad example.

By seven she still hasn't called, and I'm getting annoyed. We order out the turkey *jook* and sure enough, it's delivered to our door, or at least to the doorman, in no time. It's good, but not as good as mine.

To pass the time, I scroll through the Polish Ministry of Cultural Heritage's Division of Looted Art website again, this time looking carefully at each menorah. I can understand Walter Rosen's initial caginess — museums are horrified when something in their collection turns out to have been looted — but once it was clear that our menorah was part of a private collection and not one of the museum's own pieces, it should have been easier going. Except for the fact that their curator had absconded with the goods. That would make it tough.

I still don't find ours on the Polish site, but I'm riveted by one from the eighteenth century: a riot of trees and flowers intertwine and climb an edifice of silver suns and starbursts, while below, almost as a frieze, a fence of small cups await candles. I try not to imagine the family for whom those candles brought symbolic light, or the darkness of the day when it was torn from their hands.

At nine, Lilly's usual bedtime on school nights, she still hasn't called. She's probably fooling around with Walter Rosen. Disgusted, I go to sleep.

My phone rings at three in the morning. Damnation, she never waits until normal hours to call. I press the answer key but it isn't Lilly, it's her son. "Do you know where my mom is?" he says without a greeting. He's twenty, and home for the holiday, and not a particularly clingy kid.

"No, Francis Xavier, I don't. When did you guys get back last night?"

"That's just it. We didn't. I'm up in Vermont still. I walked into town to get some cell coverage. She didn't come back Saturday night, and I mean, I didn't expect her to, really, but she still didn't come back all day yesterday either. We were supposed to leave at three yesterday because she said she had to teach on Monday. I waited until midnight, then I walked into town. I'm really worried."

He didn't expect her back on Saturday night... He's the son of husband number two, and has managed through number three and a few boyfriends here and there, so I guess he knows his mother stays out all night sometimes. But not to return the next day?

"She went to dinner Saturday night with the Director of the Jewish Studies Museum. Obviously, she spent the night," I say cautiously.

"I'm sure she did, but that doesn't explain where she is now. It's Monday morning!"

I know. I feel queasy. "She could have tried to reach you and you didn't have reception," I say, trying to keep him from panicking.

"That's another reason I walked to town. I thought maybe she'd tried to reach me, but there are no missed calls."

"So you're still in Vermont?" I ask, my brain moving a bit slowly at this hour.

Sam rolls over in bed and puts the pillow over his ears. "Yeah. And I don't have the car," Francis Xavier says.

I get out of bed and walk to the living room. "Look, Francis Xavier, this doesn't sound very good. Hang up, call 911. Report your mom missing. And walk to the Mountain Air restaurant and see if her van's parked there. Call me back."

We hang up and I make a cup of coffee. It's almost three-thirty on Monday morning, and it's pitch dark outside. I shiver, mostly with nerves, and wait. Ten minutes later my phone rings again and it's Francis Xavier. "Her van's here. I have an extra set of keys. I can get home this way. But where the hell is she?"

"Did you call 911?"

"They say she's an adult, and needs to be missing for forty-eight hours before they can take a report."

"Bullshit," I say. I've heard that too, but when a school teacher doesn't show up on Monday morning, and her van is parked at a restaurant where she ate on Saturday night, you can't just be blasé about the whole thing. "I'll call them. Meanwhile, drive over to the Swiss Chalet Inn. Text me when you get there."

"I'm scared, Aunt Zara," this big boy says.

"Me too. But we'll figure it out. She's a smart lady, she knows how to keep safe."

I wake Sam up. He sits in bed rubbing his eyes. "Did you have him call 911?"

"Yes, of course. But they say it has to be forty-eight hours. We need to drive up there."

"And do what?"

"I don't know. But this is just one coincidence too many."

My text goes off. *Okay I'm here. No call reception but text looks good. What do I do?*

My heart is going off the rails. I'm the one who's not good in emergencies. I really don't know. "Sam? Get up!"

I call the reception desk at the Swiss Chalet Inn, but it rings twenty times without an answer. I text Francis Xavier. *Bang on the door at the Inn and ask for the room of Walter Rosen.* Francis Xavier is a big boy and he's brave, but I can feel his fear. I wish I could talk to him. All I can do is wait.

My phone rings a couple of minutes later, with a strange area code. I answer. "This is Celeste from the Swiss Chalet Inn. Your nephew has been banging on the door here and demanding to see one of our guests. What is going on?"

Her voice is tight and angry but there's fear in there too. I try to keep my voice even. "Thank you, Celeste. We're a little frightened right now. My sister, Lilly Persil, was visiting one of your guests on Saturday evening, a Mister Walter Rosen. She never came home. We're worried. Did Mr. Rosen ever check out?"

"Why don't you call the police?" she says instead of answering me.

"We have. My nephew has. But they won't look for her for another twelve hours. Can you check the room? We're terrified." I can hear my own voice rising. Sam is looking at me now, definitely awake. I hear clicking on the other end.

"I'm checking," she says.

I also am looking online and I see that the Chalet has only fourteen rooms. Celeste should know perfectly well whether a guest had checked out or not.

"He has not checked out," she says. "Hmmm...he was only booked through yesterday morning. I wonder..." I hear her clicking some more. "Damn."

"What?" I ask, breathless now.

"He must have paid in cash, there's no credit card info. We're screwed if he left without paying. I can swear we took a credit card number from him. Son of a bitch."

"Really? You're worried about your room fee? I'm trying to find my sister! Go check on that room!"

"I'll go with you," I hear Francis Xavier say in the background.

"Call me back!" I say into the silent phone. Celeste has hung up.

I pace, and Sam goes into and comes out of the bathroom before I get a text from Francis Xavier. *The room is empty but I can tell my mom's been here. Her red sweater, the one with the ribbon, is here under the bed. The police are coming. Can you come up?*

Yes, I type back. I turn to Sam. "We've got to get up there, now. Rent a Zipcar."

"I have obligations at the university today," he says.

"Fuck the university!" I scream.

"Okay, settle down. She's probably fine. They probably just went out to breakfast, or to another hotel."

"At three-thirty in the morning? Without her sweater? On a school day?"

Without her sweater. I think of Marie, found topless in a playground in Cranston, New Jersey. And the vanished reports of her death. "And I don't know how, but he probably wiped his credit card information out of the Inn's computer, too."

"What's the name of the town in Vermont?" Sam asks, buckling his belt.

I tell him. He clicks around on the computer, picks up the phone and presses a number. "This is Sam Pendleton, from the Rights Coalition. We need some folks up in Vermont. I think some serious anti-Semitic activity is going on. And we need to find a guy who calls himself Walter Rosen."

He's calling in favors. "Anti-Semitic activity?" I ask. "But Walter Rosen's Jewish. He's the head of the Jewish Studies Museum."

"Right," Sam's saying into the phone. He holds up a hand to quiet me. "I'll text you a couple of pictures, but here's what I can tell you. Rosen's about six foot seven, blond, thinning slightly on top, fit-looking, apparently has superb computer skills. And my sister-in-law is about five-eleven, sleek dark hair, buxom, brown eyes, full lips."

My goodness — I had no idea he noticed such details on Lilly. But for the moment I'm grateful. He describes what else we know. "I'll meet you up there."

I've rented us a Zipcar; we can pick it up about six blocks from here. I text Francis Xavier. *Sit tight. We can be there in three hours.*

Three hours? What am I going to do til then?

Go to the police station. Stay in touch.

That's when I get an idea. I search through my phone. There. It's Walter Rosen's cell phone number, on a picture of his card that Lilly took. I tell Sam. He smiles with tight lips, then writes a text of his own. He gets an answer right away. "Excellent," he says.

"What?"

"I sent it, and your sister's number, to Erich at the Coalition. He can track it."

"Really? I thought even the police couldn't do that, only the phone company."

"Guess where Erich works? In the security division of the biggest cell phone carrier in the east."

Francis Xavier calls me from the police station in Killington. "They took a report, and told me to go back to the cabin in case she comes back. They're at least taking me seriously now."

"So are we. Don't worry, honey. She'll be okay." He hangs up. He obviously doesn't believe me, and he's right. Why would she be okay?

· ⊪ ⋯⊰•❍◯❍•⊱⋯ ⊪ ·

The drive up to Vermont would be beautiful if I were in any mood to appreciate beauty. As it is, the intermittence of cell phone reception is driving me crazy. And every time I get an aura I have to do transcendental breathing exercises to keep from getting another newsreel vision of my mother. I need to be focused on the here and now.

Sam drives smoothly and quickly, and even though I resent having to call in the cavalry I know that this is more than anyone should handle alone. His presence calms me and lets me think. "The only reason this Rosen would want to harm Lilly is if he's somehow involved with Marie Goldberg's death. So that makes him very, very dangerous," I say.

"But it doesn't make all that much sense unless he actually killed this Marie of yours. In which case this is really, really serious and we're in over our heads already. I think you should call the police back, tell them more."

"I told them everything I could think of at the time. And there's no reception right now. Oh God, I hope she's okay. She's big and strong," I add.

"Not big enough to stop a bullet."

"Jesus, Sam."

"Sorry."

His cell phone beeps a text. "Read it to me?"

Got it. Killington, then two miles beyond the last exit, national forest. I'll send cops, I hope they'll go. Meet you there.

"Let him know we're about forty minutes away," he says. I comply. "No chance Lilly just decided to go off on a camping jaunt with this guy, is there? It'll be pretty embarrassing to walk in on them, you know."

"No. No chance at all. One, she doesn't do camping. And two, she wouldn't go off with him and leave Francis Xavier at the cabin without a car. And most of all, three, not on a school day."

"She works intermittently, I thought."

"She told Francis Xavier she was working today. She told me. She never, ever, ever misses work. At least not without calling."

"Anyone call the school?"

Oh my god. No. Not that I know of. I text Francis Xavier. *Did you call the school to see if she was there?*

No, and her car's here, remember?

Crap. It's six-thirty.

Call the school, tell them she's not coming in. We're headed outside of Killington. The national forest.

Why there?

Someone who can track cell phones tracked a signal there.

Fuck. I'm going too. Where?

Just stay there. Please Francis Xavier. We need to have you there.

He doesn't answer, but I know Francis Xavier. He'll stay put.

We reach the national park and there are two vans and a jeep parked in the parking lot. Not a lot of visitors on a Monday morning in late November. It's far colder than it is in the City and I'm shivering to the point of nausea. One van has a guy in it. Sam goes and knocks on the window. The guy rolls it down; he's eating an Egg McMuffin and the smell turns my stomach.

Sam may be a visiting professor at a university this year but he's usually a political analyst. While that's not exactly the most rugged of jobs, seeing as he sits at a desk almost all day, he still sometimes finds himself confronting some pretty aggressive and unpleasant people. His interview, just weeks after the Russians screwed the election, was on national news for a week. But no one up here will recognize him. For one thing, he's grown a very professorial beard. For another, most people don't watch real news.

Sam's easy in the confrontational role, but I'm the investigator. I watch him as he talks with McMuffin-man. "We're looking for a lady who's been kidnapped," Sam tells him. "There are going to be cops here in about twenty minutes. Any help you can give us would be great."

I figure he mentioned the cops so that McMuffin can either get excited about helping the police or get out of Dodge. Turns out he's the first kind. "I didn't see no one, and I've been sitting here about an hour." He takes a sip of what looks like a diet energy drink. He could use the calorie reduction. His pink face, framed by a ball cap, is a testament to high blood pressure.

"What about those two vehicles?" Sam asks. "They here the whole time you've been parked here?"

McMuffin nods. "Empty, too. And no one else came or left. I know the drill. I've helped searches before."

I feel the hair on the back of my neck prickle. Those people who show up for searches on a regular basis give me the creeps. I walk away, and start towards the path that leaves the parking lot. "Zara, wait for the police," Sam calls after me. I know he's right, but I feel helpless standing around. I see him check his phone and text some-one back. I head over to him. He shows me the text. *Her phone is off. His is about a mile into the park. We're five minutes away.*

I feel hope, but then I think, what if he left his phone somewhere and is long gone? I guess we'll find out.

I have no sense of direction, but Lilly's has always been perfect. Even if I got lost looking for her, she would always find me. She's the rescuer, not me — I'm ill-suited to this role, and I'm having trou-ble thinking straight. All I can think of is her red sweater with the ribbon.

When we were in high school, Lilly used to sneak up to the aque-duct to meet her boyfriend. They'd make out, or more, and I would be posted as the lookout. I hated it. I was terrified that someone would come, and resentful that Lilly would put me in that position, but I was too weak-willed to refuse. Finally I put my foot down. I had a math test to study for, I wanted to keep my A average, I wouldn't go. Lilly went on her own. When she finally returned, her glasses were gone and her school sweater was torn. *A man tried to pull me into his car. I got away but he broke my glasses, and I can't see.* She had a bruise above her eye. She never blamed me. She didn't have to.

At least I have Sam, and now two of his buddies from the Rights Coalition have arrived. One is our age, a skinny bald guy with wire-rimmed glasses, a padded ski jacket, and fingerless gloves. Sam bear-hugs him and he disappears in Sam's embrace. "Mitch," he says. "I had no idea…"

"Nothing to it, big guy," Mitch answers. He pulls a tablet computer from under his jacket. "Tracking the coordinates the whole way."

The other guy is about thirty-five, in a wool plaid hipster shirt, hipster beard, and even on this ice-cold morning I can smell the hipsters-don't-shower-daily aroma.

"Blake, of the Rights Coalition," he says to me, offering his hand.

"Zara Pendleton," I say, chattering with nerves and cold. "Allegedly the police are on their way, although we've been waiting here for twenty minutes. We drove three hours from New York City, and no one from the local police has arrived."

Sam huddles with Mitch and fixes the coordinates of Rosen's phone into his GPS. "Let's go," I say. "We can have Mr. Search and Rescue clue the police when they come."

"No way," says Blake of the Coalition. "I'll stay and wait for the cops. We can't give anyone else this information. What makes you think he's really an ally?"

Since the election, the Rights Coalition has been subject to subpoenas and official harassment, and they've uncovered violations of civil rights that we would have thought impossible in this day and age. They're paranoid, but as the saying goes, just because you're paranoid doesn't mean someone's not out to get you.

"Fine," I say, "but we can't just stand here. We need to look for Lilly. Don't they have search dogs in Vermont?"

"The cops do. But we're not there yet."

"I am."

We agree to move, the three of us fanning out about twenty yards from one another, keeping in sight but with wider sight lines. Mr. McMuffin agrees to stand guard, and I see him offer a can of Red Bull to Blake. I have the coordinates in my phone too now, but this seems like a foolish way to look for someone. The national forest is huge, and we are only three people with cell phones.

"Should we call out for her?" I ask.

"Probably not. It's not like she's lost," Sam says.

And I guess we don't want to alert Rosen, though our footsteps crashing through the forest sound more like an onslaught of bears. The thought brings me up short. There could be bears in these woods — in fact, I'm certain there are. I wonder briefly if there were bears in the forest outside of Potsdam, where Mom used to forage for mushrooms. There are definitely bears in California, and we even see them up at Lake Tahoe when we go in the summer. Their principal diet is made up of household trash and picnic coolers left in tents and poorly locked cars.

The sun is fully above the horizon now, and the light filters through the pines and leafless scrub trees and slants onto the dry leaves on the forest floor. There's always more hope when it's light.

I stop to look around for bears, one fear distracting me from the other. My phone says I'm less than a quarter mile from where the Rosen phone last signaled. I don't know enough about these things to know if the signal is continuing or if it was a one-off, and he could be in Canada or back in New York City by now for all I know.

"Hey Sam," I say, turning to ask him about that — and I realize that I can't see him. He must be walking faster than I am, so I speed up a bit. "Hey Sam?" I call out again, then hush, remembering that we don't want to give away our position. I curse and check my phone again. I'm still headed in the right direction, so I keep going until I come to a large fallen tree. The branches stick up and I can't go over it. I'll have to go around it. I choose to go to the right of it, so I'll be closer to the side where Sam was walking, but it means leaving the deer path I was on.

I scramble through the bushes, scratching my hands and face as I go. I've taken off my gloves to work the phone, but now I stop again and put them back on. My hands are icy, and the twigs are dense and sharp. My legs are feeling shaky and I wonder what the altitude is, but it doesn't matter because the longer we take the more danger Lilly is in.

I take a couple of martial arts breaths to steady myself, and move, crab-like, through the brush. I get to the end of the tree but there's no real path anymore. Sam was on a path, so if I keep going in that direction I should cross it. But if I'm wandering through the woods I may not find it, and then there will be two Persil sisters who need rescuing. I check the phone. I've strayed away from the coordinates. Perhaps best to try to go towards the goal, and meet the others there.

There's no voice reception, but obviously there's GPS and maybe enough signal for a text, so I take off a glove and text Sam. *I'm kind of turned around, my path ran out. Where are you?*

I wait a minute, but get no answer. I tell myself not to freak out, to stay calm. After all, Mom had no sense of direction either, and she found her way.

When they told us that the Americans had broken through, I couldn't hide my joy, and so they knew. But the family that had housed me for two years, who had shared their thin rations with me, who had brought me a fish on Good Friday, they didn't betray me.

The Russians came from one side, the Americans were coming from the other, and here in the town the German soldiers were making a last brave stand. I say they were brave because they were. They were fighting for their homes, they were young and scared and they knew that this was their last battle. The bombs were falling, and soldiers were shooting on either side of our little apartment. In one window the Russian bullets flew. In the other, the German bullets came. And from above the American bombs whistled towards us.

The sound of fighting was like bells, in a way. High and steady, and punctuated by deep notes that shook the floor. Or maybe it was we who shook. An explosion rocked the room, and a bullet shattered glasses in the kitchen. The family all dropped to their knees to pray.

We all knew we would die. I could not kneel with them, though if they died, I would die too. I could not die as a Christian. I prayed. I prayed the Shema: Hear o Israel, Adonai is our God, Adonai is One. I would die as a Jew, with the Shema on my lips.

I didn't die.

The Russians won the battle, and on they came. The commanding officer saw me. "You're a brave German beauty, fraulein. A shame to kill such loveliness." In Russian, I told him I was Polish, not German.

"Come," he said, taking my arm. His intent was obvious. A pack

of soldiers came through the now-collapsing apartment. He shook his head, pulling me away. The soldiers laughed.

I followed. I had no choice, but I felt nothing — no fear, no anger, no pain. For me, I was already dead.

He pulled my shirt off, saw the scars on my chest. Unmoved, he tore off my skirt. "Come on, fraulein. Move for me. Show me a little passion," he said.

He raped me, and he raped me again, he called me his whore, but because I was Polish he would not let his men have me. At the end of the day, when he was finished, he said, "Poland is that way. Start walking."

That meant the Americans were in the opposite direction. I walked through the forest, using only the moonlight to guide me, all the way to the Americans in Potsdam.

I shake myself to clear the aura that is suffocating me. Another horrible scene, another inherited memory. I want to kill that Russian officer, I want to dismember him, I want to twist the sneering conquest from his mouth. As a child, I fantasized about killing Germans, but never with the gut-level desire that I feel now to maim that Russian rapist. *Russians raped. We all knew that if they came, they would. It was what they were known for. The other soldiers did what they felt they had to. He did what he could.*

When my eyesight returns to normal I see the jacket, and the blood. It's Lilly's quilted black Uniqlo jacket, smeared across the sleeve with crimson. I run to it and bend down to touch it. The blood is wet. I start to scream for Sam, but a hand comes across my mouth and a strong arm pins both my arms to my sides. I kick and twist as I'm dragged backwards.

The hand on my mouth blocks my breathing and forces my head back, and the lower arm comes up and across my neck, pressing my windpipe shut. I know I'm suffocating, and the edges of the world are turning grey. As the forest fades I'm in a memory — but maybe because it's my own, it's in color. It's as vivid as my visions.

I'm late for my job at the discount store, I'm hurrying along the sidewalk of the road to the mall, and cars are whizzing by at forty miles an hour a foot from my side. At sixteen I should be driving already, but right and left flummox me and I can't seem to pass the test. Also at sixteen, in skin-tight bell-bottoms, I'm adorable.

A car slows to a stop and a man I think I know from work, who also works the Saturday shift, offers me a ride. Thank goodness, I say, and get in.

Those who can't tell left from right often can't remember faces well either, but by the time the door is shut and the car is moving I know that this isn't someone I know after all. And he's black, and I don't want to seem racist or offend, I'm sorry, I thought you were someone else.

Nicely brought up girls don't make scenes.

The mall is only a mile away but he pulls into a vacant lot a block before we get there. But I was born under a lucky star. He's got no evil intent. Only a lesson to impart: If you're gonna take rides from strangers, take a judo class or something first.

Thanks, I'll keep it in mind, I say as I leap from the car. I throw up at work from fear and the relief that I've been lucky again. I get a black belt in tae kwon do thirty years later, in memory of the day.

I force myself to be still, and I go completely limp. My weight drags down on the hand on my mouth. My assailant alters his footing in the brush, and both my feet touch ground. I take the moment and turn my face to the left. I see now that he's bending down to handle me, and I know then that it's Rosen. I'm a good sixteen inches shorter than he is, so although it's terrible for me, he does have to crouch to hold on to me.

As he shuffles slightly I plant both feet and push up as hard as I can. I feel the top of my head hit his chin, and the pain shivers down my neck. I'm gratified to hear him grunt and swear, but as he gets angry he pulls his arms around me tighter. Having repositioned me, he starts to drag me again, but I can breathe now, and I squirm and kick as we move. We come to a jarring stop. He has backed into a tree. He moves us sideways, and both my arms are free. As he lunges forward to reclaim his grip, I reach with both hands over my right shoulder and grab all the flesh, arm, and shirt I can, then drop all my weight twisting left.

Just as it used to happen in my tae kwon do class, he goes across my right, and his lunge takes him over my body. Unfortunately, he doesn't let go of my face, and I twist horribly and go over with him. I feel a surge of pain in my neck that runs like an electrical current down my spine. I land on top of him, and when his hand is forced away it hits the bottom of my nose. The blood spurts forth.

Beneath me, Rosen is scrambling in the brush, but I can't move. Then panic takes over and I start to claw my way away from him. My legs aren't working right, but I keep at it, like a cornered crab in a trap. When he rolls beneath me I find myself face to face with him. I open my mouth, and close down hard on his nose. Nothing in the world will make me let him go.

Except a knife.

He's somehow produced one, and has it now with its point against my neck. I put my hand up and feel its point as he cuts me. My jaws are cramped shut and I use all of my remaining energy to force my mouth to open. He pushes me away and I flop over onto the pine needles. When he moves back I see that his face is covered entirely with blood, and it's dripping from his nose down his collar. At least there will be plenty of DNA evidence after I'm found.

"Stupid bitch," he says to me.

"I'm not stupid," I say, and my voice is thick with my own share of blood, and comes from a mile away. He smiles slightly. "Where's

Lilly?" I say, and it sounds to me like a 45 record on 33. Not that anyone today would know what I mean. My mind is wandering crazily.

Rosen has somehow already gotten up, and is on his knees next to me. "You're not as hot as your sister. In fact, you're a scrawny old hen, not worth my time. Now Lilly, she was a real firecracker. What a woman!" He pulls open my jacket and drags my fleece sweatshirt up. "Not very stylish, either, and flat as a pancake." He cuts open the sweatshirt, and the knife cuts into my flesh as well, but I'm out of fight.

He said *was*. If Lilly is dead, I'm dead. I can't fight this big man, and he has a knife, and my legs aren't functioning right. I lie there, and all the will to fight seeps out of me.

It wasn't enough that Johan had died, it wasn't enough that my father had died, it wasn't enough that my mother had been taken away. I return to Potsdam with my husband, my big, strong Jewish husband who buys me silk dresses to cover the scars, who monitors my phone calls, who calls me a princess, who reads my mail and who will protect me from anyone who even looks at me. I return to Potsdam, and the friends who sheltered me, the girls I shared the room with, are still alive. They are dressed in their dowdy East German clothes, they who used to giggle at night and fantasize about the French styles they'd wear when the war was over. Their remaining teeth are barely set in their gums, and their hands are rough with work. I return to them through Checkpoint Charlie, crossing the barrier of the Berlin wall, and fall into their arms.

In my suitcase are dresses, one for each, but I'm abashed, for the only time in my life, and am awkward about sharing them. The dresses are wool, and warm, and soft, and one is garnet and the other is teal. I know they could never get away with silk, they'd be caught and accused of fraternizing with capitalists, or worse, but these beautiful frocks could remain, if they wear their aprons over them.

One has married, one has not. There were not that many men after the war, not enough to go around. But they live together, along with the one husband.

My husband is gracious, charming in his limited German, but the girls want to get away, be alone with me, and he will not let his princess out of his sight.

Only when we go for a walk in the woods — we'll forage for mushrooms like we did in the war — does he leave my side to drink a beer with the lone husband. We girls go off together, we pass by the only mirror in the house, by the door, and I see one fresh-looking beauty in her thirties and two downtrodden hausfraus of the same age, whose erstwhile Aryan beauty can only be seen in twilight, when the sun offers only one of its last golden rays.

In the forest we hold each other, we cry, we tell our life stories, leaving out bits that would break one another's hearts, until one of the sisters can bear it no more.

Johan came back after the war.

My heart is stopped. He was dead.

No. He was taken prisoner, and badly hurt, but alive.

I cannot walk. I cannot stand. I cannot breathe. Only the belief that Johan was dead had let me keep going, leave Germany, go to America, and bear my children.

When my husband gets restless he makes the man take him into the woods. His princess has been gone too long. The German man knows where his wife and her sister forage, and he brings my husband there. I am on the ground, my friends kneeling next to me, sobbing. He runs to me. She's been hurt. He should never have let her go. He reaches for me. I open my eyes and when I see him I scream.

I'm lying in the pine needles. Rosen has torn open my jacket and fleece. But I have little to offer his boob fetish and he beats me with his disappointment. Couldn't he tell? Did he think I was concealing big breasts under a flat-chested disguise?

Somewhere, my sister needs me. I am not brave, as Lev said he was. I am courageous. With all of my remaining strength I raise my knee and catch Rosen between his legs. I know that this is risky, and that his pain and fury will boil over onto me, but I also know that this hasn't been a quiet skirmish and Sam can't be far away. Rosen bellows and I scream with all of my might.

This is my moment, and in this battle I will redeem all of my past failures. I will fight, and when I lose I will redeem the tears and immobility of my youth, when I had done nothing to earn depression. I will expiate the guilt of not having suffered. With every blow, with every drop of my blood that seeps into the forest floor I will balance the blood that flowed from Mom, the pain that arched her back, the screams and cries of her own mother as she was dragged away from her beautiful, tempting daughter. *Bring it*, Rosen. *You have no idea.*

Chapter 14

I am destined for good luck. I am destined for survival, as was my mother, but my survival comes without the high price tag. The knee that connected hit home and Rosen is vomiting in pain. I scramble out from beneath him, and pull myself to hands and knees. There's no time to do more than pant and press myself up to standing. "Lilly!" I howl, and in the recesses of the trees I hear a moan. "Keep moaning," I call. "I can hear you."

And then I stumble over something, and it's a leg. It cries out and it's Lilly. She's wearing her jeans but one of her legs is bent at the wrong place, and blood has soaked the fabric near the knee, where something juts out. My brain acknowledges the protruding bone but my heart can't or I will lose consciousness. But her body is no relief. Her breasts are covered in blood. Her face is turned away and now there is no moaning.

I drop down and turn her face to me. Her eyes are open but the pupils are rolled back. That's a good sign, I think, from having read too many mysteries. I've never been able to find a pulse in my own wrist, only right on my heart, and I can't put my ear to her bloody chest, so I bend my ear to her mouth. There's faint breath. I kiss her lips. "I'm here now. You're going to be okay. I promise. Just keep breathing," I add.

I sit back on my knees and take in a deep breath. There's not much air, and I've used all I can get to keep from fainting, but I gasp in as much as there is. I lift my chin. "Saaaaaaaaam!"

"We're coming," he calls back, and I fold over in sobs of terrified relief.

"Holy shit," he says when he bursts through the bushes. "We've got to stop that bleeding." He tears off his shirt and ties it above Lilly's knee. She whimpers and I hold her hand. "Help's coming, Lilly. Just keep breathing. Talk to her," he adds to me.

For the only time in my life I can't think of what to say. *"Sen mara, Bog wiara,"* I say. It's Polish for something along the lines of *dreams are false, God is true.* Mom used to say it to us when we awoke with nightmares. And this is definitely a nightmare.

"Keep her awake," Sam says. "Talk to her." He has no rescue training, he's not a firefighter or a paramedic, he just has the emergency instincts I lack. I take off my jacket and cover her with it.

I start to tell her the story of Lev's father.

"Remember when we moved to New York and Dad and Mom went to Germany? And Mom came back and set herself on fire?"

"Change the subject," Sam said. "Talk about something else."

I have to tell her. I have to make sure. In case she dies, I have to tell her.

"Talk to her about fashion or something." He's been checking her over as best he can, mopping up the blood on her chest with Mitch's shirt dipped in water from his water bottle.

"So, anyway, I'll tell you all the details later, but Lev Zimmerman grew up just about the same way we did. It turns out that it wasn't all that unusual. Give me some water," I tell Mitch.

I dribble a little into Lilly's mouth before Sam yells. "Stop! She might not be able to swallow. She could choke."

I turn her head to the side. "There, now she won't choke." I put water on my fingers and put them in between her lips. She licks at them, and I do it again.

"Good thinking," Sam says.

"What's green, hangs on the wall, and squeals?" I ask Lilly. Rhetorically, of course, since it's a joke. Mom's favorite. "A herring," I go on. "It's green because someone painted it green. It hangs on the wall because someone put it there. And the squeals part was so you wouldn't guess it." Sam winces, but a little flicker of recognition crosses Lilly's face, and I'm grateful.

"I wonder where the asshole went," I say. It's just occurred to me that we haven't seen or heard Rosen since I got away from him.

"We didn't see him. Obviously, you did. I'm sorry, are you okay?" Sam asks.

I realize that he has no idea what happened to me. I look a little messy, my jacket is open and my fleece is torn, and I can still taste blood on my lips, but I'm acting completely normal. Or what passes for normal for me.

"Yeah. I'm okay."

We hear a commotion and Sam leaps up. Mitch puts his hand to his jacket and it occurs to me that he might be armed. Vermont allows open carry. But it's Mitch's colleague Blake, and a cop. "What the fuck?" says the cop.

"We need an ambulance, some rescue paramedics," Sam says, and the policeman glares at him before speaking into the radio. I guess he asks for the same thing in cop-code.

"What happened? Who did this to her? And what happened to you?" the cop adds, turning to me.

"She's got a compound fracture and she's bleeding from knife wounds," I say. "Can't you do something?"

"Looks like you already did," he says. "What happened?" he asks again, and I think longingly of the New York police. They would undoubtedly swing into action. Just what action, I had no idea.

"Later. She needs help."

Something finally clicks in his brain and he drops down to Lilly. He pulls on latex gloves and takes her pulse. "Not too bad," he says, and pats her hand.

"The guy that did this is somewhere in the woods," I say. "He attacked me too, but I'm okay."

"What's he look like?"

"About six-eight, about two-twenty, blond hair thinning on top, and he's in his fifties, but super-fit. His name is Walter Rosen and he's the director of…of a museum in New York."

"Are you shitting me? Some guy from a museum did all this?"

"He's really big."

"When you're attacked, the attacker always looks bigger than he is," the policeman says. I don't punch him, but I want to. "So you gals know the attacker pretty well, then?"

"We know him, yeah. And he kidnapped Lilly on Saturday night."

"How do you know this?"

"She texted me that she was going to dinner with him. And she never came back."

"She's dating this guy? And he went off on her, you think?"

I'm getting seriously mad. "Yeah. He 'went off' on her. And broke her leg and cut up her chest. And beat me up too."

"Wait, you were on the date too?"

"Excuse me?"

Sam puts his hand on my shoulder. "Zara, let's just let the policeman do his job. He just needs to know whom to look for. Officer, we came in search of Lilly, after notifying the authorities. We really appreciate your coming out on just our word. Thank God you did."

That pacifies the cop, and I hear sirens in the distance.

The rescue paramedics load Lilly on a stretcher and cover her with blankets. When we emerge into the parking lot they put her in the ambulance. "Can I ride with her?" I ask.

The older paramedic shakes his head, but tells me the name of the hospital. His partner has already started an IV and they're moving quickly. "You can follow us, or you can just meet us there," he says, and he gets in on the driver's side. I nod and they take off.

McMuffin is talking to the cop. "Yeah, you never can tell with these city types, can you, Carter?" he says.

"Nah, they come up here with their fancy cars and their attitudes and next thing you know they're fucking around in the woods and taking up our time."

"And our jobs too," McMuffin adds.

"You got that right," the cop says, and turns to us. "You're going to have to give a statement. But you probably want to get to the hospital first, make sure your friend's all right. And don't worry, we'll keep a lookout for her museum boyfriend."

"You've got to look for him! He's a killer!" They're treating this like a lovers' spat, and acting like they don't believe Lilly was even attacked, broken bones and knife slashes notwithstanding. My blood thrums behind my eyes in fury, but Sam lays a hand on my arm and leads me away.

"The lady's boyfriend did that to her?" McMuffin says as we edge towards the car.

"Yeah. Son of a bitch, you never know with these city guys, when they're going to snap. I just wish to hell they wouldn't do it up here."

"You got that right," McMuffin says, echoing the policeman. "You got that damn fuckin' right."

But we're slamming the car doors and putting the hospital's address into the GPS by then, and as far as I'm concerned we can't get away from the cop and Mister McMuffin fast enough.

———————————————

Lilly's leg is in a soft binding of some sort, and her words are slurred from the anesthesia and subsequent pain killers, but she's come 'round after surgery and can sort-of talk. "I can spot them at fifty thousand feet," she says. "I really know how to pick 'em."

Her dark hair is swept away from her face, held back by dried sweat, and the wounds on her chest are seeping bloody fluid through the gauze covering them. A tent holds the sheets away from her leg, an IV drips into her arm, and her lips are dry. I get a cup of ice chips from the nurse and feed her one.

While Lilly was in surgery a nurse practitioner checked me over. My nose is sore but not broken, I've got a couple of shallow knife cuts that look worse than they are, and I'm pretty thoroughly bruised up, but nothing more than that. She marvels that a *gal almost sixty* can bounce back so well, and I take the compliment without quibbling over a couple of years. I buy a T-shirt in the hospital gift shop to wear under my torn fleece. It says on it, Samaritans do it with Love! I think of the gal in Rosen's office. I don't buy her one.

Francis Xavier has come and seen his mother, and gone to get dinner with Sam before heading back home, while I sit by Lilly. I've already arranged for a chair to sleep in tonight next to her. Her prognosis is good.

"Tell me how I am," she mumbles.

"Good," I reply.

"No, really, I've got to know."

I'd be content with *good*. The less I knew, the better. But I know Lilly. "You've got a compound fracture that's going to hurt like hell tomorrow in your right leg. The bone came through just below your knee. You are apparently lucky that whatever bit of muscle tore along the way was fixable, and the doctor sewed it up when they were putting you back together. You've got knife cuts on your chest — " she takes a sharp breath when I say that and puts her free hand to her bosom — "and you were dehydrated but that's taken care of now with the *suero*." *Suero* is Spanish for whatever they put in IVs to make you better, and many of us, including me, believe in its magical qualities.

"Water, electrolytes, some salt, some glucose," the nurse says as she goes by.

"Doesn't make it any less magical to know the potion's formula," I say. Lilly smiles a little and that's good too.

"…I remember the knife," she says.

"Do you want to tell me? At some point you'll have to. And the police, too."

"The guy's a Nazi," she says, and tears start to roll. I hold her hand and let her cry.

The nurse comes over. "If you're going to upset her, I'll have to ask you to leave."

"I'm not the one upsetting her. Getting carved up by a bastard is upsetting her."

Lilly squeezes my hand and I know she's saying *don't make a scene.* I also know I'm taking it out on the wrong person.

"I'm sorry," I say to the nurse. "I'm just really upset that someone would do this to my sister."

"Sure," the nurse says, and I wonder if she means Oh yeah, sure you are rather than *I'm sure you are.* It doesn't matter, but it bothers me. I think of pursuing it, but for once I don't.

The trauma ward isn't the best place to get the whole story from Lilly, with no privacy but a curtain to pull around her. There are four patients and six beds, and I'm told she'll be moved to a private room tomorrow, assuming she continues to recover well from the surgery and the dehydration. I watch her drift into a drugged sleep, and start to disentangle my hand from hers. She startles a bit. "Stay," she mumbles. I sit back down, close my own eyes, and in this uncomfortable position I start to drift away.

Around midnight a different nurse changes the IV bag and gives Lilly an injection. "Ow!" she says, and I know she's still drugged. She'd never complain about a shot in her normal self. It's woken her up, though, and the nurse says, "How's the pain? From one to ten, ten being the worst."

"From one to ten?" Lilly answers. "From one to ten it's *Fuck.*"

"Well that shot should make it better. Maybe take it down to *Screw.*"

"Everyone's a comedian," I say, and Lilly smiles. Mom used to say that a lot.

Lilly closes her eyes. "You know, I figured out why Mother hated me so much."

Oh sweet Jesus, not now. "She didn't hate you."

"She did. And I don't blame her. I figured it out while I was in the woods. From your spells, or episodes, or whatever you call them, plus everything I remember her telling me, and what dad told me. I don't know why I didn't realize, but I think until you told me the part about the abortion, I just didn't want to put two and two together. Dad did tell me about Johan, by the way."

"I know. And then you told me. Mother never did. She told me that she had been in love, and that she thought about the man every day for ten years. She told me that after Guillermo broke up with me. And I understand how she felt — it's been forty years, and I still think about Guillermo. Not daily, not regretfully, but I do."

My attempted diversion doesn't work. Lilly stays on track. "I wasn't the baby she wanted. All the pain must have brought it back to her, the agony, the blood, and then instead of a beautiful blond baby — I think Johan's baby would have been blond, don't you?"

"No guarantees. Mother's skin was olive like yours, remember."

"I'm so glad you can finally call her Mother, even if she never got to hear it. She hated to be called Mom."

"It was an oversight this time. And the only reason she hated it was it sounded weird to her, okay? Not because it was freighted with anything. Speaking of motherhood, Francis Xavier was super-brave. You've got a real star of a son, you know that?"

"She suffered and bled and all she got was this huge, dark baby. She said she was shocked at how ugly I was. And the nurse, she was named Lila, she told Mother that I was beautiful for a baby. Mother always said I was named for Lila the nurse, not for her mother, not for Leokadia. She didn't even want to give me that. And it was Dad who gave me a Hebrew name. Not Mother."

So you didn't make it up on the plane, I think. You already had it.

Lilly is crying now, and I'm sure this nurse will threaten to kick me out too if this keeps up. It might be better if she did, anyway — Sam's at the Embassy Suites near the hospital, and even though it's one in the morning he can come get me. I can sleep in a bed and come in refreshed, in better shape to help Lilly.

"Do you want me to go?" I ask Lilly. I'm such a coward.

"Of course not," she says. "I need you to stay with me."

I remind myself that visiting the sick is a mitzvah. Just because it's unpleasant doesn't mean I get out of it.

"...And every day she had to look at me and remember the child she should have had. That's why she loved you. Little and blonde and you could pass, just like she did. And when we moved to San Antonio for Dad's residency it was great that at least one of her kids didn't look Jewish. Two would have been better. You just don't remember because you were too young."

The eighteen-month difference between us counts in our childhood memories: there's so much more a five-year-old remembers than a three-year-old can.

"That's why she gave you your Hebrew name. Because with you, she remembered."

Mom gave me a Hebrew name because I didn't look Jewish...the contradiction is left unremarked. It's not worth it, and wouldn't stand up to examination. So many of our actions are stretched helplessly between the beams of our beliefs, hanging like shredded cloth, barely supported yet making the foundation of our existence. I say as much.

"I'm the one on drugs, and you sound like you're tripping."

So much for midnight philosophy.

And then this big Jewish daughter ended up not Jewish at all, but a Catholic like all her friends in San Antonio, all the little girls in starched pinafores and white communion dresses in Nuevo Laredo. And she had sex because she wanted love. She lost her virginity at fifteen because her mother was setting fire to herself and her father was obsessed with himself and his princess, and this big, needy and loving girl wanted someone to caress her and tell her she was beautiful, and that her dark unruly hair was electrifying, and that her big breasts that had attracted the attention of older boys, and even men, since she was eleven, were sumptuous and sensuous…and not because she had to in order to survive on her own in a world where rape, torture and death were the fates of anyone who made a mistake, and even those who didn't.

"We had a brother," Lilly says.

"I know."

"We had a brother and Mother hated me and scalded me with boiling water because he died."

"No. You're mixing things up," I whisper.

"But we did have a brother," she says again.

And now Lilly and I are both crying. Because actually it's all true.

⁘⸎◆⧫◆⸎⁘

In the photo Mom is sitting in the grass. She's wearing a yellow dress. I know that it's yellow because I remember the day the picture was taken, even if I was barely three and it's in black and white. I remember the little white flowers in the grass, with spiky petals and yellow centers, and I remember her sitting there with me. I'm in the picture. I'm holding one of the little flowers, and the sun is shining off my ash-blonde hair.

I have dark eyes and I'm fixated on the flower in my fist, holding it out to my mother. She's smiling a bit.

On the grass on a blanket is a little baby boy. Where is that little boy now? Jews don't believe in an afterlife in the same sense of Christian heaven and hell, and many Jews don't believe in any afterlife at all, but isn't there still a heaven for children who die before their parents? Is there a place that a mother's soul can visit in the night, when neither tears nor sleep will come? And in this life, can someone who has suffered so much ever empty the well of bad luck, use up all her allotted suffering, and be spared any more? Evidently not. The well is bottomless.

But when you get to survive, when your own delicate mother is brutalized and taken away, when your own industrialist, socialist, vegetarian father is shot in front of his wife and daughter, when your pretty cousins are raped and sent to camps, or into the fields as whores for the soldiers until they die of rape and infection, or when your uncle is shot, every fifth soldier, by his own captain, and somehow you live, you are sure that you deserve to suffer. No, the well isn't bottomless, you just haven't reached its fundament yet.

We never speak of that little boy who outlived the photo by less than a year. I remember that his name was Joseph — Dad called him Joey — and Mom held him when he cried but she cried when he smiled. Mom stirred the soup on the stove and cried, and said if it would make him well she would get into the soup-pot herself. Lilly climbed onto a chair and threw her arms around Mom's neck. The soup pot overturned and the boiling soup came spilling down and Lilly screamed as the soup scalded her sweet, tender child-skin. Lilly spent a week in the hospital, an object-lesson to children who played too close to the stove. I don't remember Joey after that.

We never speak of Germany. We never say the word *Jewish*. We never say the word *rape* or speak their names, Joseph or Johan. But they live with us. And you can only break so many windshields, only put so many silk dresses on your princess. The scars, like tattoos of numbers that are not on your arm, don't fade.

Chapter 15

I hold my phone next to Lilly. She's sitting up in the hospital bed in her room. They're going to release her tomorrow, and Francis Xavier will bring the van to take her home. The police are coming to interview her this afternoon, so we agree that this morning she'll tell me everything she can remember, before she formulates it for the cops. After all, the likelihood of the Vermont police catching Walter Rosen is between zero and none. He's likely left the country by now, never mind the glorious Green Mountain State of Vermont.

"Tell me first about your date on Wednesday night," I say. Was it Wednesday? I try to think back to when she called me and woke me up. Thanksgiving seems a lifetime ago.

"You have a black eye, did you know that?" Lilly says. Yes, I do know. I tell her to quit stalling. "Okay, so he emailed me, which I thought then was risky, I mean what if I don't check my email on school days? Or if my son uses my computer, which he does even though I tell him not to. Anyway, he emailed me and asked me if I was available and interested in going for a drink that evening after work. I don't think he realized then that I live out in the boonies, not downtown."

"I guess he found out that night."

"I didn't let on. Actually, when we were out, I told him that I lived in your apartment."

"Wait — what? You gave him my address?"

"Well, I didn't know he was a conniving bastard then, now did I?"

"With your track record, you should at least have suspected."

"Hey! Well, maybe you're right, but you didn't suspect either, did you? So I said yes, but I couldn't meet him until eight or so. He agreed, and we decided to meet at the Algonquin. I got there a little late, and he was waiting at the bar. You know how cool that place is, with the blue glow, and the glass case with Dorothy Parker's book in it and the whole ghost-y Round Table vibe. I took you to see the actual Round Table, remember?"

"I do. It was great. Now, what did you talk about?"

"General stuff. He wore a really nice tweed sport coat and a dark blue cashmere sweater under it, it really brought out his eyes. They're grey, his eyes. Beautiful in the Algonquin, scary crazy in the woods."

Lilly has an amazing memory, but it's not like mine. I can recite an entire conversation verbatim, including tones of voice, nuance and intent. I may not recognize someone on the street tomorrow after an intimate evening of deep conversation and baring of the soul, but I'll remember every word they said.

"I'm not sure I'd recognize him if I saw him again, except for the height and the blond hair," I say.

"I know. You're defective that way."

I let it pass. "So, general conversation. What do you remember from it?"

"He said he was born in Philadelphia, and that his father came from Germany. Got out before the war. His father was a teenager and came over here with his uncle. Of course, now I don't know how much is true — but that's what he said. And I told him about Mother, surviving the Holocaust, being all alone. And of course we talked about the menorah. God, do I ever regret that! We talked, I told him all about how we recognized it, and how we were trying to get it back, and I told him — nothing secret of course — " I bite my tongue. "Just the part about calling and emailing all the Lev Zimmermans, and how we didn't find anything out that way. In retrospect, he was a lot more relaxed once I told him we hadn't gotten anywhere with that."

No kidding. "And then what?"

"Well, we had dinner, and then, well, he suggested we get a nightcap. So we did."

"You told me that in our two-minute chat on Saturday. What else?"

"We went...no, I've got to tell you the truth. He told me he has an apartment up on Riverside Drive, near Katrina, like I said, but we couldn't go there. He said there'd been a flood and it was a mess."

"So you made up the part about how amazing his apartment was?"

"Um, yeah."

"Why?"

Lilly hesitates.

"Look, Lilly, I don't care that you slept with him, I mean, that's obvious, right? Since you called me at six in the morning to tell me about it on the train back up to Katonah. But why did you make up the part about his apartment?"

"Shit. Because we stayed in yours."

I turn off the phone recorder, and walk out of the room. Holy fucking Christ. I walk to the end of the hall and back, and have to do it again before I can even think. The hospital is small, especially compared to the urban hospitals in New York and San Francisco, and I can cover the full length of the hallway with patient rooms in less than a minute. After the third pace I can think about going back into Lilly's room.

"Holy fucking Christ," I say when I walk back in.

"I know. It was stupid. I should have told you."

"No, you idiot. You just shouldn't have done it. I can't believe it. You took this fucking murderer to my apartment? Not only he could have killed you, but he now knows where we live."

"Well, I didn't know he was a murderer or whatever he is at the time, did I?"

No, she didn't. But still.

"All right, but...Okay, so you spent the night."

"Yeah, it was amazing. I hadn't had sex in almost two years. It hurt like hell the first time, but you've got that nice lube, that Silk, that's really high quality stuff, by the way, it was super-useful. And he's a very, very generous lover. It was all about me, all about making me happy. He left no stone unturned, if you know what I mean."

I don't answer. She used my lube. I take deep breaths instead. "Good, I'm glad. Then what?"

"I told him you were coming back that day, or might be, or maybe Sam was, I don't know what I said, but he left at five thirty in the morning, and then I left and took the subway to Grand Central and the train back up to Katonah. And I did try to talk to you from the train, you know."

"Yeah, at six in the morning."

"Well, I was up."

That, in essence, is Lilly.

"And he told you that the cops didn't think Marie was murdered. And he told you that she stole the menorah and was making a drop in Cranston when she died. Right?"

"Yeah, I told you. But then you started texting me all that stuff, about meeting up with Lev Zimmerman and how he was involved, and of course at first I was just telling Walter about it every time you sent a text, and then, well, after we dined, we did go back to his room at the Swiss Chalet for a little after-dinner mint..."

"I haven't heard *that* expression before."

"I made it up," Lilly says, pleased with herself. "But at that point you started texting more crazy shit about how all the info's been wiped from the internet, and while I'm telling Walter about that I notice that he's getting a little manic. All that good loving? It gets mighty weird."

I'm not sure I want the details. But it might be better for Lilly to get it all out. "So he reads the texts?"

"Yeah. Every one of them. And he gets more and more intense."

"About the sex or the Marie Goldberg stuff?"

"Well, we didn't talk about the Marie stuff then, and he was getting wilder about the sex. I was a little scared — not half as scared as I should have been, it turns out. I'm really not into bondage, you know. Not even a little bit, and I told him that, but he was very persuasive, so I let him tie my hands. I'm not sure you want to hear this…"

"I don't. But tell me as much as you want, so it doesn't haunt you later. I'm your person, you know."

We had established that we each needed a "person" to confide in, especially during Mom's illness, and I had Sam. She had me.

"Well, I think I'll skip the sex parts, but he's really, really talented. I'll leave it at that. So much so that I was lulled, you know? Into trusting him. Then he said, 'Let's go camping, there's something I want to show you.' And you know what I said to that, right?"

"Same as me. *No. That's why God made houses. So we wouldn't have to sleep outside.*"

"Yep. And besides, it was already Sunday around noon, and I had to get back to Francis Xavier, and we were set to leave at three. Monday I was teaching. So I said no, and started to get dressed. I went to text Francis Xavier, since we can usually get texts at the cabin, and my phone was out of juice. I asked Walter to lend me his charger so I could plug in and text, but he said he had a different brand and it wouldn't work. So I said, 'Okay, lend me your phone and I'll text my son,' and he said that would get awkward. Finally he said he'd drive me back to the restaurant where my van was parked and I could plug into my car and text Francis Xavier on my way back to the cabin, which is stupid because that's only a twenty-minute drive, but I didn't see any other way around it.

"So I start to get dressed and I go into the bathroom to fix myself up and he comes in with my phone. He says, 'Here, I think there's a little juice left,' and he lifts up my sweater at the same time and starts to kiss my boobs. This guy is obsessed, and I mean *obsessed*, with boobs, by the way."

"No kidding. He even went after mine. Or at least went looking for them."

"You're not that flat, Zara."

"Compared to a fully-grown woman I am. But let's stay on topic. The cops will be here in fifteen minutes."

"Okay, so I'm a little sore at this point, plus I want to text Francis X, so I kind of push Walter away, but he's got my sweater off again and so we tussle a little bit. Somehow he ends up with my sweater *and* my phone and he drops them both in the toilet. And you know what *that* does to the phone, right?"

This is the third phone she's gone through. "Yeah. And your texts are all gone."

"Yup. And my sweater's wet. And he's all over me again. Remember that this guy is almost seven feet tall, right? I mean, no one is *that* much bigger than I am. Eventually I say, 'We've *really* got to go,' because it's already about three and I definitely have to get back. So I just put my jacket on over my bra, I zip up and we get in his car. I just leave the damn wet sweater on the floor. But instead of heading back to the restaurant, he heads to the highway. I say, 'Hey, wait a minute!' and he says he just wants to show me something real quick. And I start to argue with him. And I may have said something about him knowing who killed Marie."

"Oh, jeez."

"I know. Not smart. I didn't think… Then he pulls over and takes out a knife. Oh god…"

She puts her hands over her face, and I lean in and kiss her head. "It's okay. It's not your fault."

"I know, I know, but I always fought them off. I just couldn't this time. He's huge. And he unzips my jacket and cuts away my bra, and I'm fighting him off, but he has that knife. And somehow he ties my hands with my bra. And cuts me up. He's slashing at my breasts! I was screaming and kicking him, and I landed one in his groin, and that really hurt him, but not enough to stop him. In the end, it just made him mad, I think."

"I think you bruised him enough that when I landed one there, it really slammed him."

"Good for you, Zara. I'm so proud of you."

What the hell is *that* all about?

"You know, you rescued yourself. Instead of me rescuing you. In fact, *you* rescued *me* this time."

I don't say anything. I've rescued her a million times, from problems she gets into because she talks before she thinks. But yes, she's been my physical guardian angel. Anyway, she doesn't need an answer — she's talking again.

"So we get to the forest, and there's no one there. A couple of pickups are parked in the lot, but not a soul in them. Even so, he swings out of the lot and parks on the shoulder about a hundred yards down from the lot. He drags me from his car and hauls me into the forest. I've got blood on my jacket but the cuts aren't too deep, I guess, since I stopped bleeding pretty quickly. But it's getting dark and I'm petrified."

"And cold, I'll bet."

"That too. We walk for what seems like an hour, and he keeps muttering, so I realize that he's looking for something and not finding it. So I say, 'Look, Walter. I'm really great at finding things. I've got a perfect sense of direction, even when I've never been someplace. I'll make you a deal. You tell me what we're looking for and I'll help you, and you untie me.' He says he's not that stupid, and he turns on his phone and fiddles with the GPS. I think, *oh thank god, now someone can find us*. So we start walking again and eventually we get to this kind of a lean-to, or a shack, and we go inside. It's gotten dark and it's cold as hell at this point, but there's a fire pit and Walter puts some sticks in and lights a fire. He heats up some water and makes hot chocolate, and offers me some. I'm chattering and I'm scared shitless, but I don't take his fucking hot chocolate. He tries to insist, says I'm shivering and in shock, but I knock it away with my chin when he tries to feed it to me. It makes me nauseous to even get near it.

"At that point I haven't peed in hours, and I realize I really have to pee. So he says, 'Yeah, me too,' and he unties me. 'Don't wander off, Liebling,' he says, which creeps me out beyond belief, and then he watches me while I pee outside. Of course he drags me back in afterwards.

"It's pitch fucking dark outside and even with my sense of direction I know I can't find my way out of the woods at night. So I just kind of hunker down. Even creepier is that he pulls me to into his arms and holds me, and amazingly enough, I fall asleep."

"Humans are amazing," I say.

"Yeah. When I wake up I'm cold and really achy. No one our age should sleep on the ground. But the sky is slightly grey and Walter's gone and I know, *now's my moment*. I sneak out to see if he's just outside. He's not, and I creep away from the lean-to.

"I don't know which way is which but with the very faint light I figure, *so that's got to be east*, and I know by instinct that the road runs north and south so I go away from the dawn. And just when I start to relax I run smack into Rosen, who's crawling around on his hands and knees like some guy looking for a contact lens. Of course he tackles me, but I know it's my last chance.

"At that point I'm screaming and screaming no matter what he does, and he's shouting at me, and he's trying to drag me and I'm swinging my fists for all I'm worth. And at one point I really connect with his arm and his cell phone goes flying, and then he really goes ape shit. He shoves me to the ground, and there's this pain beyond belief in my leg. I must also have hit my head, but I don't know that, but the next thing is this dream where I'm lying in the forest, and I keep going in and out of that dream, and then you were in the dream, and then I was here."

"God, you poor thing. But you really were brave, as always."

"Thanks, Zara. I feel like an idiot. Again."

I hold her hand for a while, until the nurse comes in and takes her temperature. "Good," she says. "Want some Jell-O?"

Lilly makes a face but then she nods. "Yeah, if it's red Jell-O."

The nurse comes back with a paper cup of green Jell-O. "Best I could do." Lilly wolfs it down.

"Well, at least you earned your right to be upset," I say, watching the Jell-O disappear.

"Huh?"

"Didn't you always feel like nothing that ever happened to you could even approach what happened to Mom, so you had no right to be upset about anything, ever?"

"What? Jesus, Zara. No. That's fucked-up. You feel that way?"

Didn't every daughter of a Holocaust survivor?

But Lilly's shaking her head. "To each his own, or her own, I guess. I always felt like I was being punished, even as a kid. I mean, Mother even poured boiling soup on me once."

"That's bullshit!" I cry. "You climbed up on the chair next to the stove and pulled the pot down on yourself!"

She shakes her head. "That's the family myth. Mother did it, after Joey died. You're too young to remember."

"That was his name..."

"Yeah. I bet he was named for Johan. Mother had to go away for a while after that."

We have never, ever talked about this. We've never said our baby brother's name. The only immortality Jews have is when people say their name.

"I don't remember Mom being gone. My god, can you imagine?" I gulp a sob and Lilly holds my hand now. "And poor dad, too." I feel the oppressive weight of pity. "His son..."

"I don't think it was his," Lilly says. "They sure used to fight about it. But he was born with some sort of leukemia. No one expected him to last. Still, Mother took it out on me."

I can't think of a way to say this gently so I blurt it. "Lilly, I think you mis-remember. Because I can see it clearly: you're wearing a blue-checked pinafore, and Mom's at the stove, cooking. You pull the chair up next to her, and you reach for her. And you knock the pot over."

Lilly looks at me under heavy-lidded eyes. "The blue-checked pinafore is from my school uniform. We didn't get them until I was seven. I was only four when the soup happened."

I know she's wrong, but this is her myth and Mom's gone, and I can't dissuade her.

"No," she says, "I've never felt like I haven't suffered. What I felt was like an idiot compared to you and Mother, both of you always thinking and planning and being so crafty and smart, and I would just get myself into stupid stuff and have to balls my way out of it. Still do."

"You're not an idiot. You just, I don't know, you just act. You *do* instead of *think*."

"I think!"

"Not enough. But if I'm ever in the hospital, you're the one I want by my side."

"Speaking of which, pass me the nurse call. I want more painkiller before I talk to the police. This all still hurts like shit."

I pass her the button. But I want to ask something before she pushes it, something that I hardly dare ask. "Let me see your chest," I say, finally.

"I already know. I'll have it taken care of after it heals. That's why god made plastic surgeons."

I gently pull the gown aside. The room spins. The slashes form three arms of a swastika.

Chapter 16

December is grey and cold in New York City. The glories of fall are a distant memory and the wind whistles down the tunnels created by the buildings, leaving me chilled when I walk more than a block. The clothes have changed too, and I buy one of those long thick camel-colored coats that cover the behind and come up around the ears. I even buy a hat with a pompom on it, like the ones I see young women wearing with everything from ski jackets to dress coats. I've never liked hats but I even wear this one indoors.

When Angie's text comes, I'm more than receptive. *I miss you, mom!* Heart emoticons race across the screen. How does she do that? *And Meghan's going to be in a recital!*

How can she be in a recital? She's only four.

She's in a little drama class. They're doing the Little Engine that Could. She's a caboose. I wish you could see it.

JetBlue flies within a twenty-minute drive of Angie's house. I'm on the Thursday-night flight.

Air travel is amazing. The flight is delayed and I indulge in a chair massage in Terminal 5 of JFK, a luxury that soothes jangled travelers and makes passersby stare with envy. I try not to moan or drool as the masseur rubs the knots of two months of anguish away from my shoulders.

Finally we board and take off, and looking at the city as we circle once and zoom away, I realize that New York has become my home again. The buildings are lit up in the early dusk. The sun sets earlier here than in San Francisco — and I don't mean the three-hour time difference — and the whole city pulses with energy, even from the air. In six and a half hours I'll be in San Francisco.

As the cabin lights dim and the rest of the plane drifts off to sleep, I think about Lilly. I pull out a notepad and try to write a poem about her. My poetry has gotten me through years of infertility and parenting, stress and loss, but I haven't written a word in New York, and the words are rusted in my mind. I cook less in New York, I don't write, I don't practice my tae kwon do, and I don't work. And yet the months are racing by. I miss Lilly. After thirty years of living without her, of visiting twice a year, I miss her now after two days.

Why did she lie about seeing Walter Rosen at my apartment? She so easily lied to the poor soul at the front desk of the museum. She spun her story to the Vermont cops so all the really important things were left out. And she, Lilly of the Perfect Memory, "remembers" the story of the soup so wrong.

And yet she was the one who wasn't crushed with survivor guilt. Like Aurora, she protected herself with her own version of the facts. I couldn't look at the facts, so I denied their very existence. Her way was braver. She knew them, she just rephrased the narrative. In the end, my visions were my way of forcing myself to face what I knew. And her fabrications were her way of living with what she'd already faced.

We're landing. Six hours have flown with the speed of, well, a jet plane. Below, the lights of San Francisco glitter, its string of bridges reaching like jewels from its core across the darkened bay. Such different energy from New York. I wish Lilly were by my side.

As soon as the wheels hit the tarmac a hundred cell phones light up. I text Sam that I've landed, even though it's three in the morning in New York. After our adventure in the woods he sleeps less than he did before, and I get an immediate response. I text Angie, too, and she's already outside security waiting for me. For once, Derek is home so she can leave Meghan to meet me at the airport at midnight.

It's chilly, but compared to New York the air is somehow lighter and less oppressive. Angie drives smoothly across the freeway lanes, chatting and steering with neither fear nor bravado. All along the road the billboards shout their modern messages, ads for tech companies that make things that no one can understand but themselves. Angie smiles. "I'm going back to work next month. It's an amazing job. Look, there's one of their ads."

I tell her I'm glad. Tomorrow I'll have her explain what she'll be doing, but for now, it's four in the morning New York time, and San Francisco looks like yet another alien planet that I call home.

———— ✦ ⋅❊⋅❂❖❂⋅❊⋅ ✦ ————

I share a room with Meghan. Angie's little flat in North Beach, the one we bought together during the recession, has two and a half bedrooms, so what used to be the guest room has become the nursery. Painted the yellow of a runny egg yolk, it gleams with light this morning when I open my eyes. Meghan has considerately crept out of bed hours ago, and I can hear her in the kitchen banging her spoon on the table. Consideration goes only so far in a four-year-old.

I lie in the guest bed looking over at Meghan's converted crib. It's the kind that progresses from crib to children's bed to single bed, with small adjustments as the child grows. Such innovation. I remember that Angie slept in a dresser drawer lined with blankets the first night we brought her home. It all worked.

At first I think there's no presence of my mother here, but my eye is caught by a three-part painting of the sun in a field of flowers — rising, mid-day, and setting. A Polish poem is written below each frame, the first in English translation, the second in Polish, and the third, under the setting sun, repeats a line of the poem in both languages: *The sun, the flowers, the sky.*

I look closely at my mother's writing, so tiny and perfect. The translation is hers, and the poem is by Leopold Staff. The sun seems to melt into the flowers, and then the sun is running, dripping into the flowers, and then melting into the sky. I squint at the rest of her translation. *Away from my mind all thoughts depart, like the child of years gone by. I think with my eyes alone: the sun, the flowers, the sky.*

She made that painting when Angie arrived to heal the family's grief. After years of yearning for a child, I had finally been blessed. And somehow, this little bundle of warm, damp flesh, born three thousand miles away from the towers of New York and the memories of half a century, had finally filled the hole in Aurora's heart. None of the three she had borne herself could do what this baby did. And the painting, the beautiful brilliance of the artwork framed by the minuscule calligraphy of the poem, was passed from Angie to Meghan, who unknowingly sleeps under its summer light year 'round.

I lie quietly in bed a bit longer, taking full advantage of the luxury of jet lag. This afternoon Meghan will be a caboose. I need to be at my best.

Angie taps at the open door and comes in with a mug of French-press Peet's coffee. I sit up in the bed and take it from her, letting the aroma of California surround me. "How's my little caboose?" I say.

"Excited. It's her theatrical debut."

I sip, and glance at the big-faced clock on the wall. Almost ten in the morning. "What's on deck for the morning?"

"We can walk around North Beach, just hang out if you want."

I'd like nothing better.

By ten-thirty we're outside, enjoying the cool damp air of a sunny December in San Francisco. The rains have already started, so the grit that hardens the air in late fall is gone, washed down to the street and into the bay. No foghorns blow this crisp morning, and as we make our way down the steep hill to Washington Square, I can hear the Powell Street cable car bell in the distance, ringing its way to Fisherman's Wharf.

In the square the Tai Chi practitioners are gone, having completed their moving sculptures with the dawn, and the derelicts have risen from their bedrolls and sleeping bags and are now congregating in pods over a shared cigarette. Saints Peter and Paul Church, the color of communion wafers, looks down on us. Angie and I buy more coffee and spread a blanket in the sun for Meghan to play on. An urban child, she doesn't think twice about carrying on her spirited dialogue with herself in the midst of this mélange of caffeine, fresh-baked sourdough bread, and filth.

"Where's the grand theatrical production this afternoon?" I ask.

Angie nods towards the church. "There's a play group at the church; Meghan goes two afternoons a week. They're doing drama this month."

I sip my coffee. "Have you given any thought to Meghan's ... well, spiritual education?"

"No more than you gave to mine, Mom."

"That's unfair," I say. "I gave it a lot of thought. And came out on *no action*. But I did think about it. And I did offer you the chance to have a bat mitzvah."

Angie laughs. "Yeah, I wanted none of that! Still don't. And Derek doesn't care. So no, I haven't."

It strikes me that Derek doesn't care about much, but I manage not to say so. Angie's happy, I'm happy. "Tell me more about this job you're taking."

Angie prattles away in a flood of computer terms I know very little about. My generation may have invented computers, at least at the personal level, but hers has made them central to life itself. I nod and smile, and as I listen I see the confident, happy girl that has grown into this self-assured woman, mother, whatever-she-does-with-software person. The shadows of the past don't reach this far.

* * *

The children are lined up in a row against the back wall of one of the church's many assembly rooms. The green linoleum and folding chairs are timeless. On the walls are posters of flowers, *Jesus loves the little children of the world, Hope Spoken Here*, and a huge cross hanging from the ceiling. No one is hanging on it, fortunately.

The teacher announces the pageant, and names each child as he or she comes forward. Every color, every race; new immigrants and descendants of slaves; war refugees and children of techies. First comes the engine, four children turning in circles. Then come the toys, including a little boy in a Viking hat and a drawn-on mustache, who looks intensely at each member of the audience, unblinking and fierce. At the end, Meghan, a boy named, I think, Tiger, and another girl whose name is long and melodious but I don't quite catch, put their hands on each other's shoulders to form the caboose. "Caboooooose!" is their opening line.

The teacher reads the familiar story and the fierce little Viking says, "We must try to get to the town tonight!" It's the longest line of the show and he delivers it with panache. The parents clap.

"I think I can," they chug, until they reach the top of the mountain. The engines let out a cheer, and go racing around the room. The toys cheer and follow, and the caboose brings up the rear. They repeat their main line: "Caboooooose!"

And then everyone in unison, "I thought I could!"

Bows are taken, parents cheer. I look around the room. At this frozen moment, the horrors that each parent lived through, or the terror of those whose mothers or grandfathers or cousins or brothers were lost in the evil of someone's war, are forgotten. The future is played out in the hopes of these little engines that can.

New York and Aurora are very, very far away.

The next day I take advantage of being back, and pay a visit to the San Francisco Jewish Community Center. An enormous modern building with a grand atrium and multiple auditoriums, the Center is the cultural hub of liberal Judaism in San Francisco. The list of performers, speakers, artists, social activists, and programs is mind-boggling, especially for a city so much smaller than New York.

After the standard security guard bag-search, there's a desk with a kind-looking white-haired woman behind it. Unlike the museum in New York, the San Francisco Center embodies the California attitude. "Let me get someone who can help you," the woman says, scrolling the screen of her computer. She sends a message, and within minutes a young woman with a dyed black crew cut and glasses approaches me. Her name tag tells me she's Tova. *Good.* What a beautiful thing to name your child. It's a name of hope, a name that carries with it the belief in *good.*

"I love your name," I say.

"Ugh. I've always hated it. So much to live up to."

There goes that theory.

"Do you have anything on inherited trauma?" I ask. She can't be more than twenty-four.

"Would you like books, pamphlets, or referrals to counseling?"

I'm impressed, but I pause. None of those is what I want. "An exhibit, maybe?"

Her eyes glitter behind her thick glasses. "We don't have what you want, but I know who does. Come with me. Watch your step, these stairs are tricky. Or would you like to take the elevator?"

I follow her up a wide staircase to a room with photos covering almost every inch of the walls. "It was a temporary exhibit," she says, "but you can see it online."

L'dor vador. From generation to generation. The inherited trauma, the inherited memory of pain, across the generations, across cultures, as portrayed in art, on display at the San Francisco Contemporary Jewish Studies Museum. The video by the exhibit advisor says it all. When the memory of trauma isn't dealt with, pain passes to the next generation. In this exhibit, it isn't just your past, you don't need to be Jewish: pain is inherited across cultures. And if you don't acknowledge the pain, it manifests in your life and in the lives of the generations to come.

I watch the video and tour the exhibit through Tova's computer. She hands me a tissue.

"California is a breath of fresh air, but it has to be earned," I tell her.

Tova shakes her head. "Every time I watch that video I wonder. Does pain need to be processed? Or does it have the right to remain, to destroy generation after generation, because of the enormity of great evil? Why should the next generation be spared? By trying to nullify it, are we failing to give it its due?"

She understands more than anyone I've ever talked to, this youth of a woman.

We walk together to the upstairs patio, where children are gathered for a story. "In Israel, they tell Holocaust jokes," Tova says to me.

"No!"

"Yeah, young people, people my age, do. It's a way of processing, and a way of saying, *hey, we suffer too. We serve in the army, our children's schools are bombed, when our wives go to the market they may not come back.* Want to hear one?"

"Maybe not," I say. "But how many generations need to suffer? When do we get to forget?"

"So, a guy's on the way to a party on Auschwitz Street in Tel Aviv. He stops another guy for directions. So the dude says, take Dachau up six blocks, turn left at Warsaw Ghetto, and two blocks later go up the hill at Kristallnacht and you're there. So the first guy says, okay, but where's Auschwitz? And the dude says, Auschwitz, my friend, is here."

I stare. "Not really funny," I say.

Deadpan, she replies, "So you think the Holocaust should be funny?"

A second or two, and I laugh.

Tova smiles back. "Your mother?" she asks. I nod. "My grandfather," she says. "I'm terrified to have kids. I have the taint of horror in my blood."

I stop myself from throwing my arms around Tova, crew cut and glasses and all. But I do touch her hand before I turn away. *The taint of horror in my blood.* What a terrible thing to carry.

Angie somehow doesn't. Did I fail? Or did I succeed beyond my wildest dreams? I think of the painting in Meghan's room. Aurora, named for the dawn, had sought the light of the sun, the flowers of summer, in Angie's birth. Maybe it's time to let that sun in.

Chapter 17

The break was just what I needed, and I return to New York refreshed. I go straight to the *Monuments Men* book as soon as I'm back at the apartment. I can use the search function on my Kindle. I was right. The head of the Führer's ERR, the Nazi looting organization, was named Alfred Rosenberg. He bragged to Hitler that he had searched all of the collections of prominent Jewish citizens and art dealers in the occupied territories for items of value that would please his Führer. He even made photo albums of the best of the looted art and artifacts to further ensure proper recognition by his beloved leader.

Originally intended to show that the Jewish people were inferior, this careful cataloging of artwork indicated otherwise, and thus provided the perfect excuse, according to the author, Robert Edsel, for moving the artwork out of countries like France, and into Germany.

I wonder where those photo albums are now.

I phone Lev Zimmerman.

"No, I don't think your menorah would be in those," he says. "It was beautiful, but not of unusual artistic merit. It was probably just looted."

"Would you ask your dad?"

"He has Alzheimer's, Zara. He doesn't know who I am, never mind what your Hanukkiah is. It wasn't a famous or historical piece. That's why I was willing to let Marie steal it. There are bigger and more significant items, not just in market value but in the uniqueness of the design and workmanship. Though I do have to say, the turquoise enamel on that menorah is just not done anymore." He's a complicated guy, this Lev.

Lev agrees to meet me in the city, and we go to the Algonquin for lunch. I get a little shudder remembering that Lilly's first date with Rosen happened there. Lev turns heads with his movie-star looks but he doesn't seem to notice. We get a table near the glass case. "Ever read any Dorothy Parker?" I ask.

He shakes his head. "Didn't read much as a kid. I still only do it now and then. I'm more visual."

"How's the trading business?"

He shrugs. "Making it work. So — any news?"

I'm still unsure how much to tell Lev. My sense is that despite the fact that he was in on the museum theft, he was ultimately Marie's, but not Rosen's, co-conspirator. In fact, poor Marie was really Rosen's dupe. And Lev hasn't tried to deny his role in the insurance scam.

Still, I'm not ready to tell him the whole horror-in-the-mountains saga. I hedge.

"No, but I've got a theory I want to test out on you. I think that Walter Rosen, the guy who heads the Jewish Studies Museum, is a descendant of Alfred Rosenberg, who was basically Hitler's chief of looting. I actually mentioned the similarity of the names to him when we first met him, and he acknowledged that his name was changed from Rosenberg when his father immigrated. Names are so important," I add.

"They are. I was named for my father, my grandfather, his grandfather, down the line. Ashkenazi Jews don't name anyone after the living, but we reached back to grandparents and distant relatives for continuity."

"Sephardic Jews name kids for the living," I smile. "But we all lie about our names. I know I do."

"Yeah, giving someone your name gives them power. Sort of like some indigenous people and photography."

I know what he means. "I always say my name is Susan if I don't want someone to have that power."

"Crazy. I say mine's Joe. I've never met anyone else who did that."

"Or at least no one who talks about it. You need to meet Lilly. She can't come into the City now because she's recovering from…um, she broke her leg, compound fracture, but as soon as she can navigate again we'll have to get everyone together."

"Poor gal. Compound breaks take forever to heal. How'd it happen?"

"Long story. I'll tell you someday."

He shrugs sympathetically. "Meanwhile, how are we going to get my stuff back?" he asks.

"Now it's *my stuff*? A minute ago it was *your menorah*."

"If we get it back I'll sell it to you." He pretends not to notice my glare. "We'll tell my sister the story and she'll understand. And some extra cash wouldn't hurt. It's expensive to keep my dad where he is, but I don't want to put him in a publicly-run home. It's hard enough getting him good care at any price, and he paid into the system for decades. I can't palm him off on some…some warehouse."

I feel for Lev, and I think of Mom's last years, her descent into unknowing blankness. If Dad hadn't left money for her care, if I hadn't been able to supplement it, if Lilly hadn't been able to visit and monitor the quality of the gentle, competent nursing home we found, the nightmare would have been even worse. We had so much, but so few do. I change the subject.

"Do you think the current political regime is the wave of the future?" I know that using the word *regime* is loaded, but I'm just exploring Lev's views.

"Well, we're not going to go quietly."

"Besides," I say, "it's a big country." Sam thinks the tide will turn, thanks to demographics, and, in no small part, the Rights Coalition's work. It's like being married to a secret agent sometimes.

Our soup comes and we eat quietly. Then a thirty-something woman comes up to our table. "Excuse me, Mr. Cruise, I'm sorry to bother you, but I'm a super-big fan, and I would love your autograph." She's pretty, slender, with long light-brown hair, and a blush that won't quit. She holds out her menu and a pen. Lev smiles and signs the menu, "Lev Zimmerman". She looks at it and frowns.

"I'm not Tom Cruise," he says, smiling that amazing smile. "But I'm honored just the same."

"Fuck!" says the girl and stalks away.

He shrugs. "Happens."

"You're going to love Lilly."

I notice he's not wearing his wedding ring. Does he think this is a date? Then I recall that he mentioned an ex-wife at some point. "Lost your ring?" I ask.

He looks briefly baffled, then smiles. Damn, he's good-looking. "My security blanket? I wear it when I go out just to keep ladies at a distance. It sounds conceited, doesn't it? But really, you wouldn't believe how often I get approached. Like you just saw, only worse." I believe it.

With dessert, I make a decision. "The reason Lilly can't come into town right now is that over Thanksgiving she met up with Walter Rosen."

Lev almost spits out his coffee. Then he makes as if to turn up the cobalt-blue hearing aid behind his ear. "No shit!"

"No shit," I echo. "The guy's a real monster. He broke her leg and slashed her with a knife."

Lev looks horrified, his lips turn pale. "No. My god. Why?"

I stop short. In for a penny, in for the whole Megillah. "Because I figured out that he was in on the scam with Marie, but well beyond what you and she planned. You thought that you and Marie were just pulling an insurance shakedown... but Rosen had a much more ambitious plan. It was dawning on me that he killed her at your temple and took the loot himself. And like an idiot, I was trying to figure this out and I kept texting her about it while she was with him."

Lev is still staring at me. Finally, he says, "Okay, wait. So Marie and I cook up this, this idea. She executes it, and, what, tells Rosen?"

"No," I say. "Rosen cooks up the scam, gets Marie in on it, and she approaches you. You fall right in line. She takes the stuff and he gets her on video, which of course Rosen knew would happen. Now Rosen has the goods on Marie, in case she decides not to cooperate in his next step, which probably involves cutting her — and you — mostly out of the deal. He arranges to meet her, gets the stuff, and somehow offs her. At least that's how I see it."

"Wow," Lev breathes, "and now he knows that you and Lilly know. What good does breaking her leg — " he winces when he says it — "what good does that do him?"

"No good at all. I think he meant to hurt her, and threaten her, and keep us quiet. The broken leg was an accident. But you're right, unless he intended . . . to kill her, breaking her leg makes no sense. But he didn't kill her, and he could have."

There has to be a reason why he didn't just stab Lilly and leave her in the woods. "Maybe the fact that she's almost six feet tall, and built like a brick . . . well, she would be a hard body to dump, for sure," I add.

"She's six feet tall?" Lev says.

"Stay on topic."

"It sounds like he wanted her alive — sidelined, scared, and maybe, to a degree, complicit. And since you knew she was with him, he couldn't kill her. But where did he stash the stuff?"

I wasn't going to tell him what we suspected. "It's been over a week and no arrest of Rosen. He's probably in Europe somewhere." But the breakdown of the events gave me an idea. "Lev, you may not actually be Tom Cruise, but do you think you could manage a little acting?"

We go to the museum, and the man at the front desk recognizes me. He blushes when Lev smiles. "Mr. Rosen's on vacation for two more weeks," he says when we ask for the Director.

"I think his assistant is going to help me. Mind if we head up?"

"We'll be super-quiet, promise," Lev says, as if it's noise they worry about.

"If that's the case, go on up," says the front-desk man. Lev winks at him. We head up the stairs. Damn, that's charm.

The assistant is wearing an RIP Fidel t-shirt today, with a picture of the bearded dictator, cigar in mouth, on the front. She greets me like an old friend even though I still don't know her name. If it weren't for the t-shirts, I probably wouldn't recognize her at all. She smiles at Lev. Everyone does. "How can I help you? Mr. Rosen's on vacay until mid-December."

"That long?" I say. "He told me he'd be back December first. Wow. And he said I could pick up the photo albums today, so that we could get a start on the research. Mr...." I stop myself in this fabrication.

"Joe Lieberman," Lev says, and I try not to laugh. But our young assistant doesn't get the joke, and she extends her hand, while smoothing her straight, colorless hair with the other.

"Nice to meet you, Joe," she says.

"Likewise — but I didn't get your name," Lev says easily. I can see how he charmed the temple board all those years.

"Oh. Sheila. Sheila MacConnaugh, that's spelled exactly like it sounds!" She grins.

"Lovely, Ms. Sheila," Lev says.

"Yeah, not exactly the most expected name at a Jewish Studies Museum, is it?" she adds. "Anyway, so Mr. Rosen never said anything to me about the photo albums, so I didn't get them ready. I wish he'd left a contact number, it's so unlike him. I've had to call him a zillion times about stuff, and his cell voicemail is full. I've emailed him, and usually he checks his emails even when he takes a day off, but so far, zippo."

"That's odd," I say. "We did hear from him right after Thanksgiving, my sister and I, and we actually talked to him, and Lilly met with him. I had no idea he'd be gone this long, and we need to get the albums. For the insurance claim."

"Oh! Now that you mention it, he did say something about meeting with Ms. Persil over the Thanksgiving break, and I know that he's been very concerned about the insurance claim, so much so that I'm really glad that he extended his vacation a bit. He was getting pretty frazzled by the end. Though I do miss my daily hot chocolate!"

"I love a good cup of cocoa," Lev says, twinkling at her.

She blushes. "Oh, yeah, we all love Mr. Rosen's hot chocolate. He makes it special, with these European tablets, Drostes, in warm milk." She casts her eyes down. "Gosh, I can't believe she's gone."

"Gone?"

"Poor Marie. She really loved the hot chocolate. Mr. Rosen used to bring her a cup at her desk. What kind of director does that?"

Now *there's* food for thought.

"I wonder when he decided to extend his vacation," I say, as musingly as I can. Another investigative technique: When interviewing employees, it's better to wonder something than to ask it — most of the time. This time, it works.

"He emailed me on the Saturday after Thanksgiving. Just a note saying he'd decided that he needed a bit more of a break, and there were some pieces of art that he thought he'd check out for our next exhibit, so he'd be back December twentieth. We don't need to worry about Christmas, you know!"

I smile at the little joke, and nod. "That would make sense, then. So we should just work on the albums until he gets back, and we can set up the insurance meeting for, say, right after New Year's. That should give everyone time to get the valuations in order. Joe, do you think you can do the estimates that fast?"

He's no dummy. "Well, if we get the albums now, and Sheila, if you have an up-to-date claim we can work off of, then we're good to go."

She looks a little flummoxed. "I don't have any updates. I only have the one that Mr. Rosen gave me right at the beginning. Was there more stuff stolen?"

"Oh, yes, at least that's what Mr. Rosen told us. But no worries, we can update the list when he gets back. We'll work off the old one, unless you think we shouldn't?"

Sheila reaches under her desk and opens a small drawer. On the back of her t-shirt it says, "We hardly knew ye..." Referring to Fidel, I guess.

"Oh, sure. I'll give you the one I *think* is the original, and you can compare it, see if anything's been added." Now that's my girl.

"Brilliant," Lev says. "That will give me a head start."

She blushes again, takes a key from the drawer, and lets herself into Rosen's office. She shuts the door behind her. She has some sense, after all. It's too bad, since I'd like to know where the books are kept, but I don't risk following her. She emerges with five thick photo albums. Lev quickly takes them from her.

"Thanks," she says.

"They're heavy," he answers, not saying she couldn't carry them, just being gallant. The guy has social skills I'd kill for. I flash on the first conversation we'd had on the phone, where he sounded whiny and disjointed. I get a chill. He looks nothing like I had originally imagined, and he certainly has charm he didn't display in that call.

Before I can let that thought get out of hand, Sheila is handing me a printout. "Here, sorry I don't know about an update. Why don't you give me your email, so if I find something newer in the system I can send it? Or should I just send it straight to GrandEquity's claims manager?"

Yikes. But I know what to do. "Both, if you want, or just send it to me and I'll forward it after we compare it with the original — if you find an updated version at all." And I give her my Persil-Pendleton Investigations email. "That way the company won't get too excited about multiple and changing claims."

She nods and jots the email down. "Let me sign a receipt for the albums," I add, and she looks grateful.

We leave quickly, Lev carrying the albums.

In the elevator, alone with Lev, the chilling idea takes root. I don't dare ask him when we're alone, though.

On the street I say, "I'll take them from here. You were great."

"Thanks," he says. "Don't want me messing with your investigation?"

How can I say that I suddenly don't trust him? Or don't trust him again? Or still?

"I just think it's safer."

"If you say so," he says. "I guess being an embezzler doesn't exactly inspire trust."

The distrust is far worse than that. "Lev," I almost whisper, "you *were* going to meet Marie that night, weren't you?"

It's almost as if the whole city stops. I feel him stiffen.

"Yeah," he says. His voice is almost a croak. He clears his throat. "She was going to bring me back the pieces that she'd taken, the ones that belonged to me. The insurance claim had been submitted, so I could have them back. But when I got to the temple," he swallows, "she was already dead. I swear to God."

I start to shiver. He puts a hand out to steady me, wraps his arm around me. "I promise," he says.

I'm seeing black out of the corners of my eyes and I have to wait until the world stops spinning. "Why did you lie?"

"I had to, Zara. I'm sorry. But I had to. I mean, I'm in the middle of an insurance deal, I have a record — of course I couldn't say we intended to meet. Don't you understand?"

"Did you lie to the police too?"

He shakes his head. "They've never interviewed me about Marie. No connection, no reason they should. Look, Zara. I've never hurt anyone in my life. I'm just not that kind of guy. Please, please believe me. She was already there, already in the bushes, half-undressed and not breathing. Scared the shit out of me."

"Did you call the cops when you found her?"

Again he shakes his head, his arm still around me. "No. Having a record changes the way you operate in this world."

"Well, it certainly doesn't help." I say it with a small, thin smile, though, and he shrugs and signals a cab. "Thank you, Lev. This will help both of us. I promise."

"I know," he says, shutting the cab door. "Keep me posted."

It's raining as the cab pulls up, and the doorman comes out with a big umbrella to escort me and my photo albums in. In the cold rain, New York is a unique shade of grey, with grey buildings, grey skies, grey water running down the gutters, and everyone dressed in grey or black. Even the doorman's coat is grey, his umbrella is black, and we track grey splotches across the entryway as I struggle with the bulky albums. Only the lights from the Christmas tree installed in the foyer the day after Thanksgiving, blinking white and red, relieve the monochrome. The doorman pushes the elevator button for me.

"Family photos from Thanksgiving?" he says. I smile and nod. It's as good a story as anything else. The old covers on the binders make me sneeze. "Bless you," he says as the elevator door slides shut.

Sam's waiting for me at the apartment. That's strange in and of itself since it's only three-thirty in the afternoon. "School get canceled due to rain?" I say when he opens the door.

"Since you've been meeting with a Tom Cruise look-alike, hugging him on the street, I thought I'd come and meet your beau."

"What?" I start guiltily, blameless though I am. "The best defense being a good offense?"

"Meaning?"

I put the albums down. "Wait a minute. First, how did you hear about my lunch with Lev?"

"That's Lev Zimmerman?"

"Did you think that every Jewish guy looks like Shylock in *The Merchant of Venice?*"

"Not fair, Zara."

"Well, yes, that's Lev Zimmerman. Isn't he gorgeous? Some gal came up and asked him for his autograph at lunch. *Mister Cruise, I really admire your work!* Apparently it happens all the time. So, what are you really doing at home?"

"I was worried about you. Since that business up in Vermont I twitch when I'm at the university. I'm petrified that something's happened to you."

"So you're not having an affair with someone there?"

"*What?* Are you fucking kidding?"

"Not an answer."

"Wow. What a lack of trust."

"Listen, Sam. You run off to the university day and night —"

"That's to let you be with Lilly. And to let you work out this stuff about your mom, which I don't blame you for one bit, as you very well know. I'm trying to do my best to let you work this through, and not, as you call it, mansplain your life to you, since I'd be wrong anyway. But no. I'm not, and I haven't been, having an affair, not now and not ever."

Of course I believe him. We've always had a solid and honest marriage. But… "So then how do you know about my lunch with Lev? Either you were hiding out in the Algonquin and you haven't told me, or you followed me there. Which is it?"

I keep my eyes focused on him, but I'm having trouble with my breathing and my heart is pounding. I wonder if I'm supposed to take an extra pill when this happens.

"Breathe slower," Sam says.

"I'm fine. Answer the question."

"You're not fine. Sit down," he says. He's right and I'm dizzy, so I edge my way to the sofa. He sits down next to me, and I model my breathing on his. "That's better. Okay. No, I didn't follow you, or anything creepy, and I swear that I'm not fooling around. This is stupid, but —"

"Are you saying I'm stupid? Or that my concerns are stupid?"

"No! Now let me finish. Because, listen, I went downtown, well it's really mid-town, but I went because I wanted to try to get tickets for *Hamilton* at TKTS in Times Square, and when I couldn't get them I thought I'd go over to see the Dorothy Parker book in the glass case — you were telling me about it the other day and I got curious — but I couldn't remember what the place was, so I texted Lilly and she said it was at the Algonquin, and that you were having lunch there with Lev Zimmerman. So I walked over and saw you with him. I can prove it."

He takes out his phone and I lean over to see the text interchange with Lilly. It is what he said, but as I lean over to I look at his phone the smell of the albums mixes somehow with the aroma of his cologne, and the combination reminds me of my dad. The room wavers a bit and for a moment I think an episode is coming on, until I realize that it isn't. What's coming on is a bit of long-needed mental clarity.

"I get it," I say.

"What? Do you believe me now?"

"Totally. No, look. These albums? They're old. They're the originals. And that's where the stuff is."

"What stuff?" he asks, but I've started to shake. This is unreal. I get up but my legs don't support me and I stumble back down to the sofa. "Bring me those albums," I say to Sam. "And a glass of water, please."

"You're not going to pour water on the albums, are you?"

"Don't be ridiculous."

I open the first album, and what struck me in the cab now makes sense. In the front of the album is a ledger, written in a lovely hand, almost calligraphy. The pages are thick black vellum, and the photos are old black and white pictures carefully glued in place. They're pictures of Jewish artifacts, beautiful even in the yellowed old photos. Some sections are labeled with dates and the names of towns and cities in France. No owners' names, alas. In the main section of this album, all of the items are from Paris. I set it aside.

My hands shake and I take a sip of water, careful not to spill any. Then I open the second album. And the third, and it's the third one that has Warsaw in it. This ledger runs four pages. The rows across are addresses, items and numerical designations. I don't read German — I'll have to get the exact translations from Lilly — but each precious thing they took, each treasure, each memory, is meticulously noted for the Führer. Unlike the Paris album, in the Warsaw one even the family name of the aggrieved Jew whose cherished heirloom was being ripped from his home was carefully recorded in the ledger, if it was known. Otherwise it was depersonalized as *Juden*.

I page through carefully. Sam has his arm around me, holding me very close. I know the name of the street. I know, because I saw it in one of my spells or episodes or whatever the newsreels or flashbacks are, and I saw them take it. And sure enough, there it is, dated February 12, 1940, and there's the menorah, and two sets of candlesticks, a Seder plate, and a silver platter. I've seen these in my vision, and I know that these platters were inlaid with what must have been precious stones in a Spanish pattern reminiscent of the patterns at the Alhambra. We were Sephardic, and the plate must have been with us from the Expulsion in the fifteenth century. What a haul.

I hold the album on my lap, barely breathing. "The soldiers came, and made my mother show them all the beautiful objects in the house, and took them from her," I said. "She was only thirteen, but she spoke perfect German."

Sam nods, watching me closely. But I stay in the present, and I realize that I haven't had an episode since Vermont. Even when I imagined the picture of Mom with the baby boy — I could not think of him as *my brother, Joey, Joseph*, since for a long time I didn't even remember him — I didn't fall into the past, or see her before me.

"I think I'm through it," I say. "The spells."

Sam nods. "Maybe."

"But meanwhile, these are the real deal. They're some of the Rosenberg albums, the ones Alfred Rosenberg made for Hitler, cataloging the artwork they stole. These albums are incredibly valuable, they're international historical treasures, and they were sitting in Rosen's office in the museum."

He must have gotten them from Old Man Rosenberg himself. *Our name was* Rosenberg *too, but it was shortened at Immigration.* "Bullshit," I tell Sam, when I relay the story of our first meeting. "*He* shortened it. It's an easy and common enough name. And I said to him at our first meeting, *It's the same name*, and he said it was an unfortunate coincidence. My God, how brazen, to be working in the Jewish Studies Museum, and as the Director, no less. He must have planned this his whole life."

"Or been doing it his whole life, at other Jewish museums. Dealing with boards filled with old Jewish art-lovers, laughing up his sleeve, scamming them, no doubt, one after the other. Museums are ashamed of any thefts, so they probably kept their losses pretty quiet. He must have had some pretty good references to get that job."

"I need to research his background. But what do we do now? Call the FBI? Do we even know whose side they're on nowadays?"

"Even I think that's a little extreme, Zara, but I don't blame you. I wouldn't turn the albums over to the FBI, at least not yet. Let's just think about this for a while. Put them in a safe deposit at the bank or something. We can't have them here in the apartment. But these prove that the menorah really is yours."

"Of course it is. Did you doubt it?" I feel a rush of illogical but heartfelt anger at him. My emotions are all over the board. Sam takes my hand, pulls me close, and his warmth, his steady, slow heartbeat, bring me into his rhythm.

"I didn't doubt your heart, but the difficulty of tracing it was on my mind. I knew you believed it was, but there wasn't any proof, any way to make a legal claim stick. There is now."

I guess I love Sam's meticulousness. I guess.

We hold hands on the sofa. The rain has stopped, and peeking from beneath the clouds, the sun sets, turning New York City golden in its rays.

⁑ ❖ ⁑

I'm sitting in an ugly little room in the New York office of the FBI, waiting for their art-theft investigator. Sam has paved the way with a preliminary report, so they know some of the basics. I have four of the five albums with me. The Warsaw one is still in the safe-deposit box at the bank. Sam is pacing.

Finally, the door opens and a gorgeous — no, stunning — blonde woman comes in. She's wearing a dark suit, a deep burgundy blouse, and her hair, pulled into a French twist, is anchored with a clip that sparkles with amethysts. Sam stops pacing.

"I'm Agent Skordall," she says, offering her hand. We introduce ourselves and she pulls out a chair across from me. As soon as she sits, Sam sits. I smile inwardly at the old-fashioned courtesy a beautiful woman can elicit.

Her hands are exquisitely manicured as she leafs through the albums. She switches on a digital recorder. "Start from the beginning."

I tell her a very abbreviated version, with the story of my mother, seeing the menorah at the museum, approaching the Director, and then, awkwardly skipping over Lev Zimmerman entirely, to Lilly's unhappy dates with Walter Rosen.

"We know all about him. Believe it or not, Interpol is searching for him too. Seems he's on a personal mission to get back the Jewish artifacts that one of his old relatives, his uncle or his father or some such thing, stole from the true owners in World War Two. He somehow got the idea that they were confiscated fair and square, so now they all rightfully belong to him. The guy's completely psychotic. I can't believe he was operating under our noses right here in New York. Thanks for the tip, by the way," she adds to Sam. "We would never have thought to look for his car at Bradley Airport."

"It was the next closest to Logan," he says modestly. I can tell he's inwardly preening, though.

"Your sister was lucky," Agent Skordall says. "It seems the gal who took the artworks for him, the curator who handled the inside job, died of cyanide poisoning. At least it's quick. Slip it into her cocoa, and minutes later she's dead."

I hear Sheila's voice in my head. *Marie loved the hot chocolate he made…* And Lilly's. *I knocked it away with my chin…*

"Cyanide gas was used by the Nazis in their gas chambers," Skordall is saying when I refocus. "It kind of fits."

Rosen's a murderer. And he knows where I live.

Sam is patting my hand like an old Irish aunt. "I hope they catch him," he says. Skordall nods, distracted. She's looking at the albums.

"This is incredible," she says. "A world treasure."

I sigh. "And it was all so very, very real."

We leave her enthralled with the albums, and exit into light snow.

"Tomorrow's Hanukkah," I say. "I wish we had the menorah for it." I'm sad; calm, but sad.

"Me too. But we'll do something fun." It begins snowing more heavily as we walk the thirty blocks uptown, to our high-rise home in this crazy city.

Chapter 18

I fill Lilly in over the phone. "The FBI lady was gorgeous. Sam could barely keep from drooling."

"Better than his students?"

"Give it a rest, Lilly." I'm not even mad about that anymore.

"So when does he introduce me to some hot professor?" she asks. "His sabbatical is almost half over already. Besides, they love women on crutches."

I snort. "Instead, how about you finally meet Lev Zimmerman?"

"You know I can't come into the City for at least another two weeks."

"No worries. Invite us up there for Hanukkah."

And so it's arranged. I give her the back-story on Lev. "We aren't the only ones who hid the second time around. Lev's family was almost the same as ours. Remember how we went to Catholic church? Even took communion? He did too. Remember how Mom used to say *one church is as good as another*, and Dad would say so sarcastically after we came back from Mass, *well, do you feel holy now?* And Mom told me to answer *holier than thou*. And I had no idea what that meant, but Dad would laugh, and that always surprised me because I thought it would make him mad, that I was actually saying *Yes, I feel holier than you.*

"But Mom wanted us to know the Catholic Mass, so that if it ever came to it again, we could pass. She was trying to protect us. Remember how we couldn't even say the word 'Jewish'? How for no reason at all in the spring there would be crackers, and in the fall there would be bread with honey and Dad would say *For a sweet year*, and there would be no explanation whatsoever? And since we didn't know any Jews, we had no idea what was going on?"

Lilly grunts and my heart pounds.

"Yeah, I know. You knew. But I was a dummy. I had absolutely no idea. I was clueless. And there was no one I could compare this to, so how could I have known? You were older. And of course, you always knew."

Sam, Lev, and I take the train up to Katonah, and Francis Xavier picks us up at the station. The town's not quite quaint; it's more classic, the way you'd imagine New England today. It's mid-December now, and it's snowing lightly. In the City there were only flurries, but as the train heads north the snow falls harder, and there's a good inch on the ground. No one seems particularly excited by it. It snows a lot here. I'm freezing.

I'm carrying the Warsaw album in a leather tote bag, and I look like nothing more interesting than a suburban matron with her big purse. No one would suspect that what I'm carrying is not only valuable and rare but of vast historical importance. We're meeting Lilly at her house, since she's still using a wheelchair and collecting disability. She meets us at her door on crutches.

"Welcome to the invalid's home," she says. She looks at Lev, and sends me *the look*. I wink. I introduce them, and he's completely focused on her.

She's wearing a stunning dark green sweater with pearl appliqués, and a long, heavy skirt. I don't think I've seen her in a skirt in a decade. "Yeah, with the cast it's easier to wear a skirt than pants, even sweats. They've changed it to a harder cast now that the stitches are out, so I'm more stable. I don't have to make Francis X do everything for me anymore, but don't tell him that!"

Francis Xavier, who's standing behind me, laughs. "I'd do any-thing for you, Ma. You know it." Like Angie, somehow he's grown up without the guilt. Our children talk to us like people. Maybe because we talk to them, too. Who knows? And we'll never know, thank God, what we would have done in Mom's shoes.

But Lilly is ushering us to the living room. Her old dog Lucy cavorts and pants, and almost throws herself into Sam's arms. I'm more of a cat person myself.

Lev offers Lilly his arm, and she takes it with a smile. She's just a hair taller than he is in her flats, but his looks make that mean-ingless. Her home is small, just large enough for her own brand of motherly chaos. Tonight there's Francis Xavier, along with two of her stepsons from husband number three, who don't officially live there, especially since she's been divorced for a decade, but who still spend large chunks of time in her house when they aren't in Chicago with their dad, and all can be found watching TV in her basement and eating her food and fixing her gutters and shoveling out her driveway and walking her dog. In Lilly's house, someone is always coming upstairs for a snack.

Francis Xavier puts out a bag of cookies and brings me coffee, and everyone else has wine. "Wine doesn't go with cookies," I say.

"Since Ma's been laid up, we finally have cookies in the house," Francis Xavier says, grabbing a handful. "I'm going downstairs. Rocco said he's coming over for dinner, but he'll shovel the walk for you, okay?"

"Just keep everyone who shows up downstairs. You too," Lilly says, pushing Lucy away. "We'll order takeout."

"Of course," Francis Xavier says. "Why should tonight be any different?"

"The Museum is closed," I say. "They say it's for remodeling, but they're reeling from this. And of course, no one's seen or heard from Rosen in three weeks. First he was on vacation, now he's on the lam."

"How was the talk with the FBI?" Lilly asks Sam coyly.

"It was okay," he answers. "Zara and I went to see them after I talked it through with one of our Rights Coalition lawyers. They went gaga over the albums."

"I don't trust them nowadays," Lilly says.

"I never trusted them much before, either," I say. "Remember J. Edger Hoover? And now I've got to worry about our own government giving information to the Russians, for Christ's sake."

"How much did you tell them?" Lev asks Sam nervously.

"Everything we needed to, Lev. We didn't tell them you were in cahoots with Marie. By the way, the cause of death was poison. So obviously, Rosen's wanted now for murder as well as art theft and all the rest."

I tell Lilly about the claim. "It's your basic insurance scam. Or at least that's how Marie pitched it to Lev. Marie was going to take some of the artifacts, and Lev and the museum would then make claims. Lev would get paid, the museum would get paid, Marie would then give Lev back the items that were his, and they would split the insurance money. So everyone would make a profit, no one would suffer, and that would be that. The only things she took were small personal artifacts, nothing that was known on the international market. I went through the list with Sheila MacConnaugh."

"Who's that?" Lilly asks. She's been out of the loop a while.

"The assistant with the funny t-shirts. But Rosen had higher aspirations. He initiated the hoax by talking Marie into the theft, but for him it wasn't really about money: Rosen was on a mission to steal back Jewish artifacts he thought were rightfully Nazi booty, and therefore his. Marie had her own little agenda — some extra cash and an interest in Eastern European art, as we learned at the Broom Closet."

"You've been to the Broom Closet? Ever see that, um, show?" Lev interrupts.

I ignore him. "Marie and Lev — sorry, Lev, but it's true — were perfect patsys for Rosen. Once he had her on video he had all the leverage he needed. After all, who would believe that a respected museum director set up the robbery, especially when Lev was also in on what he thought was only a simple scam? So I'm guessing that Rosen met up with Marie to make her give up the more valuable items he wanted to keep. And here, poor Marie thought it was just going to be a nice little insurance fraud."

"Not that she was going to die at the hands of a neo-Nazi," Lev says. We all go quiet.

"There wasn't any mention of a car in any of the reports," Sam says at last. "Did she tell you how she was going to get to the temple to meet you, Lev?"

That was one of the things that was bothering me at the Algonquin. I just hadn't put my finger on it until Sam brought it up now.

Before Lev can answer, Lilly chimes in. "Walter must have driven her to the temple, or maybe she took an Uber like Zara did, and Walter met her there."

I watch Lev closely. I cut my eyes over to Sam, and I see that he is, too.

Lev gives a little shudder and takes a deep breath. "Bastard was setting me up, wasn't he?"

"It isn't hard to find out if someone has a record," Sam says softly. "And your temple problem was in the papers. Kind of makes you perfect for the role."

"Well, fuck him. At least the insurance company is going to pay up," Lev says. "I'll get my money, even if Marie, may her memory be a blessing, won't."

"Well it's our menorah," Lilly says. I blink at her. "Our mother's menorah," she corrects herself. That wasn't the problem.

"Oh yeah, true," Lev says. "I guess you should get part of the dough."

"No way!" I say, and at the same time Lilly says, "Oh yeah!"

"That's insurance fraud!" I say to Lilly.

"Not really," she answers, and Lev smiles at her.

I shrug. Financially, Lilly and I look through the opposite ends of the telescope. But it looks like she and Lev at least share similar lenses.

"I can't believe I didn't come up with the idea myself," Lev says to her. "When Marie approached me about the exhibit, I'd just been canned at the temple. She'd seen something about it in the papers, and we got to talking. I was upset, and I wasn't being careful who I talked to, as you know from when you first called me and I thought you were my bookie with the California phone number. And I sure needed the money. I just can't believe how badly it all turned out."

"I know!" Lilly agrees. "It's so unfair. I mean, insurance companies have all the money in the world, and we get screwed by them every time. So it makes perfect sense to me."

"I should have handled more of the deal myself. I wouldn't have botched it. And yet," Lev adds, "it seemed foolproof."

"Not for the fools."

Sam kicks me under the table, but he's trying not to laugh.

"It was Rosen's idea, even if he planted it in Marie's mind. You couldn't have done it better, Lev," I say. "He's a real pro."

Lev grins.

Lilly has her Costco menorah on the table, and she hollers down to Francis X to come up with his brothers and anyone else down there. Boys, or, really, young men, troop noisily up from the basement. She hands Francis X the striker she uses to light the gas-burning fireplace.

"Zara, can you say the blessings in Hebrew?" she asks.

I'm honored and I oblige. When I get to the third blessing, the blessing for having lived to reach this season, we're all a little teary. Then Lilly hands around little chocolate coins, with George Washington silhouettes on them.

"No real Hanukkah *gelt*?" I ask.

"Not at Costco."

As I unwrap the coin I think of the Droste's tablets that Rosen used to make hot chocolate. "How did Rosen make the hot chocolate he tried to give you in Vermont?" I ask.

"He had these tablets, and he boiled some water on the fire he made."

Sam kicks me hard under the table. I don't tell my sister it probably had cyanide in it.

"Sam, we need to go back to Vermont. I know where the artifacts are."

"What are you talking about?" We're on the train back from Lilly's. Lev has decided to stay for another glass of wine, and take a later train, and then two more, to get home. Or not. I noticed that Lev wasn't wearing his wedding-ring-of-convenience tonight.

"That's why Rosen's phone was on, remember? He was looking for something with his GPS. That's how you found him. And remember, Lilly knocked his phone out of his hand, and he went nuts. That's because that's where he had the stolen artifacts — somewhere in those woods. And he couldn't find them. That's why he was still there. He was out of his mind looking for them. Otherwise, he would have left Lilly and run. I couldn't figure out why he stuck around until we found him. He was desperate to find the phone and find his stash. That's why."

I'm excited, and Sam is too, I can see. But pragmatism prevails.

"I'm sure he found the stuff eventually and took off with it. The cops didn't find him…"

"They weren't looking very hard," I say.

"True, but they still didn't."

Something else dawns on me. "Oh, shit. McMuffin! Because remember, there were a couple of cars there? And McMuffin Man said he hadn't seen anyone arrive? That was because Rosen had gotten there the night before and parked down the road. Rosen and Lilly spent the night in the lean-to in the woods. I'll bet McMuffin stuck around, saw Rosen come out. We should have taken pictures of all the license plates."

"Lilly remembered what kind of car Rosen drove. She's got that amazing memory. That's how I reported it, and that's how they found it at Bradley," Sam says. "They traced him as far as a flight to Holland. From there, it's anyone's guess, since he has an EU passport."

"I'm surprised the Vermont cops didn't even ask Lilly about Rosen's car," I add.

Sam shrugs. "They didn't ask much. Your Mr. McMuffin drove a 2009 F-150 pickup with a grey camper shell with an American flag decal on it," he adds. "We could track him down if we had his plates. But he knew the cop — the cop called him by name. I wish I could remember it."

"That's okay. It was Carson. But what's the point?"

"To find out if Rosen came out later, if Carson saw him. If he was carrying anything."

"Like he'd care, as long as it wasn't a McDonald's bag. But you think Rosen found the stuff and took off?" I ask.

"Yep. If not that day, shortly thereafter. The stuff's gone, I'm sure. I'm sorry, Zara. I really am."

I nuzzle into his arms. "Sam," I say sleepily, "we still have the coordinates of where Lilly knocked his phone down, right? So we can still find the lean-to, even without Lilly."

"True," he says into my hair.

"What time did Rosen get on his flight?"

"From what we were able to find out, about three hours after we found Lilly."

"Not a lot of time to go digging in his condition."

"I didn't think of that," Sam admits.

"We've got to go back. We have to try. We need to go tomorrow. My mother combed Paris for my ring. We have to at least go look."

Sam strokes my cheek. "It's snowing. If it's snowing this hard here, imagine up in the mountains."

He's right. It's best to let it go, at least for now. "I'm going up there when the snow melts," I say, "even if I have to wait for spring. By then, Lilly's leg will be healed."

"Meanwhile," Sam says, "we'll watch the internet for it. And we know that your mother's spirit lives on. Your ring guarantees it."

I look at the pearl in the center and try to see into the ring's past life, like I did as a child. But what I see instead is Angie's face, my own child, growing up happy. And *her* happy child. And the train rocks gently into the snowy night.

Chapter 19

'Tis the night before Christmas, and Lilly, Lev, Sam, and I are sitting at my tiny table in my tiny kitchen, while the lights of Manhattan shine in a hazy yellow glare outside the window. We are eating by candlelight because an hour ago the power went out, just as I was putting the finishing touches on my Polish Christmas Eve dinner, and when the lights came on about fifteen minutes ago we decided to go with the romantic allure of looking a couple of decades younger. Francis Xavier has flown out to Chicago to spend the holiday with his step-dad and brothers, testament to Lilly's family dynamic.

We've all had at least one shot of vodka each, Sam having bought Zubrowka, the bison-grass-scented Polish vodka my mother favored. After it sits in the freezer for an hour, it goes down like syrup.

I get up to clear the first course, herring in cream sauce. Lilly bought it at Dean & DeLuca, and I actually had a bite. I bring out the hard-boiled eggs. They're the most magnificent deviled eggs in the world. To make them, first I brought them to a boil in a big pot of salted water — with a little vinegar added, like for Easter eggs — and then covered them and turned off the heat. The trick is to keep the shells intact. I left them there untouched for thirty minutes, then ran cold water over them to prevent the yolks from getting a green rim. Once the eggs were cool enough, I carefully cut the shells open lengthwise, trying hard not to break them. After thirty years, I never break any of them. I scooped out the insides into a bowl, added a whole stick of unsalted, slightly softened butter, some finely chopped parsley, and cut it all into mélange with a pastry cutter. You can use two knives. Then I meticulously refilled the eggshells, flattening the surface of each half.

Before the electricity went out I took the biggest frying pan in the apartment and put all the eggs in, face down. There's enough butter in the eggs to grease a cruise ship, so I didn't add any butter to the pan. I put it over a low-ish heat, since the apartment stove is annoyingly electric, and let them cook. When the lights came back on I was able to finish crisping them, and now I've brought them out to the table on a platter.

"They aren't traditional to Christmas dinner, you know," Lilly says. Mom said that too, every Christmas Eve.

I put the platter down. "They're the only thing on this crazy menu that I know everyone will eat," I say to Lev. He nods as he picks up an egg. He doesn't need to be told to take his salad fork and carefully eat the insides.

"We had these at Easter," Lev says, and Lilly meets my eyes. Another crazy mixed-up Jew.

But Lilly's eyes are strangely hard; they're Mom's eyes, hard and sharp, not Lilly's usual soft, Anne Frank eyes, and I grasp the edge of the table.

So much butter. Such a luxury after the years of fear and starvation. A feast of untold gluttony. When I could order real egg tempera paints again I had to stop myself from tasting them. An egg. What my mother would have given to have an egg. So much butter.

My mother's voice fades and Lilly's eyes have returned to normal. "Should I get the soup?" she asks. "Stay put, Zara. You've overworked yourself."

"She did that at the Dunkin Donuts the night I met her," Lev says, giving away my secret. "I thought she was having a stroke."

"No," I say, "this is different. I didn't see anything. Just heard her voice."

"Oh, that's *so* much better," Lilly says.

"Second sarcasm of your life?" I answer.

"Girls, stop it!" Sam says. "Let's have the borscht."

Lilly ladles the clear, red, sparkling soup into bowls, and adds the dumplings. "*Barszcz z uszkami*" she says. Borscht with little ears. The dumplings are like little wontons, filled with sautéed mushrooms and onion. At home I make them with actual wonton wraps, a trick I taught Mom. She never rolled the dough out to paper-thin again. Lilly bought these little ears. In New York you can get anything.

Then there's the fish, not the traditional carp raised in the bathtub but a nice East Coast snapper. At home we grill salmon. And then we have kugel. "Kugel?" my mother had asked. It was the contribution of another mixed-up couple, who used to join us for "Jewish Orphans' Christmas Eve". And salad. And dessert should be a twelve-fruit compote, symbolizing the twelve days of Christmas, but in this case, it's a four-fruit cocktail in sweetened white wine. Then there are cookies. If the courses come out even, we're good. If they come out odd, coffee counts as a course. There used to be twelve courses.

"No, Zara. If the courses come out even, we count the coffee to make it odd. The twelve apostles plus Jesus. It's an *even* number at the table, and an *odd* number of courses."

Sam looks at me, and I can see he's trying not to laugh, but I charge ahead. "No, Lilly, it's..."

Sam can't hold it in any longer. "This is a microcosm of everything in your crazy family!" he says. But he's laughing. "One of you remembers something as gospel —"

"He said 'gospel'," I giggle, as if it were *underwear* or *butt*. The vodka has got me silly.

"And then it's true for you forever. And the other one remembers the exact opposite."

"True, Sam. But then it's all true, right?" I say.

"You should hear what *my* family's like," Lev says.

"There's really no objective truth to these traditions," I say. "There's tradition. That's it. But they're my truth. And Lilly's, and Lev's — and Sam, they're even yours at this point."

"We always had a ham at Christmas," Sam says. "Simple."

• ‖ ‡ ◆❍◗◆❍ ‡ ‖ •

Christmas Day dawns, at some point. The vodka from the night before has left me with a buzzing headache. Sam rolls over. "Thank God we don't have to put together a bicycle," he says, and pulls the covers up around his ears. I can hear Lilly running the coffee maker in the kitchen, and it sounds like a jackhammer.

Lilly hands me a cup when I shuffle into the kitchen. "Merry Christmas, Zarita," she says, and kisses me. I hold her close.

I get a little box from the mantel. "For you."

She opens it. It's a snow globe about the size of a golf ball with a gold menorah inside. I got it at Tiffany's. "It's beautiful," Lilly says, tipping it. Little gold flakes swirl in the liquid. She looks at me with her big eyes, and I see tears in them. I'm touched.

Lilly gets down on the floor, which — given that her leg is still in a walking boot and she's using a cane — is no small feat, and pulls a package out from under the sofa bed, about the size of a small shoebox, wrapped in generic green wrapping paper. I tear it open. It's a handbag, red, gorgeous, and familiar.

"It was Mother's," she says. "She gave it to me. It's a Lana Marks." I rub the nubby leather, and I can smell Mom's rose perfume. "You should look it up," Lilly adds. "It's a classic."

I don't care about the bag's value or its classic nature. I care that Mom held this bag, and now Lilly wants me to have it. "Thanks," I whisper.

Sam chooses that moment to emerge, tousle-headed and wearing only his pajama pants. "Merry Christmas, girls," he says. "Mind if I grab the shower first?" Neither of us answers and he takes that for a *yes*.

"Chinese food for dinner tonight?" Lilly asks.

My head is killing me. "Advil first. Takeout second."

The day moves slowly. Lilly and I take turns napping, then Sam and I go out for a walk, and it's oddly warm out. There's almost no one on the sidewalks this far uptown, and the streets are nearly empty of cars. The sky is grey but the air is thick, and I'm perspiring by the time we get back. Lilly offers to call in the Chinese food order.

"They'll deliver to the front desk," I say. "They'll buzz us when it's here."

"Why don't we go get it," Lilly suggests. "It'll do me good to get out."

"Can you walk that far? It's all the way over on Second Avenue, and then about six blocks downtown."

"I can, and we can always take a cab back so the food stays hot," she adds. "Sam, come with us?"

Sam shakes his head. "Actually, I'm going to go pick something up," he says, shouldering his coat. "I don't remember it being this warm in December when we were in school. Is it always this warm now on Christmas, Lilly?"

"We get a weird thaw sometimes," she answers. "The weather app says it's going to be even warmer the next few days. Up to the sixties during the day. What on earth are you picking up on Christmas Day?"

"Can't tell you," Sam says. "Back at six."

Lilly takes a closeup picture of the snow globe, and it looks like a gold cloud with a shimmering ghost of a menorah in the background. She posts it to Facebook: "My Christmas Menorah", and gets one hundred and twelve likes in an hour. This girl's got social media star power.

Around four, we head out to pick up our dinner. We take our time, strolling along Second Avenue. Our pace is slowed by Lilly's boot, and for once I don't have to trot to keep up with her long-legged stride. Most of the restaurants are closed, but the lights twinkle and the air is gentle. We hold hands.

"Let's get a real *goyishe* order," Lilly says once we get to the restaurant. We order scallops, shrimp, lobster tails, and pork buns. The place is packed, and not everyone looks Jewish.

"We can eat in," I suggest. "We can call Sam and have him meet us."

"Nah," Lilly says, "let's take this all back to the apartment. A little hair-of-dog vodka will do me good." Much as I hate to admit it, I could use a little hair myself.

There are no available cabs, of course, so we end up carrying the food all the way back to the apartment, and as we pass the doorman he says, "Quite a party, eh?"

"Yeah," I answer. "Merry Christmas!"

He holds the door. Sam was very generous with the holiday tips. "Always glad to help you gals have a good time."

"Weirdo," Lilly says under her breath as the elevator door closes. "He acts like we're up to something subversive."

I don't answer her. I feel queasy, and not right. I wait to see if I'm going to have a spell, or even some good old rapid heartbeat, but nothing happens. "I don't feel quite myself," I say to Lilly. "I feel, I don't know, like I'm having an anxiety attack."

"It's all that *treyf* you've been carrying," she says. "Let's get you inside."

I take my key out to unlock the door and my hand is shaking. My ears are pounding and I feel like I'm going to puke. Last night's vodka must have taken it out of me.

"Here, let me, hangover baby," Lilly says, taking the key from my shaky hand. She does the bottom lock.

"No, top one first," I say, but the door opens just with the bottom one, and as the door swings open, I stumble with the food, dropping the pork buns. Lilly's cane hits them and she slides into me, slamming the door open hard. A muffled sound comes from behind the door.

"Oh my god, Sam, I'm sorry," I say, and the door slams shut. But it's not Sam. Towering above me is Walter Rosen, holding his phone.

I start to scream but he puts his hand over my entire face and shoves me back against the door. His palm is pressed into my nose and upper lip, and I have the terrifying sensation of airlessness. I open my mouth and try to breathe, but the air rasps against my lungs. One of his fingers is over my eye and I'm starting to see stars. I'm at a disadvantage, with my back to the door and my hands full with the Chinese food, but it never occurs to me to drop it.

He says something in German into his phone, and Lilly grabs it from him. He lunges for her, never letting go of me, but his hand shifts and I bite his palm. Lilly swings her cane, bringing it down hard on his free arm. The sound of his arm-bone cracking is nauseating.

Rosen is screaming something in German, and Lilly shouts back at him. It sounds like they're cussing each other out, but German never sounds beautiful to me in the first place. "Hit him again!" I say around Rosen's palm as he digs his fingers into my face. Lilly is busy yelling at him, and somewhere in my mind I think, "I didn't know she was *that* fluent."

Finally, Lilly takes another swing at him, and this time she connects at his neck. With a roar he backs away, and slips on the pork buns scattered all over the foyer. He crashes into the coat closet and drops to his knees. I take the carton of food I'm holding and shove it into his face.

"No! Nein!!" he screams as the hot and spicy shrimp and scallops spread across his eyes and nose.

"Shove it into his mouth!" Lilly yells, and I obey without question. He struggles with one arm, and she holds his head against the food. "He's allergic!" she says, and I watch as Walter Rosen starts to gasp.

"Where's the menorah?" I say to him, as he claws at my hands. His face is reddening and he's breathing loudly. I push lobster tail in garlic-ginger-scallion sauce into his nose. I shove a whole prawn into his mouth as he wheezes for air. "*Where's my menorah?*"

"My god, you're going to kill him," Lilly says.

"Fuck that!" I say. "He tried to kill you. He carved you. I want...my...menorah!" I shout, with a shove of the prawns with each word. I feel no mercy.

Rosen says something in German. He's turning a strange shade of purple. "*Wo?*" Lilly says harshly. He says something else, but I can barely hear him. "You'd better not be lying," Lilly says. He says something else, and then his eyes roll up a bit. "Call 911," Lilly says, her voice shaky.

At that moment, Sam walks in the door.

⸻ ❖ ⸻

"How did you know he was allergic?" I ask Lilly after the police and the ambulance leave. Sam handled the police brilliantly, sparing us the horrors of interrogation. Typical Sam, he had our FBI Agent Skordahl's phone number memorized, and once she spoke to the responding officers, they were happy to make the arrest.

"The paramedic was unbelievably hot, wasn't he?" Lilly says.

"Oh, for God's sake!" He was, actually, and he gave Rosen a shot that reversed the anaphylaxis in time for the cops to read him his rights before he was loaded onto the ambulance, handcuffed to the gurney.

"Well he was. But about Walter. When we went to dinner in Vermont, he had a whole fit about my ordering lobster. I thought he was being cheap, or kosher, or something. And he was really picky about what was in his sauce, and if the shellfish was kept separate from the rest of the food in the kitchen. Then I realized it wasn't kosher, it was allergy — when he ordered the pork chop."

"Genius. But I thought you just wanted to scald him with the food."

Lilly forks up a glistening shrimp. New order. Delivered, this time. "I guess the doorman thought Rosen was a guest?"

"I asked him," Sam says. "He said that there was a whole list of people that we'd supposedly authorized to come up tonight. God knows what Rosen had planned. I'll bet he did something with the building's computers. He's obviously a hacking genius."

"I know how he got the key," Lilly says. "I lost my keys in his car. I had my wallet, the slim-carry one with just my license and my debit card, in my pocket, but the keys fell out on the floor. If he'd had my wallet he would have realized I didn't live here."

Sam raises an eyebrow. He doesn't know about Lilly and Rosen doing the nasty in our bed.

"He would have gone to your house instead, where you didn't have Zara to protect you. Only your cane, your height, Lucy the geriatric wonder dog, and maybe Francis Xavier and all his friends and step-brothers," Sam chuckles.

I put my hand on Sam's arm. "So, what did you pick up?"

"Oh my goodness! I totally forgot in all the excitement!" Sam jumps up from the table.

While he's gone I turn to Lilly. "I had no idea you were that fluent in German."

"I'm not. It was the weirdest thing. It was, I don't know how to say this, it was as if I just knew what he was saying, and could speak it. It was like...like Mother was speaking." Lilly's eyes fill with tears. "I could hear her voice, coming from my mouth. Like last night, with the eggs."

"I saw her in your eyes last night."

We're quiet a moment. "Do you remember what you said?"

She shakes her head.

"Try. Because we asked him where the menorah was, and I think he told you."

"No, wait..." Lilly says. "He asked *me* where it was! He said he saw that I'd posted it on Facebook. I told him we didn't have it. He said, 'You posted the other one. The gold one.'"

"So he thought we had the stolen items? That means he never found them. It's snowed ever since Thanksgiving, up in the mountains."

Sam emerges from the bedroom at that moment. In his arms he carries a little white and grey thing. It moves. "A kitten?" I jump up from my chair. He hands it to me and I hold it close. A kitten. "She's beautiful."

"He. Hopefully, *he*. Merry Christmas!"

"Thank you, Sam." I feel the little purring engine. "He needs supplies."

"Got them. It's all set up in our bathroom."

I put my face against the little body and feel a sense of peace come over me. A peace promptly shattered by Lilly.

"I know where it is. It's in the woods, behind the shack. Buried next to a tree where the symbol is," Lilly says, her voice far away.

"What is?" Sam asks.

With a glance at me, Lilly says, "The menorah. Rosen told me."

"In German," I add, and listen to my little kitten purr.

———— ⋅ ⋕⋛◆◗◎◖◆⋜⋕ ⋅ ————

The weather keeps getting warmer, and by the end of the week, just as Lilly said, it's in the sixties during the day. I've checked all the ski reports online. There's no snow left on the ground in Vermont, except on the taller mountain-tops. "Today's the day," I say to Sam. "We have to do this."

Lilly, Lev, Sam and I load up Lilly's van. She's still using the cane and can't hike far, but she's got her perfect sense of direction and she's the only one who's been to the shack. The whole nightmare of that ordeal starts to come back to me, and I'm afraid that I'll go into some kind of spell, one that I can never come out of — but in fact, I haven't had a real spell since that day in the woods. Little bits and pieces, but no out-and-out newsreels.

The drive up to Vermont in mid-winter is a reminder of the harshness of the season outside the City, but it has its own bleak beauty.

I enjoy it far more than that crazed dash to the mountains a month before. Sam is driving, Lilly is up front with him — her long legs would deserve the prime place even without her injury — and Lev and I share the back.

"Are you nervous?" Lev asks me. I smile a little, shake my head, but of course I am. "What if we don't find it?"

"We keep looking. What if we do find it? You'll be out the insurance money." I wish I hadn't said it. The original issue of who owns it is still unresolved.

Sam steps into the conversation. "We'll work that out when and if we do recover it. Let's not get ahead of ourselves. It's a gorgeous ride."

"I got good news from the plastic surgeon," Lilly chirps up. So like her to bring up unspeakable things. "The scarring is minimal, and she can eliminate it when she does, you know, a little nip-and-tuck. Win-win all the way around."

"I'm glad," Sam says, sparing me from responding. He knows I'd ignore the entire last month if I could.

We pull into where McMuffin and his cohorts had been, where Sam and I had parked. There are cars there, people obviously taking advantage of the warm weather to get a hike in. We'd thought of that possibility, and we were ready to move on and park further down the road, as Rosen had. I'd hoped to spare Lilly that. Her face is hard, or as hard as hers can get. Mine would have been granite.

"Do you have warm gloves, Zara?" she asks. I don't resent it, she needs to do that, to focus on something safe. I nod. "That scarf looks nice," she adds.

"Thanks. Goes with my sweater." The clothes-talk soothes her, and she closes her eyes slightly. "You don't have to do this," I whisper.

"I do things," she whispers back. "I have to."

I nod, my hand on her arm, awaiting her cue.

"Okay," she says. "Let's do it. This way." And with her incredible sense of direction, the sense that neither my mother nor I ever had, she leads the way. She picks her way with her cane, pushing dead branches and fallen leaves out of the way. Sam walks with her, correcting course with his GPS, while Lev and I follow behind.

"You think we'll find it?" Lev asks for the fourth or fifth time. We all have a dog in this hunt, as Sam would say.

"It was *tell the truth or die*," I say again. As she recalled it, Lilly had apparently said she'd let him die like the swine he was unless he told her where to find the menorah and anything else he still had hidden. Sam had quietly slipped Rosen's phone into his pocket before the paramedics arrived at the apartment, and had verified that he had the coordinates in his own GPS as well. Nothing looks familiar. I can walk to the corner store and if the weather's different I won't recognize the route, so a walk through unfamiliar woods is a complete mystery. But when Lilly and Sam veer left, somehow I know it's wrong.

Your sense of direction is worse than mine, Mom.

Really? Well, I walked all the way to Potsdam.

"No. We have to go around."

"Go around what?" Sam looks at me quizzically.

"This log. I'm sure of it."

Sam and Lilly exchange looks. "Uh, Zara, you're not very good…" Sam starts.

"She gets lost in a paper bag," Lilly says to Lev.

"I know I do," I say, "but this time I'm sure."

"Lev, go with Lilly. I'll go with Zara," Sam says. "If we don't find what Zara thinks is the way, we'll rejoin you."

I sigh with relief. "Thanks," I whisper to Sam. He nods, and I follow my instincts to the right.

My instincts are always, always wrong. This time proves to be no exception. We come to a clearing, and there's no shack in sight. Sam puts his arm around me. "I know how to get to the shack coordinates from here," he says, without judgment.

This is where we found Lilly. I know it. We turn back to the left, to head towards where Lilly and Lev have gone, when I see it — a glint. A hair clip, and as I kick away at the pine needles, a dull metal disk at the base of a tree trunk.

"Look!" I pull Sam towards it. It's engraved with a swastika, and it's been nailed into the trunk. "That's what Rosen was talking about, the symbol in the tree. I'm sure of it. That's why he was so angry. He couldn't find it and was digging wherever he thought he could remember. But after he hurt Lilly, she was lying on the spot the whole time!"

We hear voices, and Lilly and Lev are visible ahead. "We've found the shack!" Lilly shouts.

"Come!" I answer. "Come here!" Sam echoes me, and they make their way through the brush.

"This is where I saw him!" Lilly says. "Over there." She points to the other side of the clearing. "That's where I peed."

Lev laughs and gives her a little side-hug. But I'm on my hands and knees, digging with the trowel I brought. "Not that way," Lev says. "I've got hole-digging experience. From my, ah, early days."

He wields the trowel with much more authority than my chicken-scratching. "Careful," I say. "The stuff's delicate." A glint of gold comes into view. "Oh my god!" I say, and I start to cry. Sam bends down and lifts my menorah out of the ground. Lilly reaches for it, Lev reaches for it, and Sam stands holding it against his chest.

I meet Lilly's eyes, and together we put our hands on the menorah, covering it, covering each other's hands. I put my face against it, and Lilly embraces me, putting her head down on mine. We stand in the silence. A jay squawks, a plane rumbles overhead, and I look up at Lilly and at Sam. The sun comes out from the clouds and warms my back, and for a moment the world stops spinning.

It's New Year's Day, exactly four years after Aurora died. Since then, the new year always comes in with sadness. We are back at Lilly's, and at midnight we kissed, drank champagne, and I texted Angie, since it was only nine in the evening back home, but she didn't answer. Derek was still home, not off to Dubai or Brazil or wherever, so no doubt they were having their own New Year's Eve celebration and not waiting to text Mommy.

Then we'd lit the menorah. Yahrzeit candles burn for twenty-four hours, sunset to sunset on the anniversary of the death of the loved one; but Aurora got not just one candle that night, but a full menorah of candles, even if they only burned for an hour. This morning, we light them again. We sit and watch them burn, their light an eternal reminder of Aurora, of Mother, of Mom.

Then the four of us, Lilly and Lev, Sam and I, joined by Francis Xavier, have pancakes and bacon and eggs and real Vermont maple syrup.

⁕ ⁃≡❖⊙❖≡⁃ ⁕

We're about fifteen minutes from Grand Central when my phone goes off. It's a text from Angie. Meghan hid Angie's phone behind the couch, so if I'd been trying to reach her for the past two days, she's sorry.

I text back, *no, all good, happy new year!* with lots of xs and os and smiley hearts.

I scroll back to the texts I sent Lilly that horrible night, the texts that let Rosen know we were on to him even before we really were. It was my fault. I should have never sent those texts. I was the one who deserved to be hurt, not Lilly.

And Mom's voice…

Is this guilt real, or are you just pfumfing through the nose? I have to smile at that funny expression, a Mom-ism for talking through your hat.

It's real, Mom.

Well, get over it. There's plenty of guilt to go around — don't add what you don't deserve.

I ask her, *Did you feel guilty?*

Why would I? she answers.

Because you lived.

Don't be idiotic, she says. *You do what you have to do to survive. It's the others who should feel guilty. The ones who did this to me, to my mother, to my family, to my baby, to my soul. Not I.*

I look over at Sam. He's dozed off. That wasn't a spell, but a simple conversation with my mother's memory. May it be for a blessing.

THE END

Writer's

Postscript

A word here about truth: People tell stories, and those stories put the narrators in the best light possible. Memories fade, memories are colored in by other memories. Customs and expectations change and new lies are necessary. Writers gather stories and fill in the missing pieces with fiction. Fiction requires narrative, fiction requires context, fiction requires a story arc that is at once believable and incredible. Only the stories in this book that show the characters in the best light are true. Only the stories that cast a dark shadow on the narrator's character are false. I can only promise you that I never looked away from the darkness. Believe what you wish.

Acknowledgments

Everyone who knows me knows of the devotion of my husband, Clyde, to me and my writing, and my devotion back to him. Without him none of this matters. My children, Julia and Will, both feel the weight of the family story in their own ways, and it's my hope that they will carry the weight more lightly than my sister and I did.

No book of mine can exist without the steady, unwavering support of my agent, April Eberhardt. I also relied on the good counsel and literary mentorship of Tom Parker, the editorial magic of Priscilla Long, and the poetic lessons of Miriam Sagan. I owe an enormous debt of gratitude to the publisher, Kasva Press, and the brilliant editors there, Don Radlauer and Yael Shahar, without whom this book would not be nearly as good.

The memorial phrase in the dedication comes from my interpretation of a line in Pablo Neruda's *"No hay pura luz"* (There is no pure light.)

The Jewish Museum of New York City was unstintingly generous in allowing me to tour their offices so my descriptions of the emphatically fictional Jewish Studies Museum would be somewhat accurate. Any security breaches were of my own creation. In addition, nothing could be further from accurate than my description of the bad acts of Mr. Walter Rosen, who is entirely made up. No such bad acts ever occurred, or ever could occur, at the real Jewish Museum. The management and staff of the actual museum are not only above reproach, they're really nice and accomplished people. I am grateful that they let me get away with creating a story around them. On the other hand, the menorah did exist, and I did see it there in 1977.

I also owe an emotional debt to the Harvard class of '76 Reunion. They gave me the courage to write this book. The attendees know who they are. Thank you.

One weekend, about a year after my mother died, my father finally told me all he could recall about her stories from the war. I recorded them as he talked, and at the end he asked me to find a way to tell her story. Unlike the father in the book, he was very much alive as I wrote this, and though he was ninety-two years old he was still as wild and engaged as he possibly could be. Although I immediately spit three times and made all of the other superstitious gestures I could think of, my father died only a few weeks before publication of this book.

My real sister, Francesca Hagadus, is an amazing person. She allowed me to use our story, fictionalize it, explore it and offer it to you, my reader, without limiting what I wrote. She did, however, require that I submit to going to her hairstylist at least once in return. She may also demand that she get to choose my wardrobe for the book tour, and in gratitude I will submit. She cried with me, laughed and generally stared at me in amazement as we walked through the drafts of the book. My heart is full.

Books, Poems, Places

Some of the interesting books I read, places I visited, and people I talked to are accessible to readers wanting to know more about Zara and her mother's experiences.

Cecil Roth, *A History of the Marranos*

Jeremy Dauber, *Jewish Comedy, A Serious History*

Elizabeth Rosner, *Survivor Cafe*

Helen Epstein, *Children of the Holocaust*

Leopold Staff, *The Sun*

Pablo Neruda, "No hay pura luz"

The Jewish Museum of New York

San Francisco Jewish Community Center

San Francisco Contemporary Jewish Museum

Robert Edsel & Brett Witter, *Monuments Men*

Ann Marie O'Connor, *The Lady in Gold*

Claudia H. Long

Claudia Hagadus Long has written about early 18th Century Mexico, the Roaring Twenties in San Francisco, and modern-day New York City. She lived in Mexico until she was eleven, went to high school in New York, and graduated from Harvard University and Georgetown University Law Center. She currently practices law as a mediator for employment and business disputes. She lives in Northern California with her husband and far too many animals, and has a two-year-old grandson. *Nine Tenths of the Law* is her fifth novel.

Previous books:

- Josefina's Sin (Atria/ Simon & Schuster, 2011)
- The Duel for Consuelo (Five Directions Press, 2017)
- The Harlot's Pen (Devine Destinies, 2017)
- Chains of Silver (Five Directions Press, 2019)

Find Claudia on:

- www.Claudiahlong.com
- Facebook.com/ClaudiaHLong
- Instagram: @claudiahlong
- Twitter: @CLongnovels
- claudialongauthor@gmail.com